‾S UNL

/ren

Souls

CW00815878

CRAIG PHOENIX

First published in 2007

ISBN: 978-0-9557503-7-3
2nd edition

Printed and bound by CPI Group (UK) Ltd, Croydon, CR0 4YY
Typeset by Lisa Simmonds at LKSDesigns

www.craigphoenix.co.uk

Cover artwork by Trudi Couldridge

Acknowledgements

This page is dedicated to all those people who helped me get this book to where it is today enabling me to achieve one of my many dreams.

A special thanks to Leslie who has been my rock through all my writing efforts. He is one of my closest friends and without whom this book would never have been what it is. I owe him more than he can possibly imagine and for that I dedicate this book to him. Thank you.

Tina - her friendship, support, and words of encouragement through this process.

Lynne Simmonds & Lisa Simmonds for their help, advice and expertise in setting this book out and getting it ready for printing.

Trudi Couldridge you have come up trumps and it is really appreciated.

A big thank you to Robertson Family for allowing me to use the New Empire Theatre as a base for my idea. Visit this website for a list of great shows to see *www.newempiretheatre.co.uk*

For all those who read this book before it was published and encouraged me to carry on especially Jean Brown. Thank you.

Finally a special thank you to my mum who has always had faith in me whatever I do, been there when I fell, listened without prejudice to my ideas, was a shoulder to cry on, and a friend. Love you mum XX

1

"Great!" I muttered.

It was raining.

I ducked back inside the entrance of my first and second floor maisonette to retrieve an old golfing umbrella before locking up again.

The normally bright communal lobby was shrouded in a depressing gloom because of the mild storm blowing outside. Opening the main front door I was pelted by sheets of rain and a blast of cold air that sent a shiver down my spine. I thrust open the umbrella into the bleakness but it was immediately caught by a gust of wind which dragged me forcibly out into the full onslaught of the weather. I fought to get it under control, finally managing to get it to rest, securely, against my shoulder with the handle held tightly in my right jacket pocket. A typical winter's evening for Southend-on-Sea, a large seaside town thirty miles east of London. I was not looking forward to the twenty-five minute walk to the theatre for rehearsals, pelted by the rain and buffeted by the wind. Normally I took my car but dad had been servicing it for me, unfortunately he'd hit a few snags so would not be able to return it until the morning. Thankfully the brown leather jacket I was wearing would keep me warm and I let my thoughts wander to the sun and sea of Tunisia where I had bought it the previous year. I even smiled at the pleasant thoughts, of my now ex-girlfriend who was with me at the time, as I started my walk through the back streets which led from my road, Shakespeare Drive, to the theatre.

These streets were typical of the area made up of lots of

terraced houses in blocks of about seven or eight. Alleyways ran in between, weaving intricate paths around the back gardens, sometimes allowing access to unwanted guests.

I've been in the street about three years and keep myself to myself. I recognised faces; the same ones appearing day after day at similar times. My face had appeared in advertising for various shows over the last couple of years, so to some who took an interest in local theatre, it was probably one of the better known ones, for the right reasons.

Crossing West Road at the top of Shakespeare Drive I headed through the more affluent part of town where the houses nestled on larger plots and were big enough to be occupied by generations of families. Five or six bedrooms, three bathrooms, conservatories, lounges, dining rooms, sitting rooms, studies, breakfast rooms. If only I could afford to buy one of these - a pipedream.

By the time the high street loomed into view the wind and rain had chilled me to the core, eroding any impulse to browse the shop windows and delay me getting to the theatre.

Though, I did always have time for one shop, 'SoundZZZ'. My favourite as it had one of the best collections of musical instruments in the area. Over the ten years since leaving school at sixteen I had managed to spend a fair amount of my earnings as a carpenter on guitars and a saxophone. A hobby. Another dream of mine was to be a rockstar, or at least some kind of musician.

I think that's what led me to the theatre. I'd seen an add in the paper saying, open auditions to anyone interested in doing West Side Story at the newly re-opened Empire Theatre which was just off the main high street near the pier. I had nothing to lose so went along not knowing what to expect. My confidence faded as soon as I stood on the stage in front of the auditioning panel, I mumbled lines and fluffed the song, yet, somehow I passed, and before I knew it was busy in rehearsals in the part of Action, not a main role, but a very prominent supporting one.

I made lots of new friends and was taught to dance, some feat for someone with two left feet. I had such a good time, both on stage and at the after show parties, that I stayed.

Now I was in rehearsals for my fifth show with them, The New Empire Theatre Players or just The Empire Players for short.

The theatre is over one hundred and thirty-five years old and steeped in history having played many roles over its lifetime, movie house, dance hall, night club then back to cinema, and then, sadly, closing, remaining empty for nearly sixteen years where it had sat, a decaying monument of history, ignored by passers- by, including myself, who simply chose to walk by without even raising an eyebrow to glance at the marvellous detail that was slowly being eroded by years of vandalism and bad weather. The building became just another empty skeleton joining the ranks of the other empty facades that were starting to litter the main thoroughfare and the many side streets.

Then, three years ago the doors suddenly flew open, without announcement, air filled with vacuum, life pulsated through it's old rotting timbers and crumbling plaster work, lights blinked dimly beneath years of dust as the electric current surged through the ancient wiring, every now and then a bulb blinked just before it spluttered it's last particles of light and dissipated out of existence forever.

With the theatre open again it was incredible how this side street, Alexandra Street, suddenly came to life, almost a grand unveiling amid a fanfare of jubilant trumpets, like the street had never existed before.

Shops that had always struggled to get their audiences down this lost valley now bustled with life. The colours of the painted signs seemingly came to life as if a magic brush had just put a new coat of polish on them.

I rarely visited this part of town, not much of anything had caught my interest. I wasn't going to explore the far reaches of my universe unnecessarily.

A gust of wind caught me as I approached Clarence Road, reminding me how cold I was. The alley I usually took was down this street and ran along the side of the theatre, back to front.

I knew the warmth of the theatre was close, well at least out of the rain and wind. The truth was that the theatre was an old building and the Copperstone family who now owned and ran it could only afford to do essential repairs. The heating system, although ancient and inefficient, still worked although there was a large area to heat so it didn't always do a great job, especially on cold days like today.

The three sets of sixties style wood-framed glass double fronted doors, which for years had given access, stood towering in front of me. A sign had been hung on the inside of the first pair on the right saying 'STAGE DOOR'. Looking at my watch I was five minutes late. This often happened if you were late. The stage door was near the entrance of the alley at the back of the theatre.

There was always an insistence on punctuality, one thing I wasn't good at. I seem to have this 'I'll get there eventually' attitude, therefore, not endearing myself to the directors and choreographers of the group. Come opening night though, I always knew my lines and moves, this is how I justified it, and I tended to think that that bought me a little leniency. Truth probably was, they were very often short of young men in my age range, twenty to thirty-five. Either way I was there and they allowed me to stay.

Facing the stage door, I gripped and turned the cold handle of the big heavy steel-plated door and it inched its way towards me, the fire handle on the inside banging loudly against it.

Walking through, the sound of music, singing and dance steps reached my ears - the opening number. 'Oops', I thought,

'Oh well, maybe if I sneaked on from the wings they wouldn't notice that I was late. I put my jacket and umbrella down on the nearest chair and decided not to conceal my entrance by strolling confidently onto the stage to join my dance partner, Michelle, as if it was part of the routine. As she spun round she smiled at me and I reciprocated.

"Daniel." The choreographer's voice boomed over the rehearsal tape.

"Sorry Matthew just lost track of…."

"Give the other men a hand upstairs!" He scowled at me, then smiled sardonically. "If you'd been here on time you'd know this is the girl's section. Wouldn't you?"

"Mmmm." I frowned at Michelle quizzically and then suddenly realised they were rehearsing 'Run Rabbit' from the opening section of the Old Time. "Okay." I turned to leave the stage and got kicked accidentally by Tracy as she spun. I quickly dodged another kick as I hastily headed to the treads at the front of the stage before running to the back of the auditorium and through the double doors at the back.

In the foyer I turned right and went up the wide elaborate staircase that climbed to the Mezzanine Theatre, which used to be the 'Gods' when the theatre was originally built as on large performance space and before it had been converted into two cinema screens.

Each new adventure had gripped the building forcing the layout to adapt to suit each new escapade. Walls taken down, floors put in, staircases removed, new doorways made, old ones blocked up, even corridors sealed up now, lost in the mists of time.

I bumped into Adrian, who was coming out of a door on one of the intermediate landings where the staircase turned at ninety degrees.

"Wooh, what's occurring Ade?" I said, narrowly avoiding him and the door.

"If you go in there, Mark wants these seats taken into the Mezzanine Theatre."

"Whereabouts in there?" He was carrying seats similar to those in the downstairs theatre.

"Just follow the corridor, they're on the left, you can't miss 'em, they're about halfway along."

"No problem." I shrugged.

The door slowly closed behind me as I made my way along the corridor Adrian had appeared from. A string of naked light bulbs were strung along one wall and illuminated the way. I had never been in this particular part of the theatre, so I took the opportunity to study the full extent of the corridor wondering what use it had had one hundred and thirty-five years ago.

Other cast members had had the chance to explore the theatre fully, all the hidden chambers, dead-end corridors, disused basements. I hadn't been around at those particular times instead listened to the retold stories. I found it fascinating, to think that some of this had not been touched for over a century. This particular area had rarely been used for any purpose other than storage throughout its entire history. It had certainly not been decorated to any degree of grandness like the rest of theatre.

The door I had entered through had only been discovered in the last two years, hidden behind a false facade. There seemed no logical reason why it had so surreptitiously been locked away, out of sight, for so long. Mark had only stumbled across it when the plaster had fallen off after the roof had leaked one bad winter.

Access had been available to the youth of the theatre, judging by the graffiti on the walls which I started to read forgetting the reason for being there, finding it difficult to comprehend the time and effort made to place a mark on the surface of the plaster. Why bother, simply to put 'Albert Lancaster 1905', 'Harry Smith 1923'. Further along, the inscriptions read like hieroglyphics, more care being taken like a dare set to see who could litter these walls with the most intricate of incisions, without being caught. The deeper and farther the culprits went in, the darker the corridor got making it easier to spend longer periods of time making the marks. The walls looked like someone's jotter, full of doodles and poems, some a good forty lines long, cartoon caricatures, stick men, and love hearts.

Reading a couple, I lost track of time. A particular one caught my eye, drawing me to it, like a child to chocolate. I started to read out loud...

> Here in death I lye
> Never fearful of the final goodbye
> Time will see
> Me rise and return to thee
>
> Ever so sweet
> Revenge will be neat
> Make the ends mine
> Blood runneth like wine
>
> My shadow will rise
> To the sound of human cries
> Ash from the ground
> I will scourge this town
>
> Rid it of all ill
> O' such a sweet pill
> Be the cure
> Death thee endure
>
> Carry me from night
> 'Til the time be right
> Steal the breath of life

Cold steel, the knife

Rise I say and breathe
Be flesh and bones that are strong
Rise I say and take your place
Once again setting right and wrong

Hadien contien nadya fortrey
Kootra dietra feil hoodray

A strange carved symbol had been placed below the poem and only just visible under years of dust. I brushed carefully at it with my fingers and let my eyes scan the words again. I started to recite them, following their patter. As I cleared the dust from the symbol the fragile plaster crumbled away. I noticed a red blotch below where the symbol had been and looked more closely at it, caressing it with the tips of my fingertips, tracing the edges trying to decipher the mark before deciding it was probably just a blotch of paint or something.

As I read aloud the last two lines of the inscription for the second time the air around me turned cold, sending shivers coursing down my spine, goose pimples rose on my arm, the tiny hairs standing to attention. The light bulbs spluttered as if to go out. A gentle breeze swept around me like a mini tornado, twisting and turning, rippling my clothes, tousling my hair. My ears became like radars, aware of any little sound. Instantly all fell eerily still.

My imagination kicked in and I became wary as an ominous feeling congealed around me. I wondered whether I was making a situation exist that didn't. My mind was whirring through a kaleidoscope of films I had seen, churning up unsavoury images that I didn't want to see.

Warmth instantly returned soothing my hyperactive imagination. The goose bumps settled. I looked again at the inscription. There was a signature below H High...

A suffocating tightness gripped my body, clawing at me. My throat became tight as if caught by a cramp. Seconds passed feeling like minutes as I struggled to get my breath, the corridor was blurring as I became disorientated. My legs grew weak. I scratched at my neck trying to ease the cramp in my throat, tears started to form in my eyes as I felt life ebbing away. My body became like lead as the muscles started to seize yet something was stopping me from falling to the ground. My Fingers and toes started felt like stalactites. The corridor faded from view.

Every organ was heavy and felt like a lump of rock. Like nothing I'd ever experienced before I was alive, yet the feeling of death imminent, held in a frozen second. My skin crawled, tightening, constricting over the flesh underneath.

Nerve endings twitched and my body didn't feel like my own. My confused mind was overloaded with electrical signals. My brain pounded against my skull.

A force penetrated my body like a hand entering into a semi-solidified substance, sucking out my life.

I couldn't tell if I was screaming in pain or not, the internal sounds were too great. Scratching, tearing sounds, sounds you hear when you put your fingers in your ears, joints moving, bones creaking against one another.

My heart was held in a cold grip, like two frozen hands round a ball, squeezing it, chilling me, squeezing the breath out of me. No longer could I differentiate between the cramp in my throat and the burning in my lungs. I expected my heart to be squashed into oblivion. I made one last valiant effort to breathe but the world faded from view.

Then, with the force of a bullet being shot from a gun, I was thrown against the wall two feet behind me, my feet leaving the ground. I felt like a rag doll discarded by a petulant child. Sliding down the wall I ended up a crumpled mess barely conscious, face up on the floor but still awake, somehow.

Before my eyes finally closed I watched something, or some-one, looking at me. Their eyes were luminescent saucers in a sea of blackness, studying me inquisitively. I tried to stare back, but any fight had gone and I gave in to unconsciousness.

2

Absolute darkness surrounded me when I came to and, with it, an unearthly tranquillity that threatened to send me into a panic. I blinked, at least I thought I blinked but there was still just darkness. For a moment I wondered if I'd lost my sight. In vain I desperately tried to orientate myself, even touching my eyes to make sure they were open, they felt strange, numb as if not there. I tried a trick taught to me for use on stage after a blackout; close your eyes, count to two and then re-open. This normally allowed your eyes to adjust to the sudden dimness, making moving round the stage easier, especially when exiting into the wings.

Two attempts, still no change. I sat up. In the blackness the corridor seemed like a huge cavernous space. I was afraid to move in case I hit an object hidden in the blackness - stubbed a finger or banged an elbow. I was in unfamiliar surroundings. A little more disconcerting was that I didn't feel any ill effects from the force by which I had been thrown against the wall, no obvious bruises, no scratches, just an uneasy sense of peace and tranquillity.

The floor was soft underneath me almost pliable to touch. I wondered briefly whether I was in bed. No, it was too dark for that.

Extending my arms out in front I reached into the darkness and found only a massive void. A nervous energy crept through me and I had to fight it to keep it in check. I didn't like where I was. I had never been scared of the dark but something wasn't right and I hated not knowing. I turned my shoulders through ninety degrees, letting my hands feel for solid objects. There was nothing. I didn't understand. In my mind I tried to recollect the corridor, I didn't remember it being that wide, only an arm's span width.

Panic threw its blanket over me and my breathing became laboured and heavy. Knowing I had to keep calm didn't help me achieve it, it was overwhelming. I was fighting a losing battle. I tried to re-focus, control it. I closed my eyes again, doubting they had been open, despite checking. I was getting confused. I started to think about my breathing, talking to it, reassuring it, telling it to slow down, concentrating on deep, meticulous, breaths. The pounding in my heart subsided.

I listened to the silence all around me and thought back to when I had entered the corridor. Recalling what I had seen before this event had unfolded, the walls, the graffiti, the seats. With these images firmly planted in my head I focussed my attention on finding them using my fingers as my eyes, willing them to find something. The coal-like blackness made me question everything, the hardness of the objects if I should connect with them, how much space was between me and the wall? Moving my hands slowly around in a big arc either side I brushed an object. I retracted my hand instinctively before tentatively starting the process again, this time, assured, I would make contact with something. There it was again. It was large. The more I believed in what my fingers found the larger it appeared to become. It was within distance of where I sat, two feet maybe. So how come I had not found it the first time? Sighing with relief I placed both hands on what felt like chair seats and relaxed further as their firmness reassured me.

Although they didn't feel cold or rough as I expected, they were there and that's all that mattered.

Putting one hand against the wall to the side of them, which itself felt strange, pliable, and the other against the floor I stood up slowly so as to not bang my head on anything I couldn't see. The more I moved about the more I realised that I didn't feel in anyway concussed or drowsy and nothing ached. I had expected some small pain at least.

Everything seemed fine, with the exception of sight, although I couldn't hear the scraping of my feet as I shuffled about, which only enhanced the eeriness.

Turning on the spot I tried to decide which way I should go. Without sight I was left with only touch to guide me and, therefore, lacked the sureness of movement. 'My fingers are my eyes', I recited like a mantra.

Using the wall as a guide I headed in one of the only two directions I could, gingerly taking each step, sliding one foot slowly in front of the other, at any time expecting to kick a solid object or trip. Still I didn't hear the sound of my shuffling feet and it didn't sit right. I spoke out loud 'hello' just to confirm that I hadn't lost my hearing, I thought I heard it, but did it again to be sure. Yes, there it was, I was sure of it. Maybe I had concussion after all?

An eternity passed in this dark abyss as I inched forward, feeling the wall. My mind became more focussed as I got used to using my sense of touch instead of sight. Gradually things felt more real, more solid, I could feel the roughness again, the indentations of the plaster, some of the graffiti carvings from years before, and that made me feel more relaxed as my imagination created a picture in my head.

Finally reaching the end of the corridor I felt for the door, nothing. 'Damn'. I rotated carefully through one hundred and eighty degrees and headed back the other way. The door had to be at the opposite end.

I made my way more confidently this time, sure it was the right direction and aware that I had not encountered any obstacles. I even picked up my pace a little, every step gaining a little more confidence. My mind drifted to the unanswered questions that were filling my mind.

Why had no one come looking for me? Surely they would have missed me? They knew I was here. After all, they had directed me in here, I was meant to be helping carry some seats out. Also… the lights had been on. Maybe there'd been a power cut.

In the back of my mind a nagging thought was caught, an uncertainty, a wrongness, yet nothing obvious stood out. I pushed my way forward through the blackness as I became un-easy about being lost in the corridor, not caring whether I hit a solid object. I wanted out, and fast.

'I must be near the door', I uttered.

Panic was starting to turn to fear. I repeated my mantra 'my fingers are my eyes'.

At the other end of the corridor I scrabbled around in the darkness feeling for the door handle. Was there a door handle on the inside? The door had opened towards me when I entered, so maybe there wasn't. I felt for the frame, it had to be here.

Found it. Relief coursed through me.

It was gone.

Found it again. It was gone again.

'What the hell is going on?' I said, frustrated and annoyed. Then using both hands I searched for it again, there it was. This time I pushed hard. I wanted out. And now!

With relief I found myself back on the landing halfway up the stairs. 'Thank god' I exclaimed, as I started to calm down.

To my disbelief this was in a kind of half-darkness, vaguely lit by the light that filtered up from the foyer and the street lamps beyond the glass doors. I'd expected to find myself back in the artificial light of the fluorescent tubes, on the stairwell amongst a throng of people. Silence was all that greeted me.

Was I dreaming? Did I really go to rehearsals tonight? Today? What day was it?

Standing still, I listened, listened to the theatre breathing. Expecting to hear some sort of noise, people chatting. If there had been a power cut, everyone would still be here, somewhere!

Mark would be walking about with a torch to make sure all were safe, including me. Surely?

Maybe I had touched a live wire. Knowing how old this building was, and with so many places unexplored properly that would certainly explain how I was thrown so brutally across the corridor and why darkness had taken over the entire building. But... it didn't explain the quietness with which I was surrounded.

If Mark was trying to fix the problem then Fiona would be looking for anyone that was missing. They both knew this place like the back of their hands, not even the darkness could fool them.

What of the lack of voices?

I puzzled over whether to proceed up to the Mezzanine Theatre or down to the foyer? The foyer would provide most light as it danced over the marble floor and that was probably my best choice.

Descending the stairs I started to relax. Turning left at the bottom I expected to see a sea of familiar faces, people sitting around, some on the floor others on the only bench, a pew donated by builders converting a nearby disused church, that occupied the area.

Nothing!

I frowned, transfixed, surveying the scene, convinced that I was in a nightmare. What was going on? Where was everybody? Taking deliberate, hesitant steps I examined the front doors more closely, the wire grills that protected the glass when the theatre was closed for the night were firmly in place, padlocked signed and sealed on the outside.

Thoughts came fast, speeding into focus then spiralling away in a myriad of other ideas. Not one remained in focus long enough to fathom an answer. Then, one thought shone like a beacon in the fog, 'I am stuck here for the night'.

I looked at the wall clock, one of the original features,

amazed it was still working ninety-seven years after it was constructed and put in place. It read three thirty-five, it was dark and quiet outside so I knew it was a.m.

I didn't understand. Why hadn't someone looked for me? Surely they must have noticed I hadn't made it to the Mezzanine Theatre and then back down to the main auditorium for the remainder of the rehearsal. I'd seen so many people. Wouldn't it seem weird to turn up and not be seen again? Am I in some sort of parallel universe?

Rational thought was in danger of making a hasty exit. Where was everyone? I decided to find some way to leave the theatre. Despite it being like a second home, it was rapidly becoming uncomfortable to be there. I walked to the auditorium doors knowing if I went that way I could leave through a fire exit. Damn, the alarm would go off. But hey, they locked me in here.

The grand double doors that opened up to allow you to take the journey into the auditorium were locked. A massive chain secured them.

Now what was I supposed to do?

Turning on my heels and throwing my arms up in exasperation I caught sight of the box office. Yes, it has a phone, I could ring Mark or Fiona, I knew their mobile numbers by heart. They insisted on people having to ring them if you couldn't make rehearsals or were going to be late.

The foyer was L-shaped, at one end and next to the first set of double glass doors, waiting to serve the clientele, was the sweet kiosk. On the left and at right angle to this was the box office, then to the left of this, opposing the third set of glass doors sat the entrance to the auditorium, the chained doors. The stairs I had come down earlier were segregated by a wall to the left of these, with a large double width bland archway cutting through the stonework. The bar was in the basement accessed via another door, which was also locked, to the left of the archway.

Entry to the box office was by way of a door between it and the kiosk. Proceeding with urgency I thrust my hand towards the handle, fingers at the ready to grab the round metal handle and pull the doors towards me. I was taken aback when my hand seemed to pass easily through it, as a stone passes through the surface of water.

I froze in astonishment, unable to comprehend what had just happened.

Blinking a few times I tried to clear the image from my mind. Then with trepidation I tried again. This time slowly reaching for it and closing my grip.

Again it passed right through.

I staggered backwards and studied my hand. Again and again I tried, panic like acid rising inside, believing this was someone's sick joke and that they were laughing at me as I played right into it. One hand! Then the other! Both hands! Still I remained there, not being able to grab a hold of this supposedly solid object.

I examined the things protruding from the sleeves of my grey sweatshirt, deciphering them, contemplating them, like a scientist might study a new life form. Were they still there? Had they been cut off in some horrendous accident that I'd forgotten about, and my imagination made them seem real to my eyes.

This was a nightmare, it had to be... I rocked back on my heels as a queasy feeling washed over me and my vision blurred.

I was outside. I could see the pavement glistening with the rain. I could see warm breath rise like a cloud in the night sky.
My view slowly panned left. Was this an out of body experience or a dream? I'd known people who'd had them, describing in great detail what it was like and this was it.
I willed myself to wake up. Nothing!
Where was I? The place looked familiar. I wanted to look around

but couldn't. Only viewing it from the direction I appeared to be looking, straight ahead. I had no control. My peripheral vision seemed to be limited, as if I was wearing blinkers.

The cold night air didn't seem to be affecting me. I didn't feel it. I tried to look towards the ground, but couldn't. I could see, from the light of a near by street lamp, the arm of a jacket outstretched in front of me. It looked similar in colour, texture and design to the one I had been wearing earlier. I was standing in the shadows somewhere. It was a garden, a public garden. I couldn't make out much more detail from the limited viewpoint.

My vision sharply changed direction towards a young girl...

I was back in the foyer. Looking round in every direction, questions raced around my head like angry bees. Too many to answer! My legs turned to jelly and I slumped to the marble floor, weary and fatigued, although it didn't feel as I remembered.

3

I moved to rub my eyes, clarify what I was witnessing, but there was no contact, just like in the corridor. I couldn't feel my face, I couldn't feel my hands. Nothing. What was going on? This was a nightmare, it had to be, yet it all seemed so real. Then like watching a speeded up eclipse, the evening's events replayed in my mind. Every little snapshot, from arriving at the theatre, entering the passageway, reading the graffiti, the suffocating pain, being thrown against the wall, to coming round in the darkness. The haze that shrouded me was starting to clear.

I retraced the evidence in my head, exiting the door on the landing. The one I'd gone through, not remembering seeing it close behind me. Not really feeling the weight of it as I pushed it open. I had been anxious at the time. My mind must have played a trick on me, made me believe I had felt its weight, that I had met some resistance. At the time there was no reason to believe it was any other way.

I tried to clasp my hands together, confirm what was happening.

I couldn't feel any contact yet I could see myself doing it. I didn't understand.

I wanted to feel sick, sick to the core, but with no physical substance to back up the emotion it was in vain. The more I wished to be sick the less it was real. I wanted to feel that uncomfortable feeling of the bile rising in my throat, the foul taste that lingered afterwards just so it would make me feel real, alive.

Was I dead? The question flashed away in bold neon in my head.

The more I thought about it the less I could get my head round it. This was a bad B-Movie and I was the star, I didn't have a script and didn't know the plot, or how it was going to end. Would I be saved by some miracle? Or, was I not the star? Just some movie extra, playing the first character to leave the set?

None of this seemed wrong. I was caught with my furtive imagination writing the script as I went along. A ghost. Maybe that was it? Still with some mission to fulfil, before I could finally depart this world, and rest for all eternity.

Had I died? This question appeared like a spike of lightning in the sky. Up in the dark corridor had I left this planet without realizing? Not wanting to go.

I didn't remember incurring any lasting pain of the final breath. Was it really that painless to pass on?

I rotated on my heels and faced the street doors. I was lost. I didn't know what to do next. Where to go?

I must have stared at the doors for an eternity, my whole life cascading before me. A bus passing the theatre broke my thoughts. Yet I couldn't remember a damn thing that I'd been thinking about. The time was lost. Gone. Just like my life.

My life – gone! Just like that.

I went reeling to the floor.

A notion gripped me that I was still able to think clearly which seemed to contradict everything I had ever read or heard about ghosts and their continued role in the world, replaying situations, again and again, without comprehension or thought to change the act. A sudden strength and sobering rationale took a hold of me, a determination to do something and not just let my time be wasted. What though? I had no clear idea, although there had to be a purpose.

Leaving the theatre was the first step and judging by earlier events, if I was thinking clearly and all was true, I should be able to pass through the glass doors and the wire grills without a problem. I looked at them, they still looked so solid.

Tentatively I moved to the doors and pushed my hand towards them, it didn't meet any resistance. I smiled briefly before realising it only confirmed that I must be dead. Oh my god!

I stood looking at the doors as if they were a formidable barrier, my heart sank within me. My life was over. Gone. I couldn't take it in. I had to get out and I wasn't going to go gingerly. I was going to charge at it, either successfully exiting the building, or spectacularly failing. "Here goes," I said aloud working up the courage, wondering whether it had been aloud and not just in my head. Taking a deep breath - for all the good that it did - but it felt the right thing to do, and although I couldn't actually feel my lungs taking the breath in, it gave me the resolve I needed.

Screwing my hands into little fists, checking that was what I was doing. Normally I'd feel my fingernails digging into my palms. Nothing. I could see them clenched, dread and fear consumed me, then I took one last look at the doors, rocked on my heels and pushed forward with the thrust of a big cat about to strike at its prey.

Bam!

Less than a split second later I was out in the early morning air, studying the familiar surroundings with a new interest. Expecting to feel the cold, remembering how it had been when I arrived earlier for rehearsals. I couldn't. In a strange way, I was relieved as I suddenly realised I didn't have a coat.

Although I'd seen the bus go past, everywhere was quiet, only the street lights indicating that there was life down this side street.

I pondered what to do. Should I go home? Should I go to a friend's house? No they wouldn't know I was there if I was dead.

What do I do? I didn't know. I didn't have a purpose - that I knew of.

Work? What about work? My family? What was I going to say to them? How would they find out?

So much to consider. So much to take in and I couldn't change a damn thing. My heart sank again and I began to feel alone and helpless, emotions that I didn't think possible as a ghost.

Wearily and thoughtlessly I wandered towards the high street. I'd lost the dogged determination I had gained only minutes before but with no purpose or reason anymore there was no point heading anywhere.

At the junction of Alexandra Street and the High Street I turned left, as if to go home, out of habit rather than reason.

Time neither went fast, nor slow as I milled around lost, glancing in shop windows not registering what I saw. Nothing held my interest anymore. Why should it? My eyes followed the ground, trying to find some magic line that was going to lead me somewhere! Anywhere. Then with a start I stopped and looked once again at the nearest shop window. I had no reflection – so I was definitely dead.

Dead!

But how could I have doubted that anyway?

The whole situation perplexed me as I still felt alive inside, in my mind. Is this how real ghosts feel? I had a strange sense of foreboding, a sort of consciousness that I believed shouldn't be there. I'd seen many programs on the paranormal, none of which ever explained what I was experiencing. If death was really like this, contrary to all my beliefs, then there was a consciousness afterwards. No purpose though. A living hell! An inexplicable existence, an eternal view of the world with no participation allowed, watching from the sidelines.

After wandering around I eventually found myself standing outside 'SoundZZZ', my church. A place that encapsulated everything I was, my heart's desire, a place where nothing else mattered, I could go, forget my troubles, and dream.

A sense of playfulness gripped me. There was nothing to stop me entering the shop out of hours, not any more.

Out of habit I checked the coast was clear, not that anyone

would be able to see me anyway. Or could they? More questions.

Slowly I approached the chain-mail type shutter, with its many crafted links. Bracing myself once again, I pushed through, unsure whether my presence would set off the alarms, cringing in anticipation.

Nothing! No sound.

Inside I was a kid in a sweet shop with endless amounts of pocket money to spend as my mind was temporarily distracted from my troubles. Floodlit by the street lights outside the sight was awe-inspiring, light reflected off the shiny instruments that hung so perfectly on their stands. Even if I couldn't touch, there was nothing to stop me from pretending to gently caress the instruments which I adored. Imagining what they felt like in my hands, the USA Black Fender Telecaster I always promised one day I'd buy. Beautiful. This was heaven, yet it was also torture.

Wandering round, I took in every detail of the finely crafted Saxophones, Yamaha, Yanagisawa and Trevor James all hung so enticingly on the wall. If only I could play them all.

Hours must have passed without me realising as the noise of the rising shutters broke me from my revelry. Slowly they rose, allowing access to the front doors of the shop.

I had to get out. What if I was seen? I still didn't want to believe that I was dead and just a ghost no matter how much proof I had.

A shop assistant brushed through me sending a shockwave of truth hurtling to my core. It made me feel scared as if I had needed reassuring that this was really happening to me.

Leaving the shop, I gave way to a person walking in the opposite direction and then heeled my way home for want of a better place to go.

Fascinated by ghosts, I always believed they weren't able to go just anywhere they liked, instead they were tied to the spot where they had died, 'The Dead Spot', held by some invisible chain destined to replay that scene of their life until the Earth dissipated in a spectacle of explosions. Was I an exception to the rule? There has to be exceptions. Rules are made to be broken. I firmly believed that. Then what was I?

Heading up the High Street I avoided making physical contact with anyone, preferring to make for the big open spaces, as if I had some contagious disease. I had a couple of close calls, but at the last second I always managed to evade it, much to my relief.

Why was I bothering to head home? What could I do? My pace slowed to an amble, there was nothing there that could help me, I was sure of that. I didn't know what else...

Where was I? I recognised this place. It was my flat. I was inside my flat. But I was still on my way home, here, How? What? No, this can't be. I didn't understand. It was the same as before.

Viewing things that I had no control over.

It occurred to me that I was viewing the world through someone else's eyes. But how?

My vision was restricted as I could only look in the direction they wanted to look.

They explored each room. My rooms. Trying to uncover what? My life? But why? What was going on?

Up in the bedroom on the second floor they opened the window seat and lifted out the blankets one at a time, putting them neatly down in a pile on the floor. They seemed to be searching for something, it was not a random exploration, they knew where and what to look for. I tried to think of what I had in there but nothing came to mind.

Removing the bottom of the window seat they lifted out a box from under a loose floorboard. Opening the box slowly...

Whoah! I was back out on the street.

What was going on? Why was I seeing these things? What did it mean?

I began to feel even more disorientated than I already was. I was only two streets away from home, where now I hoped I would find some answers, so quickened my pace.

All the way I puzzled over what I kept in the box? This should have been obvious but try as I might I couldn't remember. 'What was in the box?' I repeated hoping the answer would suddenly appear. 'What was in that damn box?' I said aloud to myself.

Approaching my flat on the opposite side of the road I stood looking up at it, the top two floors of the building, hesitant about entering for some inexplicable reason yet it was my flat, my home.

"What do I do now?"

"Hello," came a voice that broke me out of my thoughts.

Glancing round I saw a girl of about sixteen or seventeen holding on to a harness attached to a sandy-coloured Labrador, just like one we used to have at home when I was a child. Her eyes were hidden by dark designer sunglasses which I found odd as it was grey and cloudy.

"Hello," she repeated. The dog patiently sat down and looked at her.

She couldn't be talking to me I thought, although her face appeared to be looking in my direction and there was no one else around, unless she speaks to her dog. She was about five feet seven inches tall with long brunette hair tied neatly back, and an encapsulating smile that I found hard to tug my gaze from.

"Hellooo," she re-iterated, extending the 'o' sound as if trying to make a point that I was being rude, which I wasn't. Not intentionally

"Hi," I retorted, not expecting to get a reply.

"Are you lost?" She promptly replied.

"Sorry?" This was more a question than an apology.

"Are you lost? You seem to be lost. I can't help but sense you feel lost."

"Mmmm... No... I... don't..." I didn't understand. No one had paid any attention to me in the shop or on my way home, no eye contact, smiles, anything. Or had I just not noticed? Suddenly I'm having a conversation with a complete stranger, who seemed to know I was there.

"Why are you just standing there then? Don't you have somewhere to go?" She said with a voice as sweet and soft as I had ever heard before.

"Are you a ghost?" I asked hesitantly.

"No." She smiled showing a line perfect white teeth. "I am blind though. I'm Ann-Marie, this is my guide dog Mojo." She patted Mojo's head affectionately. "He knows you are there too, he can sense you." She stated everything so matter of factly as if it was an everyday occurrence.

"How? Why are you talking to me?" My questions sounded rude, almost aggressive.

"You felt lost. I don't know how I know, I just do. Are you?"

"What?"

"Lost?"

"Oh. Mmm... I... suppose... I must be. But how do you know I'm here. I was in a shop this morning and no one gave me a second glance. I didn't think anyone could see me."

"I can't, I'm blind," she said, sighing heavily.

"Sorry."

"It's not your fault. But I can feel you, or rather I can sense your presence. Mojo can too, animals are very sensitive to spirits. I can talk with the dead. It used to be scary, but now." She shrugged her shoulders and frowned. "I've had some really good talks with spirits, they don't judge me like some people."

Amazed. This all seemed so bizarre. "I suppose."

There was a pause before she added, "you seem too solid."

"What?" I had no idea what she meant.

"I mean. Ghosts that I've spoken to normally don't have any

sort of substance as such, but you do." She pursed her thin lips. In a strange way she compounded my own thoughts.

"I'm not sure that I understand," I replied.

The door slammed and I was looking at Ann-Marie and Mojo. She was alone.

But I was just talking to her.

Turning to face down the road I was heading away from her. A hundred yards farther along I stopped in front of a blue car. It was my car! I was seeing everything and was there. Yet there was nothing I could do. I had no power, no control.

Maybe I would catch a glimpse of the reflection of the person whose life I was viewing in the glass of the car.

Damn, the angles were all wrong.

Sitting in the car, the person was familiar with everything, the krooklock, the ignition, starting the car, he, I surmised as his hands looked too manly to be a woman's, rammed it into first gear, the grating sound of clashing cogs was followed by a thud as the gear found it's footing. The man planted his foot firmly on the accelerator and, almost too late, turned the steering wheel and glanced the bumper of the car in front. He didn't appear to care speeding off up the road. Every gear change was worse than the one before as the sound of crunching gears echoed along the road. I took a cursory glance at the girl with the dog.

I was watching the car disappear up the road standing with Ann-Marie again.

"Hello. Are you alright?" I heard her say, but it took a while to register. "You were gone for a minute. You alright?" she said with a friendly, inquisitive manner.

"I don't know," I stuttered, still not sure what to make of the situation.

"What happened?"

I looked at Ann-Marie, questioning reality. "I don't know." I paused to compose my thoughts. "I get these visions." I started sounding like a patient talking to their doctor. "Well, they are not exactly visions. I don't know how to describe them. It's strange, one minute I was standing here, then, I could see you from over the road, but through someone else's eyes." I paused, realizing how absurd it all sounded.

"What do you mean?"

This strange girl was talking to me as if I was some old friend she known for years and was just going through a tricky spell. I continued. "I came out of that door, my front door." I animated my speech with hand motions forgetting she was blind, but it clarified everything to me. "Not me, them. I think. I looked over here, then went to my car…" This was beginning to sound even more bizarre but I continued anyway. "… got in and drove away." As an afterthought I added. "My dad must have returned it, he must have posted the keys through the letter box earlier." I looked at Ann-Marie. "Then I was here again, with you." I half expected her to turn and walk away at this point. I would have done if it were me.

She stood thoughtfully digesting all the information. "I'm getting cold. Why don't you come back to my place and tell me more. I'm not sure I can help but I might be able to explain. Home Mojo." She commanded before I had time to answer. Mojo sprang to attention. "Was it a bad storm last night?"

I stood for a second in puzzlement looking at her walk away. Then I remembered the storm last night, it had been yesterday, so it was only the next day, Monday, and the late autumn sun was doing little to warm the day, not that I could tell, only the warm wisps of breath that had risen as she spoke gave it away.

I was still stunned by the fact that she thought she could explain my predicament. She seemed nice enough and in the short time I'd been in this state I had tasted loneliness and it was nice to share my thoughts and feelings. I walked with Ann-Marie and Mojo to West Road.

She seemed warm and caring with a way about her, a patience, a curiosity that wasn't overpowering, a genuine wish to help. I found myself wanting her to. What could she do though?

"Thank you," I said, somewhat lamely catching her up.

"It's okay." She smiled.

We walked in silence until she asked me to tell her what had happened, so I started relaying the events of the last twelve or so hours.

All the time I was talking, I watched her. Fascinated by the way Mojo was her eyes. I wouldn't have believed she was blind if I couldn't see the dog, intuitively they acted together, pausing at the edge of a road until Mojo gave the all clear, so natural, a perfect partnership of trust. Occasionally this fascination of mine would break the flow of my story, just for a split second before I would continue.

Ann-Marie appeared to have an awareness of her surroundings that most sighted people took for granted, after a while I realised that she would wait until she felt we were not within earshot of anyone before asking me any questions.

She didn't live that far away from me, Tickfield Avenue, a ten minute walk for me on my own. It was so named because it used to be the site where three clockmakers were situated at the beginning of the century. One of them, Browen and Sons, had made the clock that hung in the foyer of the theatre. He started to make it before his death in 1883, whereupon his eldest son finished it and presented it as a gift to the theatre, a way of saying thank you for the good times his father had enjoyed there. Gradually the clockmakers disappeared one by one. After years of the factories being empty they were bombed out during the World War II, a row of terraced houses took their place.

Ann-Marie's house was typical of these with the exception of a small porch which clung to the front of the house differentiating it from the others. Double glazing had changed the overall look of the place, the standard sash windows were gone replaced with modern openers. The house went back a long way and was immaculately decorated, warm and inviting - it felt like a home, if somewhat a little busy with patterns.

4

Ann-Marie removed Mojo's harness before going into the kitchen. She made tea for them both, placing a bowl of his favourite watered down treat on the floor where he lapped up whilst I watched both, admiring their friendship.

We then went into the lounge leaving Mojo to join us a few minutes later, when he curled up at Ann-Marie's feet, resting his head on his tail and closing his eyes. Ann-Marie bent over and stroked him affectionately, a sign of her appreciation that he was always there for her. Mojo briefly lifted his head and licked her hand before settling down again.

As I watched I reflected back to that morning, coming round in the dark corridor, alone. Although that didn't bother me, it was the fact that no one had even missed me. I'd seen nearly twenty people that evening when I arrived for rehearsals, my supposed friends, yet I had not been missed. It was like a knife in the heart.

I looked at Ann-Marie as she sat in the armchair, her eyes danced around lazily as if trying to focus on a point in the distance, a point she couldn't see, yet she appeared unaware of it. She had dull brown eyes and I wondered if that was as a result of going blind.

Everything she did seemed so effortless as if she had a virtual map in her mind, the layout of the house. Her tea was on the coffee table next to where she sat, her hand moved instinctively towards it only briefly fumbling for the handle.

"You're watching me?" Her words startled me.

"Sorry. Yes!" Although she could not see, she had great perception of the world around her.

"Why?"

It was such an innocent question. Yet I found myself feeling guilty, guilty for watching, being curious about her world, of what I didn't know.

"I… I… mmm… just amazed at how easy you find your way around. I…"

"It's alright," she said, trying to ease my obvious nervousness. "I have been blind for about five or six years now. Kinda familiarise myself with my surroundings." She replaced the cup where it had once stood. "My mum makes sure she doesn't move furniture around, so it's almost instinctive. After all we've lived here for," she paused, feeling for the answer, "about four or five years."

Finding my voice again. "I just find it incredible. I mean you're blind yet you move around so easily. I've seen normal sighted people be more clumsy."

She smirked.

"I was eleven when I lost my sight. I've never seen this house so I've had to build up a picture of it in my head, a map. I use patterns, the wallpaper, the feel of the carpet under my feet. We moved here when I was twelve. I think there were too many memories in Staffordshire. That's where my dad died." She stopped to think, her face showing the loss. "I was ten at the time…"

I was out in the open, a wooded area that I didn't recognise, and I wasn't alone. Yet I couldn't hear or see anyone else.

Somebody was there, somewhere.

There was blood on my hands, the hands I was seeing. I could feel my heart pumping adrenalin round my body, energising every muscle. It was all real yet I had no control, a puppet being controlled by the hands of its maker.

I didn't understand.

Looking round I checked the scene. Something had occurred.

But what?

I gathered some leaves and wiped the knife being held in my right hand. I'd seen it before yet couldn't place it.

Why did I recognise it?

I started to run slowly through the trees. Now I could hear heavy breathing and the slurping of the wet mud underfoot. Occasionally my feet would slip throwing me off balance making me use my arms to steady myself.

A dirt trail stretched out in front of me, a faint path between the blanket of wild nettles covering the ground, trees spearing it and reaching for the sky, some short, some tall, ivy wound its way up the trunks, trying to reach the canopy that loomed up above.

Stationary again, I rotated on the spot, looking at the fauna that stretched out in all directions. There was nothing except woodland. If it had been any other time I would have enjoyed the outing but I didn't know what was going on. Didn't know what it meant. Where was I?

There are many woods in the local area and to the untrained eye, mine, I couldn't tell one from the other.

On the move again, I was walking this time, kicking my way through the bracken and undergrowth, grabbing more handfuls of leaves trying to clean my hands. I wanted to look, to see if I could find a cut, so much blood, there had to be a cut somewhere, but I was forced to look where I was going.

In the distance I saw a couple walking hand in hand with a dog off its lead and poking its nose into anything and everything. I looked at them. They saw me but didn't seem to register me. I quickened my pace towards a junction of paths ahead.

Looking all ways I saw a gate to my right in the distance. Walking towards it I slowed my pace as if on a Sunday stroll, enjoying the…

"… Daniel… Daniel…"

"What? Sorry." I said with a start. I was back in Ann-Marie's lounge.

"You'd gone again, I mean you were here, your soul was, but your spirit was," she searched for the word, "distracted."

"I don't understand what's happening." Agitated I walked to the window hoping to find the answers to all my questions staring back at me. I looked through the glass into the street beyond, not really seeing it. I turned again to face Ann-Marie, who was staring at me. It didn't matter where I went she always knew where to look.

Silence filled the room. I didn't know what to say. I wondered if this was the only person I'd ever be able to talk to again.

Ann-Marie got up and immediately Mojo was alert and ready by her side. She rested her hand on his head. "Ann-Marie's room, Mojo." Grabbing her tea they left the room, leaving me standing perplexed.

"Daniel, you coming?" she called from the hallway. It took me a couple of seconds to realise what she had said. Bemused, I followed.

I caught her up at the bottom of the stairs where she had slowed, although still making it all look so natural, Mojo was to her right, her left hand resting on the banister, just in case she should slip or loose her footing. She didn't. I expected her to and followed in muted curiosity.

At the top of the stairs we turned back on ourselves heading towards the front of the house. Family photos littered the hall walls. I studied them, recognising her in some of them. One in particular caught my eye.

A picture taken on a canal boat, a bright sunny day, she must have been eight or nine, the man in the photo I took as being her father. He looked young, mid to late thirties, slightly greying hair with a good physique judging by the biceps protruding from the sleeveless t-shirt that he wore. Ann-Marie was laughing. I could almost imagine myself there, listening to father and daughter playing happily together. They looked so close, so blissfully unaware that his life was going to be tragically cut short.

I smiled. Then I thought about my own parents. Up to now I had only spared a brief second to think of them.

My parents lived relatively close to me. I could walk it in forty-five minutes. They had a small, well kept bungalow, downsizing after I moved out, a bit of a hint that they didn't want me to move back. I didn't mind, I didn't want to move back, I was… had been happy in my flat. I tried to see them at least once every couple of weeks calling in on my way home from work. Sometimes though, I found myself too busy, wrapped up in my own world. Now, although I can see them, will they ever see me? I thought a chill ran through me but then doubted it was possible in my current state of being.

Solemnly I walked into Ann-Marie's large and sparsely furnished room. The large bay window, hiding behind heavy net curtains, dominated it. There was a smaller single window to the left of this, in front of which sat a wicker chair with two cushions placed neatly on it. A small desk stood in the bay. There were two large wardrobes built into the alcoves either side of the chimney breast.

Ann-Marie was sitting on the edge of her double bed opposite the bay window, she grabbed a remote control from her bedside table and turned the stereo on, which sat on a chest of drawers to the left of the bedroom door, Robbie Williams' 'Angels' was playing.

What irony I thought.

"What's it like?" she enquired, laying back on her pillows hands behind her head and Mojo with his head resting on the bed looking at her.

"What's what like?"

"Being… you know. What you are."

Not sure how to answer I stared at her. It was a simple question and one I hadn't given much thought to.

"It's weird. Mentally I feel nothing has changed." It occurred to me that I hadn't eaten or drunk since it happened. "I don't need to eat. I think I don't, I mean, I don't feel hungry or thirsty." I started to pace the room, wondering how to explain what I felt. "It's hard to explain exactly. I know I'm here, but I'm not..."

I was in a car, travelling fast. The sun hung low in the sky like a fiery disc piercing my eyes. I guessed it was mid-morning.

The speedometer showed I was travelling at fifty miles an hour.

I could see the hands on the steering wheel clearly, they were streaked with grass stains. The knuckles were white from gripping the steering wheel so tightly. Occasionally the fingers on the right hand flexed open as if they ached from physical exertion.

I could sense an air of arousal, but it didn't feel like it was of a sexual nature, more out of a feeling of completing a task, a feeling of being alive, the whole body pulsing with an electrical charge.

Looking ahead I hoped to see a sign, some indication of where I was, where I was going. Typical, nothing.

Flashing blue lights appeared on the opposite side of the dual carriageway. The sirens got louder as they drew closer before hurtling past without hesitation.

A hand reached up and adjusted the rear-view mirror I hoped I would catch a glimpse of the driver's hair, face, eyes, but it happened too quick and the image was a blur.

The blue lights disappeared in the distance behind me.

"... not what?"

"Sorry."

"You went again."

"Did I? Yes." Then I mumbled. "But where was I though?" I thought of how to best clarify. "I'm seeing things. Feeling things. Sort of. I don't know how to explain, it's weird. I don't know who and I don't always know where. And I don't have any control." Ann-Marie looked confused. "Like this morning when I met you. That time when I wasn't with you. I could see you from across the road. It's like I'm in two places at once, but can only focus on one situation at a time. I have no control over it when it happens. I don't know what any of it means or if it is real."

Ann-Marie sat there, silent, obviously thinking I'd gone mad, or she had by listening to me.

Mojo's head lifted sharply, ears pricked. I could hear the sound of a key entering a lock.

"That's my mum." She reached over to the bedside table and picked up her clock, it didn't have any glass covering the analogue face. With her fingertips she felt the position of the hands. "She usually gets home about now for lunch."

There were footfalls on the stairs and within a minute a tall slender woman with rosy cheeks walked through the doorway, undoing her overcoat and taking off her scarf. She must have been nearly six foot in her heels. Her brunette hair was cut into a neat bob. Her complexion deceived her years. A pleasant smile greeted us, she had a warm look in her eyes. Unfortunately for Ann-Marie, only I could see it.

I wondered what images of her mum were planted in Ann-Marie's mind, from the time when she could see.

"I'm going to do some lunch. Do you want some? Or have you eaten?" Her dulcet tones echoed round the room like a warm summer breeze.

"No I haven't. Yes thanks."

"Aunt Rose said she might pop in later..." She turned and walked back towards the top of the stairs. "...as she's got to go the chiropodist. Said she might take a breather and call in, take the weight off her corns."

Ann-Marie looked pensive. "Yeah, okay," she called back, then clicking her fingers, turned and faced me. "Yes," she exclaimed in whisper. "Aunt Rose, of course, she should be able to help."

I looked at Ann-Marie who had 'an air of the cat that had got the cream' expression. That this one person was going to solve everything. That she could help with my predicament.

She didn't elaborate, but left me to fill in the blanks. I remained clueless, my brain throwing up all sorts of suggestions; maybe she was a spiritualist, a psychic, a witch. All seemed too far fetched to be for real, I'd only ever been interested in anything spiritual or ghostly from a fictional point of view, pure entertainment. But I was experiencing something completely unknown, so anything must be possible.

Downstairs we heard the radio go on, a sudden blast of noise, before being turned down to a more lilting background sound quickly followed by the 'Southend Local Radio jingle'.

"I'm going to have some lunch, you can come if you like, or you can stay here." Ann-Marie got off her bed, Mojo ready at her side.

"I'll stay here if you don't mind."

"Whatever, I'll leave the radio on. Come on Mojo, kitchen. I won't be long." She walked out of the room, one hand on Mojo's head, the other searching out the door frame, then the banister that would lead her to the top of the stairs and guide her safely down.

Left by myself, I surveyed the room more closely, relaxing and taking in the surrounding details.

It was a plain-looking room, one colour seemed to dominate, beige – a warm but boring tone. Yet, on closer inspection, the room was not as plain as it initially appeared, more thought had gone into the décor than met the eye. The detail was in the textures and I recalled what Ann-Marie had said earlier about patterns being her virtual map. That is what made this room different. Looking more closely at the patterns, each wall had different textured wallpaper, I wanted to run my hands over them and feel what Ann-Marie would feel. I tried, but felt nothing. Four walls, four patterns. The carpet had a heavy circular pattern on it. Even the duvet had bold braiding round the edges. Anything that could be done to bring this room alive to touch had been done. The minutest of details, patterns were the colours for this room and for Ann-Marie.

After thinking about the love and affection with which this room had been furnished, my mind drifted back to the question of Aunt Rose. How was she going to help?

5

I sat down in the wicker chair and for a moment questioned whether I was actually sitting in it, or just levitating over it, it was a strange concept that I couldn't fathom. I could walk through solid things, yet still manage to sit on them or was it that I just believed I could, I didn't know and it was confusing me to try and solve the riddle.

I reflected on my own parents. What will they do when they don't hear anything from me? It would take a while, but they would miss me eventually. What exactly would they find out? Sadness wafted over the good and bad memories. I wanted to cry, yet the emotion didn't seem real enough, more sort of disconnected, somehow half hearted. I sat feeling cold and isolated, lost in a world I didn't belong to, not knowing where I was meant to be or what I was meant to do.

I was awoken from my melancholy by footfalls as Ann-Marie and Mojo entered the room. She paused for a split second as if remembering an important piece of information before continuing to the bed where she sat down, casting her eye in my direction.

"That's my favourite chair. I sit there whenever I need a hug and no one's around." I looked at her surprised by her openness. "When I was young my dad used to sit in it with me on his knees reading my favourite stories to me." She smiled reflectively. "He did all the voices too. Aunt Rose!" She broke from her thoughts as if finding the answer she'd been looking for. "She is a spiritualist and a white witch. Although, she won't tell that to Mum."

"A white what?"

"A white witch." Without seeing me, she must have sensed my reaction. "It's alright, she's a good witch."

I sank deeper into the chair, despair smothering me. What was happening? I looked across at Ann-Marie who looked so normal yet was talking about witchcraft as if it was an everyday occurrence. Then I caught what she had said about her Mum.

"Why won't you tell your Mum?"

"She doesn't feel comfortable about that sort of thing. I remember once when we were having a chat and the subject just sort of came up…" She thought for a second, then continued. "… can't remember why. Never mind. Anyway this was before we knew Aunt Rose. But the subject came up and Mum said she didn't believe in that sort of thing, it's all gobbledy-gook and gave her the creeps, so what she doesn't know won't hurt her. She's not really my aunt though, Aunt Rose that is, just someone we met one day in the doctor's surgery."

"A doctor's surgery!"

"Yeah, we hadn't been down here long…"

"Sorry… what was that Ann-Marie?" came the voice from the hallway.

"Nothing Mum, just singing along to the radio."

Her mother poked her head round the door. "Aunt Rose's appointment's about two-thirty, she will probably call in about four. You know what she's like when she gets talking. I'm off now, be back about sevenish, want to get a couple of bits of shopping on the way home."

"Okay Mum, see you later." Her Mum vanished from sight. She seemed to glide silently down the stairs before we heard the catch of the door click securely in place.

Ann-Marie continued making herself more comfortable on the bed, Mojo laying on the floor. "Where was I. Oh yeah… we hadn't been down here long, we were just sitting there in the doctor's surgery. It was so weird. I can't even remember why we were there." She paused looking for the answer, but nothing came. "Anyway we were sitting there waiting quietly when this lady just turns round to my Mum."

'Terrible to lose someone so close dear, always hard on the young ones.'

'Excuse me,' my Mum said, astounded by the woman's sudden interest.

'It's always hard when you lose someone so close.'

"Aunt Rose spoke so softly that you couldn't help but feel at ease. The waiting room was empty, only us three. I didn't have Mojo then, not that we would have taken him anyway. The whole situation was so surreal, I'd never seen my mum talk to people she didn't know. Then without warning she just looked this lady straight in the eye. There must have been a connection 'cos, without warning, the sluice gates just opened. All Mum's pent up feelings came rushing out so fast I thought she wasn't going to take a breath. Up to that point, after Dad's death she'd always been so focussed, sterner that she had been before.

"Then, for some unknown reason, this woman, Aunt Rose, seemed to hold the key to unlock Mum's deepest feelings, everything she'd ever wanted to say, but couldn't." Then Ann-Marie added more reflectively, "the doctor's face must have been a picture when he came out to call her in, my mum that is, he said, 'Mrs Lewington?'

'Yes... no...' She blew her nose and then added. '... I'm fine now, I think... Yes, definitely. Much better', in between wiping her eyes and regaining her composure. 'Come on Ann-Marie let's go home. Thank you,' she said to the woman. And then she did something which I would never have believed, if I hadn't witnessed it with my own ears, she invited her back to our house for a cup of tea. Aunt Rose accepted quite readily.

"Stunned, the doctor continued, a little put out, judging by his voice.

'Miss Davies, you're next then.'

'No I'm fine thank you Doctor.'

'What? If all my patients could be cured so easily, I'd be out of a job.'

"Then he huffed and went back into his office totally perplexed." Ann-Marie smiled to herself and sniggered, "I was astounded."

I sat quietly listening.

"Well you had to be there. When we got back to our house Aunt Rose and my Mum must have talked for hours. I was starving but I didn't want to interrupt, I think Mum had felt so isolated up to that point, but now felt relaxed, at ease with life again.

"When I did go down to the kitchen because my stomach couldn't hold on any longer I felt Aunt Rose give me a knowing stare, it was quite eerie at first. Then when Mum left us to go to the toilet she spoke to me.

'You feel things don't you dear,' she said all mysteriously.

'I'm not sure what you mean,' I replied defensively.

'I can sense it dear, you feel the spirits. You talk to them sometimes don't you? It's okay dear, I'm not going to hurt you. You don't know what to make of your special gift.' She emphasized the word 'gift?' 'I can help you master it. If you want to that is?'

"I stood there silent not knowing what to do, I wanted to confess but it was so strange, how could a complete stranger know things about me, things I wasn't even sure about..."

I was holding something close to my face, it was difficult to see. It wasn't something. It was someone. The back of someone's head. I was holding them tight, against their will. Their hair was in my face. My hand over their mouth I could feel their warm breath.

I felt the cold on my face or the face I was seeing through. Before, it had always just been pictures, a blinkered view, but pictures. Now,

I could feel, sense, the coldness of the air.

There was struggling, we were awkwardly walking, moving forward along a path I'd never seen before. From my perspective it seemed secluded but I couldn't tell.

I dragged the body I was holding to the ground, eventually laying 'the someone' in front of me. Surveying the area, I noted we were definitely in a secluded area, close to a cropping of trees that I didn't recognise. A field stretched out in front of me as far as the eye could see.

Suddenly there was a shot…

"What the …" I stated as suddenly I was back with a jolt, shaking "What's going on?"

"Was that another one?"

"One what? Yes. But worse though." I was trying to calm my shaky voice.

"What? How?" Ann-Marie sat bolt upright on the edge of her bed looking at me.

"It seemed more real. The cold. The hair. The person." I saw the images flash through my mind again.

"What happened this time?"

I explained as best I could what I saw, and what I felt yet visualising the images just made me feel more agitated. "I don't like this," I exclaimed. I wanted to scream, rake it all from my mind. I was living a vivid nightmare and it grabbed me when I least expected it. I stood up and paced the room as if that would help placate my racing mind. "What did it mean? What am I doing here?" I almost shouted. "This is ridiculous I'm dead, yet, these feelings, these visions." Ann-Marie sat listening to me as I vented, "I always believed when you died you became a ghost. You don't have feelings. Just roam the earth, day in, day out, the same place. But no, it has to be different." My sarcasm wasn't lost on Ann-Marie.

"Aunt Rose might be able to explain things. She knows things, she helped me…" Ann-Marie said, trying to ease my anxiety. I could feel her looking at me.

"How will she be able to help? I'm dead," I said punctuating the last words with venom and stepping towards Ann-Marie, Mojo sat up and bared his teeth ready to protect her.

"There's no need for you to be like that." Ann-Marie's hurt voice penetrated my own thoughts as she patted Mojo, reassuring him that it was okay. "She will. She knows things, can tell things… just give her a chance. It took me a while but once I let her in she helped me develop my 'gift'." She lifted both hands, flexing the first two fingers of each to emphasize the phrase. "Believe me, Daniel, she will help you sort this out." She let the last sentence settle and, reluctantly, I knew that I didn't have any other option.

I stepped back and Mojo once again lay down on the floor. The radio filled the room, easing the slight awkwardness. I turned to the window to watch the world outside again, hoping to clarify answers to questions I wanted to ask.

The impulse to leave was compelling yet I fought the urge, even though I was uncomfortable and felt this was all futile. I didn't know where I'd go anyway so what would be the point. Ann-Marie was my best and only option and that was an injustice to Ann-Marie, she had befriended me, she didn't have to, I would never have known. I couldn't understand why she was trying to help. I was ashamed that I'd even questioned her.

"You're not a normal spirit like the ones I'd usually speak to." She'd relaxed back on the bed, resting her head on the pillows pushed up against the headboard, feet outstretched.

"What do you mean?" I found myself facing the wicker chair and tried to picture Ann-Marie and her father sitting there, him reading her a story.

"You feel things far too passionately. Spirits I normally communicate with don't feel the way you do. They know things, sure, but feelings they once felt. Now they are just stuck here in this world waiting for their purpose to be fulfilled." She paused, swallowed slower, then looked directly at me, I could feel her eyes digging into my back, I turned and looked at her. "My Dad had a purpose. To guide me when I first went blind. His spirit didn't crossover... just hung around, although he didn't know why at first. His purpose wasn't clear, that was until I suffered Meningitis... that's how I lost my sight. He... we started to communicate just after. It was like losing one sense and gaining another. I was scared at first, of the blindness, and a little of him, but for the wrong reasons. He helped me come to terms with being blind. I s'pose I believed I'd gained something through losing my sight. I'd been able to speak to my father again, tell him that I missed him. He told me he couldn't stay, and until then he didn't know his purpose, once his task was done he went... for good." Ann-Marie gulped hard biting back the sadness.

She twisted awkwardly and reached for a small bear which sat near her pillows. Her hand fumbling around until she held it tight, squeezing it affectionately, a tear formed in the corner of her eye.

I was touched by her sign of affection and shaken by my own disrespect for all she was trying to do for me.

Once again the radio was the only audible sound to break the silence that rested between us. I knew I was bad company on a one to one basis, it was only now that it was hitting home just how bad I could be, how thoughtless.

Mojo's head perked up before the sound of the doorbell reached us.

"That'll be Aunt Rose," Ann-Marie stated with certainty, placing the teddy bear back down on the pillow. "Come Mojo."

I followed them to the front door in silence where I stood in anticipation of the person I was about to meet. Even a strange nervousness settled on my shoulders. My imagination started firing random images of films that I'd seen, putting together a formidable picture of an old hag, dark dirty clothes, a slight stench of some strange concoction that she'd been mixing in her cauldron. A picture of a woman who walked with a stoop, had a humped back, buckteeth, and long black straggly hair.

Instead, the face that greeted me was that of a very well dressed, pleasant looking woman in her mid-sixties with bright young eyes and weathered skin. She walked with a stick although she didn't appear to need it. She didn't have a stoop or a hump. Her demeanour was stern yet when she spoke the softness of her voice blew away that facade.

"Hello Annie dear," she said, then suddenly sensing me. "Ahh," she looked in my direction, "you have a friend with you."

I turned, expecting to see someone else standing behind me like a shadow.

"This is Daniel." Ann-Marie closed the door, allowing Aunt Rose to walk towards me.

I was running through a field of overgrown grass and weeds, breathing heavily as the cold air hit my warm face. There was no obvious destination in sight, just hedges to my right and ahead.

Looking down at the ground, it was muddy, I glanced at my shoes caked in mud.

A shot rang out.

Then another, this time it hit something solid to my right.

I didn't like this. I couldn't fathom what was going on?

I saw the ground loom closer.

My face was in the mud. I'd fallen. Slowly I got back up, my limbs weary, my breathing laboured. Each gasp deeper and longer than the previous, I could feel it. My throat was dry from the exertion. The exhaustion.

I heard a shout from behind, a long way off. I was expecting to turn to face it, but no, whoever I was, was determined to outrun the danger, battling on, step by step until finally reaching a hedge. I dived through a gap and out beyond the field into a country lane.

Walking, I tried to control my breathing. After a few steps I walked more assuredly, I coughed occasionally as the cold air reached the warm cavities of my lungs.

A car horn sounded...

I was back in the hallway again.

"Oh dear!" said Aunt Rose, putting her hands to her face, fear in her eyes as she studied me. I felt like an exhibit in a museum.

"What is it Aunt Rose?" Ann-Marie asked anxiously.

"This is not good, Annie dear, not good at all."

"What isn't Aunt Rose? Aunt Rose?"

Aunt Rose's face had filled with a deathly paleness as she took a faulty step backwards putting out her hand to steady herself.

"I sense death, Annie dear, death." Aunt Rose's voice trembled as she pointed to me.

I didn't understand. I glanced from one to the other bewildered waiting for an answer. Anything. Ann-Marie looked at me. Aunt Rose stared at me as if caught in headlights of a fast approaching car, her hands still at her face, one covering her mouth, the other at her cheek, her eyes still wide, her stick had fallen to the floor.

"I nee... glass of water, please Annie dear." Aunt Rose choked on the words.

"Mojo, kitchen," Ann-Marie urgently commanded. She walked straight through me and I shuddered although I felt nothing.

Aunt Rose and I stood there, a stand down before the fighters drew their guns.

"Need to sit down," she muttered to herself but loud enough for me to hear. Wearily she turned placing her hands on the door frame that was to her left, before heading into the lounge, where she sat down on the sofa.

Ann-Marie came back with the water.

"Aunt Rose?" she called out.

"In here dear. I had to sit down." Ann-Marie followed the voice. "Just to your left." Aunt Rose reached up to clasp the glass held in Ann-Marie's hands. "Thank you Annie dear."

Ann-Marie sat down in the armchair she had occupied earlier in the day, Mojo by her feet, her hand resting halfway down his back.

"Are you okay Aunt Rose?"

I had followed Mojo into the room and was standing next to the open door. Not sure if I should stay, the reaction by Aunt Rose caused me to feel awkward and question my presence in the room. Was I evil and didn't know?

"What was your name again?" Aunt Rose enquired regaining her composure.

"Daniel," I answered as if talking to a school teacher.

"Whatever I felt has gone... but it's connected to you... I could feel death. A very strong association." She focussed on me, her voice taking on a more definite tone. "The touch of death and it was through you. Wherever you went for that short time, you were in the presence of evil." She drank some more water.

Shell-shocked I didn't know what to say. I could feel Ann-Marie's stare penetrating me.

After a few minutes Aunt Rose asked me to explain what I had seen in the vision, which I did, in as much detail as I could remember. Both listened intently without comment. I also detailed my earlier visions and even though Ann-Marie had heard them before she still took in every detail as though it was the first time.

A thought occurred to me and as if reading my mind Aunt Rose said. "If you are wondering, yes I can hear you, like many who have the gift."

6

Aunt Rose settled herself on the settee beckoning me to her. "Now Daniel, come and sit next to me dear." Her warm enchanting voice broke down any resistance I might have had.

Sitting down I didn't appear to make any impact on the soft, pillow-like cushions, still she knew I was there.

"Yes," she said in the stereotypical way that I'd heard many a palm reader use in films and I began to wonder what I was letting myself in for. "You have a strong aura, a very strong, powerful force. I can see why you felt Daniel's presence Annie dear."

"It's like nothing I've ever felt before, I knew there was something different I just couldn't put my finger on it," Anne-Marie replied, pleased.

"Daniel, please rest your hands on mine." Aunt Rose held out her hands, twisting her body slightly towards me. Tentatively I responded. I had always been sceptical about this sort of thing, believing it was just mumbo jumbo. Now all my beliefs were being tested, pushed to their limits.

As I acquiesced to her a charge drove through me like an electrical pulse of energy, coursing its way to every fibre of my ghostly being. In an instant Aunt Rose was in a trance-like state, eyes glazed, pupils dilated. She stared directly at me penetrating my inner self.

Her presence grew stronger within me as she explored and searched for clues. I became relaxed and comfortable as the process continued, all my initial scepticism fading.

Aunt Rose's eyes gradually widened in enlightenment, an understanding, followed by bewilderment.

With a weak voice she spoke. "A strong powerful force is consuming you, making you weaker. You can't fight it. It's becoming stronger... and..."

Her body slumped backwards into the settee, her hands breaking the connection with my own. Her arms flopping onto her lap before her left arm twitched momentarily sending the glass of water she had rested on the arm of the settee crashing to the floor. The contents floated initially on the deep brown pile before rapidly soaking in. Aunt Rose's head flopped down to her chest and she lay there motionless.

I glanced over at Ann-Marie, who had been listening intently, expecting her to jump up to attend Aunt Rose, but she sat there. I was stunned at the lack of compassion being shown and stared from one to the other, not knowing what to do.

"Ann-Marie!" I exclaimed, more alarmed than I intended.

"What?" she said nonchalantly.

"Your Aunt." The urgency made my voice break which surprised me as I wasn't real. "She's not moving. I think she passed out, or something."

Ann-Marie sat coolly looking towards her, her face contorted in concentration. Then she announced, "she's fine." Stunned, I sat dumbfounded. "Sometimes when she feels things, it can take a lot out of her. Sort of saps her mental energy. She'll be okay in couple of minutes."

"How can you be so sure? How do you know?" The questions came in quick succession.

"If I concentrate hard enough I can feel her aura. She taught me how to tune into her. She'll be fine."

"Oh. Okay." I wasn't sure as I learnt more and more about Ann-Marie's surprising talents. "She spilt her glass of water on the floor," I added lamely.

"I didn't hear it break."

"No, it's in one piece."

Ann-Marie got up and moved towards the settee to pick up

the fallen glass, letting her hands feel their way over the carpet to locate it. Then, leaving the room, I heard the sliding of her hand along the wall as she walked towards the kitchen, Mojo following a second later. When she returned a few minutes later the glass had been refilled. She placed some kitchen towel on the carpet and proceeded to soak up as much of the water as possible.

Groggily, Aunt Rose came round, placing her hands on her forehead. "Oh dear... my, I haven't felt anything like that before." Her voice shaking as the words rattled out of her.

"What?" I said anxiously, desperate to know anything she had discovered. "What happened?" I pleaded not letting her answer. "What is it? Please. Tell me," I couldn't contain the fright in my voice imagining all the possibilities, concerned and worried that she'd felt something, but what?

Ann-Marie proffered the glass of water to Aunt Rose which she took gratefully although she was still pale and a little confused about her whereabouts.

I wanted to shake her, making her come round quicker. I wanted answers. I wanted them now. In my frustration I got up and paced the room. "Come on, what was it? What did you feel?" Impatience was something I always had as a child growing up and it had driven my parent mad, it almost sounded ungrateful. "Please. Tell me..." clenching my fists in frustration.

Ann-Marie looked at me. "It's no good talking to her. It takes her a while to recover. She won't be able to hear you. Give her a few minutes and then she'll re-focus on you. Aunt Rose?"

The room fell silent, both Ann-Marie and myself stared at the drowsy figure on the settee like expectant parents as she drank from the glass, one large continuous gulp.

The waiting was frustrating. I wanted to know more. Find out about me. As I pondered that thought a pain took a hold from deep inside me, a biting pain that I'd never felt before, the nerve endings in my fingers and toes electrified...

... I was locking my car door, watching for any prying eyes in the shadows. It was a street that was familiar to me, yet I couldn't place it. I heard the thud of the central locking, clicking securely in place. I turned around. Scanned the street, no one about, a cat was crouching on a wall, its tail flicking gently in the breeze. It stared at me, him. Us!

I walked along the road about a hundred yards towards a block of garages at right angles to the street and set back slightly from the path. As I drew level with them, I glanced around, once more checking all was clear before entering a narrow alleyway that ran along the left side, behind the garages. It was overgrown with brambles, overhung with trees and climbing shrubs which created a sort of natural tunnel. Without hesitation I plunged further in, brushing aside anything that was in my way, not caring whether I was scratched. There was somewhere I was heading, but I didn't know where.

At a 'T' junction ahead I turned right and carried on, ploughing through the thicket ahead of me. A noise to my left caught my attention. I stopped and listened for a second before searching the undergrowth for something to stand on to gain a view into the garden where the noise had originated. I found a broken chair buried in amongst the weeds and, tugging it free, I placed it next to the fence and peered over.

I could just see over it. Through the trees there was a child playing in the garden, she was about six or seven years old. I was never much good with ages.

"Psst," I heard. Where did that come from? It was someone trying to attract my attention.

It was from me...

"... ack within minutes. Daniel! You're back... see Aunt Rose, that's what happens."

"Yes," Aunt Rose said thoughtfully. "I've never come into contact with this sort of thing. Personally that is. Meg, my friend on the other hand, has told me of encounters like this.

I'm sure, yes, I'm sure I remember her telling me. Mmmm. I can't quite remember all the details. Let me think." Aunt Rose disappeared into her own world, lost with her thoughts for a second. "There is a reason you're experiencing the 'Visions'. What was it that Meg said once? Oh fudge, memory's not as good as it used to be. I know I'll give her a ring."

She pulled her mobile phone from the pocket of her cardigan. Then squinting at the tiny screen scrolled through the numbers that appeared one by one, all the time muttering to herself. Finding the right name she pushed the dial button. I could hear it ringing as I stood looking on impatiently.

After five rings it was answered. I could hear the voice but not make out the words.

"Hello Meg... it's Rose."

Ann-Marie and I listened while Aunt Rose continued her conversation with Meg, relaying all she knew so far and asking me any questions that required answering.

"Daniel, how long has it been now?"

"Less than a day. Why?"

"Less than a day, Meg." She paused.

"When you first had these visions was there anything different about them than now?"

"They were silent..." I said hesitantly before thinking a bit harder. "... just pictures like a silent film, I couldn't hear... or feel anything."

Again she passed this information to Meg.

"And now?"

"And now I hear things... and feel things. Each time they seem to be more realistic." I started to talk faster as it all became clearer and my slow brain recognised the changes that had taken place. "I feel heartbeats, adrenalin rushes. I have no control. I can't look where I want to, or turn round."

Aunt Rose quickly relayed all this to Meg, there was a long silence.

"Thank you Meg. See you at bridge on Thursday. It's at Maud's isn't it?" She cut the call and looked directly at me. After a moment's contemplation she added, "Meg says that what is happening to you is that you are becoming at one with the other being, two sides of the one coin joining together to make the whole thing. Eventually you will become one." She leaned forward clutching the glass tighter. "Then the stronger half takes control." She paused, as if more bad news was to come. How bad could it be? "That unfortunately will be the other half of you. You will lose everything you were, and everything you are. You, as you know, will no longer exist. And that will occur in only eight days."

"But how can she be so sure?" I was full of despair.

"My dear friend has experienced this twice before."

"What?" I was gobsmacked. "It happens all the time?"

"No dear. That is not what I said." She corrected.

"But it can't be. It can't be." I was reeling from the shock. I didn't know what to make of what I was being told. I saw the events of the last day flash before me. A well of emotion flowed up inside, I wanted to punch out but knew I couldn't. The only two people who seemed to understand and wanted to help were here. I couldn't offend them and yet the desire to run, to try to outrun this situation grew within me and before I had thought about the consequences I'd bolted from the room, from the house. I was running for my life.

What life? I was dead already.

7

I had run as fast, and as hard, as possible from Anne-Marie's house and now found myself caught in the impending dusk wondering what I was to do. Finally I stopped because running was not accomplishing anything only fuelling the fire of frustration. It didn't help that I felt nothing from the run, no exhaustion, no weariness. It was like I hadn't been running. Instead I was experiencing the emptiness that epitomised how alone I now felt.

The people around me were wrapped in scarves and hats, with collars fastened so tightly round their necks it looked as if they would choke, I guessed it was cold and wished that I could sense that feeling once more.

I walked the streets aimlessly. Streets I'd known for years, familiar sights, places filled with memories, the alleyways my friends and I would race our bikes down, the brooks where we would build dams, the sweet shop where every Friday I spent my pocket money. What was going to happen now? Inside a mix of emotions battled with each other, anger, rage, emptiness, loss. I wanted to punch something. Hit out. Strike someone, something. 'WHY ME?' I cried at the top of my voice but it didn't make any difference, no one heard me.

I wanted to speak to my parents but they wouldn't be able see me, they wouldn't be able hear me. I didn't exist to them anymore and I wondered if they knew yet.

Again I ran, I didn't know why, just a compulsion to run. I hated running. Street after street, I crossed roads without looking, head down, wanting to be hit by a car, to feel the end, the reality of a collision, end all the frustration.

Without realising how I'd got there I'd stopped outside my parents' bungalow, my security blanket. Somewhere I'd always felt safe, a haven where I could find help and good advice, even if I didn't take it. A friendly face and a kind word, reassurance if I was ever in doubt. They had always been there for me, I couldn't remember a time when they hadn't, every fall, every knockback. I was lucky to have my parents.

What now?

That thought echoed inside my head. Parents are meant to go before their children, one of life's hardships, an unwritten rule, not the other way round. I would never get the chance to speak to them again, not even to say goodbye. I could see them but they couldn't see me. I could listen to every conversation they had, they'd never know.

What would they learn about their son? How I went? What happened?

It occurred to me, like the sun melting away the mist on a frosty morning, that I didn't really know what had happened to me. Surely, I should know how I died, if I died! I did die didn't I? I questioned. Yes I should because ghosts always re-enact how they died, that's what I thought, what I believed, so they must know. But I didn't. I had a conscious awareness, stronger feelings, Ann-Marie confirmed that. Why?

How did I die?

I needed to know all the facts whether I liked them or not. I had to find out everything I could.

My father's car suddenly turned into the driveway, the headlights cutting through me like searchlight beams, my mother was in the passenger seat. Pulling up in front of the white garage door, they got out, chatting casually, as I had heard many times before.

My parents – both in their mid fifties had taken early retirement. My father had worked in the post office since leaving school. He had been quite lucky as well, occasionally having a flutter on the horses when he felt the urge. One time he'd won £35,000 on a five horse each way accumulator, each horse coming in first. This had enabled him to invest modestly in property, buying and renting, their retirement plan. They now owned six properties mortgage free, plus their bungalow. My mother still did the occasional bit of teaching. She always enjoyed giving back to others what knowledge she had.

I was watching a TV reality program unfolding in front of my eyes. Except I was physically present in a strange sort of disconnected way. I smiled forlornly.

"Matthew, you can be so rude sometimes." My mother closed the car door and walked to the boot where my father was lifting out carrier bags full of groceries. "That checkout girl had probably just had a busy day, and you know what it can be like sometimes when it's busy."

My father replied in what I knew was his condescending way. "Well what do you expect? It was a stupid question anyway."

"There's no need to be rude though." She shot a glance at my father before walking to the front door. "Have you got the front door key handy?"

"No." My father put the last carrier bag on the ground before closing the boot and locking the car with the remote key. "Hello... I handed her the credit card... and she goes, 'Do you want to pay with this?'... errr no I want to pick my nose."

"Everyone's entitled to get a little confused."

"Mary, I think you've got to be alive to get confused. Where do they find these people?"

"You can be so sarcastic Matthew James." My mother always called my father by his first names when she was annoyed with him.

"Haven't you got that door open yet?"

"Pot. Kettle. Black." My mother stated whilst searching her handbag for a set of keys. "That's such a stupid question."

"Touché." My father laughed opening the door with his keys. They smiled warmly at each other and went inside.

I stood a while longer enjoying replaying the banter they'd shared, the picture of my parents together. I walked to the now closed front door and then tentatively stepped through it to the entrance hall where I stood behind my parents almost feeling like an intruder.

"It's turned cold all of a sudden. Did you turn the heating off before we went out?"

"No," my father said, looking at the thermostat situated on the wall by the telephone a little farther down the hallway. "Still at fifteen."

"Strange, just feel a chill in the air." There was a pregnant pause and my mother's expression became deadly serious. "Something's not right… it's Daniel. Don't ask me how I know, I just know."

"What do you mean something's not right?"

"I don't know for sure. I need to ring him."

I watched as my mother quietly and efficiently went about the task at hand, trying to contact me, ignoring the shopping defrosting on the floor. In one swift movement she'd picked up the handset from its cradle hanging on the wall and pressed speed-dial, all the time muttering to herself.

"Answer the phone, please answer the phone…" She repeated willing it to happen.

My father carried the shopping through to the kitchen letting my mother console herself, believing there was probably nothing wrong at all just a mother's intuition working overtime.

I felt guilty standing there. There was nothing I could do to ease her anxious mind. Knowing that when I didn't answer the phone she would fret until she heard news, a word, anything from me, about me. This was too much, I had to go. I about turned to leave.

As I passed through the door I felt the pain that I had felt earlier, and I knew what this meant…

I was in a hallway. My hallway. I was staring at the wall. Standing, staring, in a daydream, either that or I was admiring the previous owner's choice of wallpaper.

I could just make out the aerial to the phone in my hand.

I felt a sense of mischief and a wry smile oozed across my face. I didn't know why.

I stood there a little while longer, letting the phone ring.

The doorbell rang out its pretty little charm. It always did sound dreadful, one of the small jobs I'd always meant to do, but had never got around to.

I turned to look down the stairs at the front door. I could make out the shape of a young person behind the frosted glass panel in the door, the paperboy.

I began to fear for his life. I couldn't justify why, a sense of uneasiness about the possible ways forward for this situation. Damn, why didn't I leave the money for him last week?

Slowly, purposely, I walked down the stairs. I still felt the wry smile on my face as the phone now lay silent in one hand. Turning the catch on the door I pushed it outwards making the paperboy dance awkwardly around it to avoid being hit.

"Excuse me, you haven't paid your papers for a couple weeks, and I was told to come and collect it, it's £6.32 with the magazines, only if I don't get paid, it'll get deducted from my wages." The words were fired out without a chance for rebuke.

I didn't say anything, just looked around. I felt the urge to shout out 'RUN', but couldn't, I opened my mouth, I heard another voice, a strange unfamiliar voice.

"Yes, sure. Come inside and I will sort out the money."

"No it's okay I'll wait here" the boy took a step backwards

"I see." I looked at the boy for a long second. "You are quite safe. I do not like leaving the door open." I shifted my position in the doorway to get closer to the boy.

He stepped back, a look of suspicion on his face "I've got to keep an eye on my bike mister," he said nervously.

Reassuringly I spoke. "It will only take a minute or so. I am quite sure your bike will be safe." I reached out to grab the boy's shoulder. The phone suddenly sprang to life again.

The boy looked uncomfortable with the situation. 'Allelujah', I said to myself, just when you want a kid who stands up for himself.

"No, I'm alright here mister," he said, taking a further step back towards the communal door.

I felt myself start to lunge forward, ignoring the phone, when my neighbour's door opened.

Safe I thought.

"Evening...

I was back outside my parent's place.

For the first time since finding myself in this half-existence I knew what I had to do, I had to go back to the beginning. The theatre! I needed to discover what had happened to me, solve this riddle. Piece together the pieces and solve the mystery in which I was trapped.

I walked quickly to the main road and the quickest route to the theatre. Monday night, I knew the theatre would be closed as there was no show on this week, not that it really mattered anyway no one could see me.

It didn't take now I had a sense of purpose driving me along, strangely I felt alive again. The imposing building stood as a formidable barrier in front of me and a reluctance to enter seep into my pores.

I was scared yet wanted to know and, at the same time, I didn't.

I rocked about on my heels before stealing the moment. I was re-entering the beginning of the nightmare that had begun only twenty-four hours before.

Once in I observed the lobby like I'd never been there before walking over to the stairs from which I had descended the night before, so innocently, only to discover the truth of my predicament.

The light from the street lamps outside spilled in enough yet the stairwell remained cloaked in a terrifying blackness that filled me with dread as I walked over to it to return to the beginning of my hell. As I moved up the stairs I became unnerved and lost my grip on the positive attitude I had acquired only an hour before. I stopped.

What could be the worst that could happen? Nothing more than had already occurred, I laughed nervously to myself, not that it would have made much difference if I had laughed out loud.

I proceeded gingerly, taking the steps one at a time... pain again...

Blackness. Nothing but blackness. A shimmering sheet of nothing.

For the briefest instant I thought, I hoped, I was back in the corridor again, where it first happened, I couldn't make out anything.

This felt different though. Something new. I tried to re-orientate again. But all I could sense was that I was lying down. I was in bed. Sleeping? Vaguely feeling the covers moving around me, I was not in a restful sleep.

I was caught in the dreamworld and I started to see the images of lifesize characters as I started to move amongst them.

'I was in a street I recognised it but not from physically ever being there, maybe a picture I'd seen somewhere. Buildings looked new, dated but new.

I was in the past.

Cobbled streets, gaslights. Looking around, I surveyed the shops, Mr Ridley's hardware store looked so different, so new, yet so old. The new UPVC facade was gone.

I found myself spun round like a top at high speed, looking at a commotion going on about twenty feet away.

A carriage was stationary with its horse agitated and rearing up on its hind legs. There was someone lying on the ground. A crowd gathered, blocking the view. A policeman ran to the scene blowing his whistle pushing his way through the people, brushing them aside like toy soldiers.

I caught a glimpse of some blood. Almost fluorescent as it stained the white blouse the lady was wearing. The horse was still rearing, the driver trying his best to get it under control. The crowd, wary of the horse, stayed a safe distance away. Slowly, it began to settle, it's head making an occasional pull to one side, as if trying to break the reins, another man started to stroke the horse's nose soothing it further, the horse snorted its acquiescence.

My sight was drawn to a girl standing just away from the scene, she was crying, sobbing her heart out, there was a lady comforting her. For some strange reason it didn't look like a parent, maybe a friendly passer-by.

Walking towards the scene, I could see a woman lying on the ground, motionless. I wanted to cry out. But it wasn't me this time.

I was bolt upright in bed. My bed. Pearls of sweat dripping from the end of my nose onto the sheets. My breathing heavy, my chest rising and falling, I could feel every muscle, every heave as my lungs tried to fill with air, my hand clasped the duvet tightly, screwing it up into a ball. I looked at the clock beside the bed, it read 3.39am. I gulped down water from the glass on the bedside table.

As my breathing returned to normal I looked around the room before lying back down again, pulling the covers up to my chin, I felt a tear pool in my eye...

I was on the stairs again in the theatre, falling down them. At the bottom I didn't move, just laid still trying to decipher the images, wondering which me I was?

8

Contemplating the divide between fact and fiction was getting harder. A part of me regretted running out on Ann-Marie, she was the one anchor that I needed in the real world.

I had to discover the truth, the truth of how I died.

Getting up, I marched up the stairs with renewed vigour. I reached for the handle of the door, forgetting that I didn't need to use it, but that in itself made me hesitate. The door represented a magical barrier, stopping me from entering the playing field I knew I had to cross. I couldn't hold back if I was ever going to find out, maybe this was what kept ghosts re-enacting the same moment again and again, the thirst for knowledge of the truth behind their demise. I thrust forward and beyond.

In the vast void of blackness that I found myself I could not see despite being a ghost and I should have remembered the first night - I still needed light. The limited sense of touch that I possessed would not enable me to find the answers. I couldn't feel what I was looking for, I needed to see it.

Again I thought about Ann-Marie, she may be blind but she could have held a torch for me.

Frustration started to grow inside like an infection, every step forward I'd take two steps back. My frustration started to turn to anger and I knew that wouldn't get me anywhere. I needed to think calmly and racked my brains for a soothing image. I remembered one of the after show parties.

These were a tradition that I liked about the theatre. Some of us would get together and put on an after-show show, we'd spend time between the Saturday matinee and evening show discussing what we would do and then about five minutes before actually doing it, rehearse it. On stage it would turn into a farce as we made up bits on the spur of the moment whilst performing what had already been discussed. Normally, we'd be taking the mickey out of the show we were doing, sometimes it was past shows. One after-show show in particular sprang to mind, our summer show the previous year and the number 'Black Velvet'. This held a lot of special memories for nearly everyone, as the men took the women's roles and tried to copy their routines with hilarious consequences even to the point of wearing fishnet tights. I was just glad to be part of it. The evening's entertainment was usually recorded and the laughter from the other cast members was most apparent when played back.

Smiling to myself, the calmness enabled me to think more rationally.

I needed Ann-Marie. The irony was not lost on me. I needed a blind girl to help me see.

Why would she want to help after I'd run out on her? She had been trying to help then, and I had disregarded her, threw her to one side as a piece of waste. Guilt racked me and I knew I had to go back to apologise.

Leaving the theatre, I wondered if I'd be turned away and, with good reason. I had to put things right. I didn't know how. I needed to convince Ann-Marie to help me again. I doubted this would be easy. I ran different explanations of my behaviour around in my head, none of which really justified my actions. How could I apologise? This occupied my mind for the journey back to her house.

Ann-Marie's place was twenty-five minutes walk from the theatre. The closer I got to her house, the further away a plausible explanation seemed, an apology was all I could offer.

'How was I going to get Ann-Marie into the theatre unnoticed?' Bearing in mind that she was blind. It hadn't occurred to me on the way, but now it sprang to mind.

Ann-Marie's house was shrouded in darkness. I had no idea what the time was and didn't know how long I would have to wait for her to get up.

"More waiting," I muttered. "Nope it's no good if I wait I won't do it." I had to act now. I walked through the front door and marched up to Ann-Marie's room. For an instant I felt I was invading her privacy, but it was necessary.

Outside her open bedroom door I stopped and thought about what I was going to do, deciding it was rude to just waltz in and wake her from her slumber.

Ann-Marie hadn't closed her curtains as there was no need, and in the shadowy light I saw the door move slightly, rocking briefly on its hinges before opening wider. Blinking I thought I was hallucinating until I saw a hand appear at the edge.

Ann-Marie stood in her pyjamas. How could she have known?

Then she walked straight through me, and for those few seconds I felt uncomfortable, I turned to say something but instead watched as she headed down the hall. Suddenly she stopped, turned and faced me, whispering, "go and wait in my room, I'll be back in a minute, I need to pee."

Stunned, I did as instructed, taking up residence on the corner of her bed. Mojo lifted his head in recognition, then lowered it again and carried on sleeping where he was at the foot of the bed.

When Ann-Marie came back a while later, she spoke to me in hushed tones without any sign of anger or annoyance, instead, seemingly more pleased.

"I hoped you would come back." She was a little drowsy as she climbed back into bed, pulling the covers over herself.

"Why?" I answered in an imitating whisper. Had I blown everything out of all proportion?

"There's no need for you to whisper my mum can't hear you."

"Sorry, habit I guess… you know? When someone whispers I start to…" I didn't bother to finish the sentence, she knew what I meant.

Timidly I spoke. "I'm sorry about running out earlier." My feeble apology sounded even worse out loud.

"It's okay. I sort of guessed you were upset." She spoke without the slightest hint of displeasure.

"I didn't know what to think. I needed to get my head together." I started speaking, not thinking, just talking. "You know everything that has happened in the last twenty-four hours, my parents, the visions and what they mean?"

"I understand. I sort of understand where you're coming from." She yawned. "I'm sorry, I'm tired."

"Of course. I'll let you get some sleep." I stood up.

"It's okay, carry on."

I didn't know where to start. I felt the need to tell her everything that had occurred since we last spoke and proceeded at a pace whilst she listened intently. Pacing the room, I vocally, and visually, ran through everything, my ideas, the theatre, my parents.

At the end I turned and saw Ann-Marie was asleep her head nestled in her pillows with one hand underneath them.

I walked over to her bed, Mojo lying beside it, he lifted his head warily.

"It's okay Mojo, I'm not going hurt her." I looked at the clock on her bedside table, I could barely make out the fluorescent pads on the hands, nearly five in the morning.

I went to the window and studied the street below, an empty stage waiting for its actors to take up their positions for the opening.

I wasn't tired, I didn't need sleep, time moved slowly. It did give me the chance to ponder the problem ahead. How was I going to get Ann-Marie into the theatre?

★

Ann-Marie's Mum called up as day ascended over Southend-on-Sea. "Ann-Marie, its eight o'clock, breakfast is on the table."

Sluggishly she roused, yawning and stretching before throwing back the covers, hiding Mojo – who had moved onto the bed during the night - temporarily from view. He fought with them playfully before nuzzling her.

"How are we going to get into the theatre though?" she said putting her face to Mojo's.

Surprised, I looked at her, my mouth open wide. "I thought you'd fallen asleep."

"I sort of dozed off, but caught most of what you said." She yawned again.

"Oh. I've been racking my brains all night trying to think of all sorts of ways." I paused. "I'm not sure but I think I've come up with a plan."

She yawned again. "I'm sorry."

"I shouldn't have disturbed you last night."

"It's okay. What's it like outside?" she asked.

"Dull and cloudy, looks like it might rain again later."

Ann-Marie unhooked the dressing gown that hung on the back of the door, putting it on she tied it loosely about her waist. "Oh yes, Aunt Rose said, after you went, that she needs to make contact with you again. She thought that if she made contact with you when 'IT'." She punctuated the air with the first two fingers on each hand. "You know, when it happens, you seeing things, she reckons she'll be able to identify who it is… whose eyes you are viewing things through, when you see things. Does that make sense?"

"Kind of, I think, but I don't have control over it. When it happens, it just… happens."

"We might have to spend some time with her and wait then." She left the room, Mojo at her right hand.

"Ann-Marie, who are you talking to?"

"No one Mum, just Mojo." She hunched her shoulders up

realising that she had been quite loud, forgetting her Mum was still in the house.

"I'm going to work now, I'll see you lunchtime."

"Okay 'bye."

A few moments later the front door clicked into place.

Ann-Marie disappeared into the bathroom and closed the door, Mojo went in with her.

I waited in the room for her return.

★

"That's better." I hadn't heard Ann-Marie re-enter the room she was dressed now, her long hair neatly tied back.

I turned to face her. "Before we see Aunt Rose I think a trip to the theatre would be good. I need you to help me see, so I can find out as much as possible about what happened."

"So what's this idea of how I can get in?"

I became more animated as I explained my plan. "There is a show tonight and tomorrow night, a dancing school, so the stage door will be open so everyone can dump their costumes as stuff, it always is. You can pretend you're one of the performers, as it's a dance show there are lots of girls so you'll fit right in. No one will notice as they will be coming and going all day."

"How about Mojo? I'm sure they won't allow dogs in there," she replied, a little sarcastically.

"You'll have to trust me to be your eyes."

"But what about Mojo?" She stroked his back as he sat obediently by her.

"We'll have to leave him here." Ann-Marie looked justifiably horrified. Mojo looked up at Ann-Marie. He seemed to know.

"I won't be able to move as quickly without Mojo even if you tell me what's where, it'll take ages. It took me ages to build up a picture of my way around this house. And, it took a long time for me to be able to rely on him. I don't know if I can go it alone by relying on someone else who can't physically guide me." She paused, "and another thing, how will I get to the theatre without him?"

I thought for a second. "Look, I don't know any other way of doing it." I was losing the battle. I understood her reluctance and, if the situation were reversed, I'd probably feel the same. I sighed. "Well if you can think of a better way."

I slumped into the wicker chair whilst Ann-Marie sat on the bed, both in silence.

"How about if we take Mojo with us, I can tie him up outside. We won't be that long? Will we? He'll be ok for a while."

"Can do I s'pose." Mojo glanced at Ann-Marie as if he'd understood every word. I sensed her displeasure at the thought of leaving her beloved friend alone outside, especially if it rained.

"I'm still not sure it'll work but I'll give it a go." With that she got up and touched Mojo's head then left the room. "I'm going to get some breakfast. What time do we need to leave?"

I called down the hall. "If we go about ten, it'll take us about half an hour or so, they should have all the set in by the time we get there. We need to wait until the cast arrive anyway."

I decided to join her downstairs and followed at a slower pace, taking another look at the photos that adorned the wall. While Ann-Marie ate her breakfast I looked out of the kitchen window at the garden. It was small and compact, mainly concrete with a flowerbed and a shingle footpath to the fence at the back. I heard the radio being switched on but was lost in my own daydream.

A while later Ann-Marie exclaimed. "Did you hear that?"

"What? Hear what?"

"There have been two murders and an attempted murder, all in the local area in the last twenty-four hours. Police wouldn't release too many details as they don't want to create a panic, but believe they are hunting a single male in his late twenties. They are warning everyone to be vigilant. All the victims were young girls."

"Yeah, so." I didn't see the relevance, I never did unless it involved me.

"Don't you care?"

I detected a hostile tone and tried to play it down. "Yes. But what has it got to do with me, I can't do anything to stop a killer. Especially not as I am."

Ann-Marie obviously had a clue. "Didn't you say in the vision you had yesterday you were in a field and there were shots? Well. One of the girls was abducted and taken to a field, the only thing that saved her life was the fact that a farmer had spotted two people in his field and fired warning shots thinking they were vandals."

I thought for a second, I'd completely shut out whatever I could of the visions, when it suited me.

"Oh my god." A swathe of sickness that I didn't even think was possible washed over me. All the pictures in my head became clear at once - everything I'd seen - everything I'd felt. I'd viewed life through the eyes of a murderer! More questions ransacked my head like random explosions.

Then a pain shot into my body, cramps in my hands and feet crippling me...

I was walking down an alley. This time I knew why. It was clear to me what I was seeing. It was a slow torture as I could only watch in horror as the play continued to unfold.

At the entrance to the alley I halted, ducking back enough to be hidden by an overgrowing bush from a neighbouring garden. I was viewing a scene in Victoria Drive. I recognised it as it was where I used to go to school.

A cold feeling flooded my heart quelling any possible beat that could have been there. A mixed up stew of emotions, anger, hate, love, came to me at once. I knew the outcome of this venture without seeing it unfold in front of me.

I was waiting, waiting for stragglers.

There had to be something I could do, I felt so helpless, a lifeless being, sapped of all strength, being guided by the power of a force that controlled me.

I heard a voice, a young girl's voice, and I knew what was going to happen next. I tried my best to shout out, yet nothing came out.

It was no good. Before I knew it the girl had been dragged into the alley kicking, she was trying to scream but my hand was tightly over her mouth, I could feel her saliva on my fingers. She was weak in comparison to me. She tried in vain to break free, kicking, writhing, all to no avail. Her bag fell to the ground and I managed to drag it behind me with one foot.

I watched the grizzly scene unfold, every motion, every thrust of the knife into the body, the struggle of the girl to fight for her freedom in this no win situation. I couldn't avert my gaze or close my eyes, forced to look on.

It was all over so quickly. The body was still in my arms. The warm blood was sticky on my hands. I wanted to break free.

Back in Ann-Marie's kitchen I was crying without tears, the emotion was real.

Ann-Marie moved from the table towards me, like a friend would. "What's wrong Daniel?"

It took a while for me to find my voice. I was choked.

"I've seen the next victim... I was... there... I couldn't stop it. I feel sick."

I saw Ann-Marie stretch out a hand for comfort. A hand that would not be felt.

9

As Ann-Marie tried to console me more feelings of guilt and inadequacy took over. Could I have prevented this if I had interpreted the visions correctly, realising that they had in fact been real? Although I was angry and frustrated Ann-Marie was quick to point out that there was nothing I could and I had to focus on the task at hand. She was so rational and it was good to have her on my side.

It was eleven o'clock when we started for the theatre. The cold outside was biting but luckily it looked like it wouldn't rain, which was good, as Mojo was going to be outside for a while.

En-route I explained the procedure that most groups operated backstage. It was a simple one, only requiring the relevant person to place a tick in a box next to their name upon entering the theatre, and another when leaving, this was mainly for fire regulations but it also let the stage manager know if any of the cast were late.

I did my best to describe the back stage area that would lead us up to the dressing rooms, the many different levels she would encounter. It was an old theatre and many additions had changed its layout - you would walk down two steps only to go up three steps a few feet further on, and, then there was a slope. It sounded complicated and judging by the look on Ann-Marie's face she was daunted by the task ahead, she had my sympathy. She was lucky in one respect that most people wouldn't give her a second glance as she passed each dressing room, too busy sorting themselves out, hanging up costumes and claiming their small bit of counter space for make-up and other paraphernalia for the forthcoming show. However, she did need to appear competent at walking the corridors otherwise she might attract unnecessary attention which we wanted to avoid.

Suddenly it occurred to me that a teacher would know their own pupils and I wondered why I hadn't thought of it earlier. Betraying her confidence, I decided to keep that information to myself not wanting to alarm Ann-Marie. I felt guilty for doing so but I needed her to go along with this plan. Silently I prayed that it would all be fine and that the teachers would be too busy to notice one extra girl. I hoped she didn't think of it either.

On the way we stopped at the library gardens, in Victoria Avenue, so we could try and build what trust we could between Ann-Marie's interpretations of my instructions. That way we'd have an idea of what to expect. Mojo sat on the grass looking with concern at his companion braving the first tentative steps without his guidance.

Her first few steps were hesitant and very deliberate. She listened diligently but struggled somewhat with balance as she became disorientated and hesitant. I didn't know we were going to make it once inside with people, walls and steps. Time was against us and this process, whilst very important, was eating away at what little we did have.

From where we were I could see the clock on the library further down the road, an hour and a half had passed. Ann-Marie put a brave on face when I asked if she was ready, she wasn't, however determination drove her on. We left the park in silence, remaining that way until we neared the theatre, both praying for success.

Ann-Marie reluctantly tied Mojo's lead through some railings on the main high street. Then kneeling down held his head in her hands tenderly reassuring him that it was okay. Affectionately she stroked the top of his head. Mojo licked her face in return. She stood up still resting her hand on his head.

Ann-Marie had left the traditional harness at home to avoid any unnecessary attention it would have brought but still Mojo looked anxious for his mistress and friend.

Clarence Road and the backstage door was just a minute's walk away. These early steps were tentative and slow, Ann-Marie tried to relax as I verbally guided her, telling her what obstacles were nearby, but the tension was palpable. Stopping outside the pub next door she already looked exhausted from the effort and I was concerned that I was asking too much of her.

Allowing her a chance to rest I went through the back stage door to see how many people were mulling around and to estimate how many footsteps there were to the list that was hung on the notice board and, where the pen was in relation to it and the stairs. I was uncomfortable leaving her alone yet this was quite a revealing exercise. I'd always taken my eyesight for granted. Now I was beginning to realise how adverse things could be, I'd never had to worry about such trivial details, my reactions were automatic according to what my eyes saw.

Back outside I relayed the information to Ann-Marie. She looked worried and apprehensive. I reassured her it would be fine, trying to hide my own anxiety.

We set off as I noticed some of the cast starting to arrive. The scene was a familiar one, groups of two or three, walking down the street carrying bags and hangers with costumes on. I'd forgotten about the baggage. Ann-Marie would look out of place. However, there was nothing I could do now and if I didn't say anything she would never know.

I told her to wait a moment longer, as we neared the actual gate that accessed the stage door, until a small group of girls, who were carrying costumes and chatting excitedly about the pending performance, came within range. After they'd gone in we moved towards the stage door. A solitary girl appeared suddenly from the alley swamped with costumes, barely able to see where she was going and struggling to keep hold of it all. She would be the perfect one to follow in. I alerted Ann-Marie to the fact and to go on my command.

"Ann-Marie, start walking forward. There are no kerbs and it's a level surface, you have a lamp post on your right in about three paces, the gate you need is on your left about five paces after that." She walked slowly and steadily, every step with utmost concentration. "Now turn ninety degrees to your left... bit more, move forward, there's a slight step that's been worn down; it's about six inches high. Then walk forward" Ann-Marie followed my instructions implicitly, grazing the stone post of the gate that I forgot to mention. She gave the appearance of someone who'd had a drink and was feeling unwell. "Another two paces and you are at the door, it is still slightly ajar. It opens towards you. The handle is just above waist height to the left of the door but further to the left and slightly higher, bit more. That's it. Grip and pull open to your right. I realised I should have instructed her which hand to use as she initially grabbed it with left instead of the right and had to change hands for ease. As you go through there is another step of about three inches up, then your feet will be on carpet."

Although this was working well so far I could feel the pressure building and knew we both had to remain calm and focussed. The lead girl was a few feet in front not taking any notice of Ann-Marie.

"Right, now, move forward slightly, turn to your right. That's it. Lift your right hand up about shoulder height and touch the wall. It is about two feet away. Move your hand slightly further right, up a bit, bit more. The pen is at your fingertips."

She fumbled using both hands to find the pen and the correct end to write with. The cast were all too busy chatting and laughing to pay any attention to her. There was however, a security camera to fool.

"Now just next to that on the left you'll feel a piece of paper. That's the cast list."

With her left hand she felt for the paper, she had great co-ordination putting pen to paper. "There is no need to mark the paper, just make it look real." With this task accomplished I guided Ann-Marie up the stairs which were concrete and worn away by the years of performers trampling up and down to get to and from the stage.

"Why was ticking myself in necessary? Why didn't I just walk straight up the stairs?" she whispered, sure that no one was within earshot.

"There's a security camera pointing at the back door. Although they don't know what every performer looks like, they might question one who doesn't sign in."

"Oh!. But how abou..."

"Shush, there's someone coming. Look to your right and smile."

She did so. A girl coming towards us passed straight through me, and ignored Ann-Marie.

"Sorry about that," I said when the coast was clear. "I'll answer the rest of your questions in a second. Another four steps and we are at the top of the stairs, you need to turn left, then you have about, mmmm, fourteen or so paces before you reach two steps down. The steps down are quite steep. I'd say about eight to ten inches." She moved swiftly, gaining confidence with every step, only slowing to take the stairs. "Go forward another ten paces and the wall narrows from your right. Just go to your left a touch. That's it. It's wide again now, this corridor is quite long... aarghh."

I was somewhere dark. I could hear water dripping. Hear splashes as the footfalls landed in puddles. I was upright and marching at a brisk pace. Seemingly I knew where I was going.

There was a damp, musty smell in the air. My hand was on one wall, using it as a guide, it felt smooth and cold. Occasionally my hand would brush over a furry line of something but it didn't seem to bother me.

I continued unabated until the wall skewed at an angle, guiding me in a different direction. I caught sight of an illumination in the distance. Daylight. As we got nearer, we entered a larger chamber. I could barely make out the size in the dim light that seeped in.

Walking towards the light, at the end of the chamber, a large wooden door came into view separating us from the outside world.

It was thick and covered in green slime which squelched under the pressure of my hands. I pushed hard to try and get the door open, but it stayed in place. I butted my shoulder against it and pushed until eventually it started to move inching open just enough to allow me to squeeze through.

I had to shield my eyes from the glare of daylight until they acclimatised. I recognised where I was. Ambleside Sunken Garden. First opened in 1843 by Mayor Bridgewater in memory of his wife, who died in childbirth.

I heard a rip as I emerged from behind a thorn bush.

"Damn." I looked down at my trouser leg. A tear about seven inches long had appeared. I noticed my clothes were dirty and as a breeze blew past I caught the stench of myself. I needed a bath.

Back in the corridor Ann-Marie was crouching against the wall fiddling with her shoe.

"Are you okay?" I asked, for an instant regretting getting Ann-Marie involved.

"Thank god you're back," she stood up. "I didn't know how long I was going to be able to stay here without someone asking me..."

"Shush," I said, putting my finger to my lips, even though she wouldn't have seen it.

"What are you doing? Do you know where you should be?" said a harassed looking woman in her forties, wearing black, top and trousers.

"Yes thank you I was... was just doing my shoelace up," said

Ann-Marie, thinking fast. The woman nodded and carried on about her business.

"Technical run-through in fifteen minutes. We want everyone on stage in ten." The woman called out sternly as she walked off repeating it as she passed each dressing room.
Ann-Marie whispered, "I thought she might start asking me a few awkward questions."

"No. That's the beauty of show weeks. Everyone's so wrapped up in the show you can get away with a fair bit. But before you do start getting some funny looks let's get going. Turn to your right then you've got another three paces before the corridor turns through forty-five degrees to your right and up a slight but constant incline, it gets a little bit narrower." I watched. "When you get to the top you'll reach a door which opens the same side as the stage door but this time away from you. When you go through turn immediately right and the door we need is just down some steps about, I don't know, fifteen paces away from the last step."

Reaching the door I sighed with relief. We'd not encountered any people-problems except the woman, even then due to Ann-Marie's quick thinking we'd got away with that. As we went through the door I saw our goal. My goal!

Ann-Marie rested her hand on the wall finding the dado rail to use as a guide for walking down the stairs. When it changed elevation she knew she was at the bottom not far from the door I had told her about. Soon she stood in front it and I let out a sigh.

"If you reach out your right hand, just about waist height, you should feel a handle, this door opens towards you and from the left. Have you got the torch?"

My heart sank as she opened the door to the corridor where it had all begun.

"Yes, it's here in my pocket." She got it out and switched it on. "Is it on?"

"Of cour... yes. Ah that's better."

Now there was light I could see the corridor stretching out before us. I described to Ann-Marie where exactly to step. The corridor was full of various toot stacked up against the walls and I advised her to move carefully along, feeling with her hands just in case I missed anything. She did so, sliding each foot forward just like I'd done previously when searching for the exit.

I asked her to direct the torch in certain directions. There was no sign of any struggle and nothing looked out of place. Everything was still a mess, but the same mess, it was when last I saw it with the light on. Then I felt a familiar twinge of pain, I tried to fight it, knowing the possible danger I was leaving Ann-Marie in.

Once again I was outside, this time sitting down on a bench, watching people go by.

I wasn't feeling anger anymore, or arousal of any sort, just calmness. Something I hadn't felt up to now. This was almost restful.

It went dark. I'd closed my eyes. I felt myself recline deeper into the bench. Again the picture I'd seen the previous night flashed into my mind. A woman lying on the ground with blood everywhere, the little girl standing at the side of the street crying, commotion going on all around, the hustle and bustle of the people as they looked on.

I felt a tear start its journey down my cheek. Slowly at first then quickening as it rounded the outline of my cheek.

I brushed it aside and got up, walking towards to Pier Hill.

Disorientated I found myself in the corridor. Ann-Marie was not visible at first. I noticed the torch lying on the floor, frantically I turned until I saw Ann-Marie on the floor, she'd fallen. I knelt down beside her, scared as she wasn't moving and there was nothing I could do. I wanted to gently prod her shoulder or check her pulse to make sure she was still alive, to touch her hand, anything. I couldn't do anything. I growled to myself, flexing every muscle in my body. What had I done? This was not what I had planned.

I heard movement. It was Ann-Marie, she was alive.

"Are you okay?" I couldn't get the words out quick enough.

"Yes, I think so," was the weary response. Ann-Marie rubbed her head with one hand and clutched her ankle with the other. As she moved, the torch rolled about on the floor. In the flicker I saw a hole near the base of the wall where Ann-Marie had landed. It looked as though when she'd fallen she had knocked some of the chair seats, stacked against the opposite wall, down and they had toppled over and dislodged a few loose bricks.

"Ann-Marie can you shine the torch over here please."

"Where's…"

"Sorry, straight ahead of you."

"No. Where's the torch?"

I turned to face her. "Sorry, it's about two and a half feet from your right foot." She reached out fumbling on the floor. "Can you shine it to your left. A bit more."

She did so. I heard her make a noise of pain. "Are you okay?"

"Yeah, I think so. I'm just going to have a nice bruise on my leg."

"There's a room or something behind these bricks." I said excitedly. Where one brick had almost completely dislodged I could see the space beyond was cylindrical in appearance and plunged into a dark abyss.

"Can you bring the torch a little closer, please?" I asked inquisitively, staring in to the blackness.

"What have you found?"

"Hold on. There's something attached to the wall. It's a ladder, it goes down. Can you come over and remove some the loose bricks."

Ann-Marie joined me and carefully started to move a brick

at a time under my guidance. Finally the hole was big enough to shine the torch down the well-like shaft which just kept going and going like a bottomless pit.

10

I clambered through the hole onto the ladder and it was as if I were still alive, my imagination making me think I could feel everything, the cold metal of the rusted rungs, the roughness of the brick. Ann-Marie directed the torchlight down the shaft as I descended. The light was not strong enough and soon I found myself surrounded in blackness even though I hadn't reached the bottom.

Looking up I could see Ann-Marie holding the torch and momentarily forgetting she was blind I called up "How do you feel about climbing down here? It's just that I can't see a damn thing, its pitch black and I could do with the torch to…" I stopped. My heart sank as I realised it was too much to ask, it was dangerous and rightly, I expected Ann-Marie to baulk at the idea. Another obstacle in my way. I wondered how I was going to continue in the dark.

Astonishingly Ann-Marie replied without even a pause.

"What are the steps like? I should be able to do it." Ann-Marie didn't let her disability stop her from doing anything and I admired her courage.

"It's basically a ladder, the rungs are about twelve inches apart. It's quite a narrow shaft and goes down a long way." Pausing I thought about what exactly I was asking her to do, it was risky for a sighted person. I relented "It's okay. Don't worry about it. I'll find another way," my voice and thoughts trailing off.

"But you need the light, right?"

Reluctantly I replied, "unfortunately yes." I climbed up

nearer and saw the apprehension on her face.

After already falling down on a relatively flat surface I could see the inherent difficulties in trying to get her through the hole in the wall and onto the ladder.

I studied the opening I'd climbed through. It wasn't big enough for a person to get through. I'd forgotten I wasn't real. The expression of her face showed she was torn between helping and baulking, but then gripped by determination her hands fumbled at the loose bricks, measuring the size and shape of the hole. A pang of guilt nagged at me, I was putting her in danger.

"It's okay, don't worry about it. It's too much." The words were like a challenge to her.

"No, I'll do it." She said, forcibly.

"I can't expect you to climb down…"

"I said 'I'll do it'. Now tell me what I need to do." Her voice commanded obedience and I was taken aback by her tenacity and courage. I doubted I would have done it if the situation were reversed.

Before she could enter the shaft Ann-Marie removed more of the loose bricks enabling her to ease through whilst relying on my instructions to guide her onto the ladder, a situation which, due to its nature could prove fatal. She had put her trust in me and, in turn, I would not let her put a foot wrong. Although her sense of touch was very good and she moved intuitively for the most part.

Why did she trust me so much? I hadn't exactly done anything to earn this trust.

After a few precarious moments she was standing on the ladder, hands gripped tightly on one of the rungs, torch clasped in her mouth. I continued to talk to her constantly, reassuring her and her footing, which I could just make out in the dim glow of the torchlight. Efficiently she descended the ladder, one step at a time. Visibly she relaxed as she got used to the way each rung felt under her feet, quickening her descent, hands continually clasping the next rung down before allowing her body to rest fully on the one she was stepping onto.

"Aaarrgh." I saw myself falling away from her.

I was strolling along the seafront watching the wind blow in gusts that whipped up the rubbish, whirling it around in the air before allowing it fall to the ground when the next gust would pick it up and start the cycle all over again. There was no one else about.

I detected the same calmness as earlier but this time it was tinged with loneliness. I felt a little unnerved after only experiencing the violent nature of this person, this murderer. Now I was in an emotional well that made this person complete, and feel more human.

It was easier for me to deal with when I didn't understand. Now I was confused. This was a real person, real feelings, and real emotions. So, why the killings? Was I in the body of a deranged madman? No, it was too controlled.

I was trying to feel empathy with this person.

Here I was viewing life through the eyes of a stranger, a murderer, and I was starting to empathise, starting to know my character.

I kept looking around taking in the scenery, the leisure centre built in the sixties and where I had cracked my head open once by banging it on the edge of the swimming pool. Then there was the doughnut stand, the public house, and confusion yet understanding and recognition. Why?

I was at the foot of the ladder with Ann-Marie standing over to me. For a second my mind was awash with anxiety as I remembered how I was meant to be helping her down then instant relief knowing she had made it by herself proving, once again, that she didn't always need other people's help.

"Did you see another murder?" she said calmly.

"We're at the bottom?" I was still a little confused by what I'd felt. "Can you shine the torch around?" My speech was disjointed as I kept going over the emotions of my last encounter. "Please. Thanks. No, I didn't see another murder. It was strange."

"Stranger than seeing murders committed?" I detected a note of sarcasm.

I looked around as Ann-Marie swung the torch in a slow arc. "No, that's not what I mean. I was walking along the seafront, just observing, not looking. There was a sense of confusion but I'm not sure why.

We're standing in a tunnel, similar to the one I was in earlier, but only viewing." I paused. "We can go left or right." As I looked both ways I tried to work out our location according to the streets above. "If I've got my bearings correct, left we head towards Clifton Parade, right we go back towards Clifftown Road." Still turning over the last vision in my head I looked one way then the other.

"I don't know where they…"

"What?" I snapped benignly. "Sorry, I didn't mean to…"

"It's alright."

She turned on the spot and lost her footing, as she fell I instinctively went to grab her hand but mine passed straight through hers. Unlike before when someone passed through me and I felt nothing this time it was a tingle like pins and needles, the nerve endings in my fingers alive with electricity.

"Ouch!" I said.

In the dim light from the torch I could see Ann-Marie sitting on the ground.

"You alright?"

"What was that?" Panic rose in Ann-Marie's voice.

"What was what?"

"I saw something, briefly, a bright light. It shone directly into my eyes."

"What? I don't know. I tried to grab your hand as you fell"

"But I saw light." She paused, thinking hard trying to decipher the moment. "Where's the torch?" Ann-Marie started to get up, brushing the dust from her clothes, her hands searching the space around herself for any hazards. "You tried to grab my hand?" It was a question and I was puzzled by it.

"Instinct I suppose." I spoke apologetically. "The torch is just a little to your left… bit more."

She shook her head dismissively. "I must be imagining things. Where are we going?"

"I don't know. I don't know which way to go."

"Err. The ground is wet. You're lucky you don't have to worry about it."

"Lucky," I scoffed. "Hmm s'pose that's one way to look at it. I thought maybe we'd head towards Clifton Parade, that's not far from the seafront, and that's where I last saw me, him. Oh, you know what I mean."

"Okay. Don't go too fast though the ground feels a bit slippy."

"I noticed." I saw her smile briefly.

The tunnel was mainly dry with just the odd puddle of water on the ground. Some of the smooth-looking bricks that reflected the light had luminescent slime over them where water had run down them over the years.

I could hear Ann-Marie shuffling along slowly behind. As we went further into the darkness I turned to see if she was alright. With one hand against the wall to guide her she was still a little slow. I tried to convince her that the ground was even but after her little fall she was understandably hesitant.

The tunnel turned right and the passage became narrower, I was amazed that it was so tall, but glad. We continued following the path it dictated. After a while I saw another ladder in the dim reaches of the torchlight. This second ladder was just leaning against the wall as if placed deliberately. As we got closer I could see it was an old wooden one covered in cobwebs looking as though it hadn't been used in years. Asking Ann-Marie to direct the light I saw the ladder stretched up about twenty-five feet to what looked like a tiny manhole cover.

"Wait here. I'm going up to see where we are." I climbed upwards. As I couldn't feel the rungs I wasn't sure of their actual condition or whether Ann-Marie would also be able to use them. At the top of the ladder I expected to bang my head on the metal drain cover still surprised by the ease, as a ghost, with which it went through. I took my time as I studied each layer as my eyes transcended the metal, mud and roots, it was a strange view of the world, a totally new perspective on things that I'd never given any thought to.

Suddenly daylight struck my eyes.

I was in someone's garden. I could see the back of a house, there was a patio area with garden chairs leaning against the table to keep the rain off the seats.

"Aargh." I was falling again.

I was walking along a road, Cambridge Road. I knew this road. I'd often parked my car here when we had to bring costumes as it was close to the theatre and free parking, if you could find a space. Something I seemed to have the knack of.

I was looking round me, a dim recollection of a distant land.

I stopped at the junction of Cambridge Road and Capel Terrace. There had been some bombing in this area during World War 2 and although the layout of streets and gardens had remained unchanged, houses had been rebuilt. Turning on the spot I surveyed the area trying to asses where I was.

A good few minutes passed when a couple of young lads passed by, they seemed to be staring at me. I didn't know why.

I turned down Capel Terrace and headed towards Alexandra Street and then into Clifton Mews and the flats at the end of this dead end street. There was an alleyway to the left of the block and I headed for that.

It was a short red tarmac cut-through to Royal Avenue Mews with a light at each end as well as the bars the council put in the ground that look like small 'n's to prevent cyclists heading in and out at breakneck speed.

I stopped about halfway along. The fence on my right was six feet tall with a trellis along the top. The other side was made of bricks cemented together to form a lattice pattern, each brick just overlapping the ones underneath by barely an inch, leaving a gap between the two ends of about four inches, plenty of room to get the toe of a shoe in without too much trouble.

That's exactly what I did.

Placing my hands on the top of the wall I put my right foot into a hole, two feet from the ground and eased myself up and over the wall. In a matter of seconds I was in the garden. I headed towards the rear of the house, keeping a careful watch for prying eyes. I made my way to what looked like two apple trees standing twenty feet in height.

Slipping around behind them I started to scrape at the dirt.

I was on my back looking up at the manhole cover.

"Daniel. Daniel… what's that noise?"

It took me a minute or so to focus and listen. Then I realised exactly what I was listening to.

Whispering, my voice full of urgency. "We've got to get out of here quick, back the way we came." I tried to grab Ann-Marie's hand but missed, not that it would have helped.

"Why? What's going on?"

"That noise you can hear is me, him… trying to get in here." My heart sank deep within me. What had I done? I'd led Ann-Marie almost straight to him and now if we didn't get out of here quick I would be responsible for her death. I felt sick. Without thinking again I reached for Ann-Marie's hand. This time I felt the twinge of pins and needles again. I retracted my hand immediately.

"I just saw myself!" Ann-Marie said, shocked.

"What?"

"I just saw myself. I wasn't dreaming. Just then. I saw me," she said in awe.

"Ann-Marie there's no time. We have got to get out of here now, I can't protect you. You know that?"

"Daniel I know, but I saw myself. How?"

"I don't know." I heard the sounds of stones on metal above me. "We need to get moving before it's too late."

This was insane. I was in a dark tunnel with a blind girl that I couldn't help and any minute now she would have a murderer breathing down her neck and all I would be able to do would be to watch.

Ann-Marie slowly made her way along the tunnel following my guiding dialogue with one hand on the wall, moving as fast as she dared. It was so frustrating. A snail's pace compared to what I wanted to be doing and I couldn't speed her up. If she fell it would slow our progress and she could hurt herself in the process. I willed her on silently.

Behind us I heard the sound of a metal clang.

"He's in... move." I tried to sound calm, knowing that I didn't.

In the flickering of the torchlight I noticed a hole in the wall on our left as large as a doorway, I didn't know where it led but it didn't matter. I just hoped it would provide somewhere to hide. It wasn't a proper entrance. It looked as though it had been smashed through leaving a gap big enough for a crouching person to get through. It would have to do.

With no time to get back to the theatre we took a chance. I guided Ann-Marie to the opening and through it as quietly as I could to avoid letting the person that would soon be passing this way know we were there.

The chamber we entered wasn't massive, a dug-out, a primitive cave-like structure of earth and rock. There was a place we could hide behind, a mound of fallen earth and stones, without being seen. Unless the chamber was searched thoroughly, which I prayed it wouldn't be. Ann-Marie settled in the dirt and I rested my hand on Ann-Marie's to reassure her it was going to be alright. She flicked off the torch and we were thrown into darkness.

The minutes passed like hours as we sat in the darkness. Every sound we heard was magnified as we waited with bated breath, her breathing, the slightest movement of her feet or hands, the rustle of her coat. I feared for Ann-Marie's safety and was regretting involving her in my stupid idea to come down here. It was too late now.

Heavy footsteps approached the entrance to our hiding place. A light haphazardly glanced off the tunnel walls.

As the source of the light became level with our hiding place I went through the motion of holding my breath.

I could almost feel Ann-Marie trembling with fright, sense her fears, her dread. I was helpless here, yet I was still cowering with her in hiding as if it was serving some purpose.

The light passed without actually entering our hideout. Relief filled my body even as we continued to sit there without moving, for what seemed an eternity.

"I saw the light, Daniel," Ann-Marie whispered.

"What?" I almost wanted to laugh. As it sounded like something church goer might say and to my ears sounded contrived.

"I saw the light as the man passed. I saw him. Well the shape of him." Her voice was rising with excitement.

"How? You're blind."

"I know that, thank you," then she allowed hope to rise in her, "but I did."

11

All the time I'd been holding Ann-Marie's hand I had been staring dead ahead, praying the person, whoever they were, would not find us. The more I contemplated Ann-Marie's words the more I became aware of a tingling in the fingers of my left hand. Automatically I went to rub it with my right not thinking logically about my lack of physical substance.

"Are you alright Daniel?" Ann-Marie asked concerned.

All the time danger had loomed it had been as if I had been real again and could feel the adrenalin pumping through a mortal body.

"Daniel, Daniel. Are you still there?"

I composed myself and nodded my agreement forgetting that it was pointless on two counts, it was pitch black and Ann-Marie was blind.

"Yes. Yes, I think so. Come on let's get out of here." I went to grab her hand instinctively and felt the shock of the tingling again.

"Ouch." Ann-Marie cried.

"What? What is it?"

"I felt something shock my arm."

"Where are you?" It was a stupid question. "Turn on the torch," I asked. "Please." I added as an afterthought, letting the tightness slip from my voice.

I heard her fumbling around on the ground for a few seconds followed by the click of a switch and our hiding place was filled with light.

"Are you okay? Can you see now?" I quizzed her.

"Yes. No… but I could. What was that shock I felt?" she asked puzzled.

"I don't know. Look we need to get out of here." I reached for her hand again.

"Daniel I can see. I can see. I said I could, didn't I?" I withdrew my hand again. "It's gone again. What did you do?"

"I didn't do anything I just went help you up."

"How?" Her question was urgent and excited.

"I held your hand." As I said the words, enlightenment dawned on me.

"That's it," she said loudly.

"Shush. He could still be in the vicinity." We both sat still and quietly listened, the coast was clear.

"Grab my hand again." I did so and felt the tingling sensation again. "Ouch!"

"What is it?"

"That's it," she said trying to contain her excitement in a controlled whisper. "When you touch my hand I can see. It's like an electric charge, it feels funny. Hold on a second. That's me." It sounded so strange I turned to look behind me. "Oh my god. Turn to face me again." I did as requested. "I am seeing through your eyes. Wow. This is awesome." She sat trying to comprehend what was going on. The tingling seemed to subside slightly as I took in the implication of what she was saying "This has never happened. Physical interaction! I've got to tell Aunt Rose."

"This is weird." I stood up, letting go of her hand, not sure what to do next.

"This is so strange. Hold my hand again Daniel, I can't believe this is happening." Reluctantly I took her hand and we stood there in our hiding place whilst she asked me to turn my head this way and that so she could take it all in.

I was pleased for her, although a part of me was tinged with sadness, but I didn't know why. This could only make things easier for us. "Come on, we'd better get going, the coast must be clear by now." My way of dealing with things was to ignore them and carry on as though nothing had happened.

We made our way back to the main tunnel.

"Daniel."

"What?"

"It'd probably be easier if you held my hand," she said tentatively. There was a brief awkward pause. Why did I feel so strange about it? It was a good thing, surely.

She only tripped a couple of times on our way back. Seeing things from the different perspective, to her left, made her judgement a bit skewed. She adjusted as well as she could.

Arriving at the bottom of the ladder, I stated matter of factly, "you're going to have to be blind again for this."

"Yes. I know," she sounded uneasy. "I'm a little scared of when I get to the top, how I am going to get back through the opening."

"Look if you climb up after me I'll hold your hand at the top. That way you can see what you're doing first hand, second hand, you know what I mean."

"Okay." I could see her shallow smile in the dim light of the torch.

Ann-Marie had no problem ascending to the top and, once there, we did as planned, except for the initial metaphoric leap of faith, it worked well.

Our way out of the theatre, I hoped, wouldn't be a problem either. I had no idea how long we'd been in the tunnel, so hoped that the theatre was still open.

I checked that the coast was clear before Ann-Marie left the security of the corridor.

There was no noise anywhere and, for an instant, I thought we had been underground longer than expected. We made our way down to the foyer hand in hand as it was the nearest exit. No one was around. There was a monitor on and we could see the show in full flow.

We walked briskly to the front doors, Ann-Marie starting to adjust to her skewed vision, I could sense that she wanted to study her surroundings yet knowing there wasn't really time. Suddenly I heard a familiar voice behind us.

"Oi! Where did you come from?"

I'd forgotten about Mark, he often did front of house. He must have been in the back of the ticket kiosk.

Before I had time to think Ann-Marie answered.

"I was just looking for the toilets. Sorry I just really needed to go, I just dashed in. No one was here so… I went looking for them. Found them upstairs. Hope you don't mind?"

He looked at her, sizing up her story. "Just this once, we are not a public convenience though." His eyes followed her out the door.

Mark was generally a nice guy but he did hate people taking liberties.

It was dark outside the theatre.

"Mojo," Ann-Marie announced with great urgency and walked briskly forward, I lost track of her hand. She was fine for the first few steps then grazed the outside wall of the theatre. "Sorry I forget, but I've got to get to Mojo, he'll be worried."

We hastened our way round to the back of the theatre where Mojo was sleeping, patiently waiting for his mistress' return.

When she came into view he sat up wagging his tail with delight. Ann-Marie knelt down, put her face to his and nuzzled him, whilst fumbling to untie his lead. As we walked back towards Ann-Marie's house she asked me to hold her hand again. She hadn't lived in the area when she could see so she wanted to know what the place looked like. Occasionally she'd ask me to face certain buildings not realising that she was talking quite loudly as people were starting to look on curiously, they probably thought she talking to her dog. She didn't care she was enjoying her new found sight.

I was in a tunnel, just barely lit by a torch I was holding, the battery was fading fast. It was like the tunnel we'd just left. Maybe it was the same one? It was difficult to tell in the gloom.

I stopped, turned to my right and felt the wall with my fingertips. I was searching for something. I had a feeling of recognition. Then brushing away the dirt and dust from the wall, I felt the smoothness of the brickwork, the coldness. Running my hands over it I found a wooden frame, then within the frame a round metal loop. Scraping away the dirt with my fingertips I tried to ease it up. It wouldn't budge. I tugged at it as best I could, it was awkward to grip, and finally I raised it enough to get my index finger through the loop to pull. Nothing happened. I tried again, still nothing.

Scraping away more of the dirt from the wall I searched out the rest of the frame of the door, which was about three feet square. There seemed to be nothing visibly obstructing it. Placing the torch on the ground, I tried again to open it. It still wouldn't budge. Again, and again I pulled. The metal loop started to make my finger smart. It wasn't big enough to put more than one finger in at a time, even though I tried.

I looked on the ground for anything that could be used as a lever, there was nothing.

"Damn it." The deep voice reverberated round the walls.

I tried kicking the door, which was about waist height, and almost lost my balance. Then I grabbed the loop and pulled again getting frustrated. I repeated this, until finally the door came away. It wasn't hinged, just a piece of wood blocking a hole, and I let it fall to the ground.

Shining the torch inside there was a knife lying in front of a big canvas sailor's type duffle bag. I pulled the knife out, studying it, before placing it in the waist band of my trousers. Behind the bag I noticed a picture frame, I couldn't see it clearly, but it was large, the glass cracked and covered in thick black dust.

Lowering the bag onto the ground, I rested the torch next to it, and untied the knot of rope that was holding it closed. I reached in.

"… you ok? Hello," was the unfamiliar voice.

Back in the main shopping street I still had Ann-Marie's hand in mine. I turned to her, the look on her face gave away that she knew something.

"Sorry. What? Yes," Ann-Marie replied uncertainly. "Yes. Thank you…" she continued more politely, moving away from the old lady dressed in a raincoat, her head wrapped in a purple hand knitted scarf.

"I saw Daniel, I saw," she whispered.

I was silent in response.

"I saw what you saw." She repeated more eagerly.

Marching on, her pace quickened, excited and intrigued by what she'd seen, finally she knew exactly what I meant by the visions.

"Stop looking at me," she said.

I turned away not realising I had been, her expression was one of puzzlement, intrigue, and excitement.

When we reached Ann-Marie's house her mother quizzed her.

"What time do you call this young lady? And you're filthy what have you been up to?" Ann-Marie's mother asked sternly. "I was beginning to worry."

"Sorry, we were at the park, I fell over and just lost track of time."

"Give me a ring next time you're going to be late." Her mum reluctantly relented.

"Okay. Sorry." Ann-Marie said, gingerly.

"Your tea's in the oven. Now go upstairs and get cleaned up. Do you want a cup of tea?"

"Yes please," Ann-Marie called, walking up the stairs, Mojo at her side.

In her room she turned the radio on low whilst she went down and had her tea, then turned it up when she came back to cover our conversation.

"How was your tea?"

"Alright, mum had done her spaghetti bolognaise, it's really nice, you should try…" She stopped. "Sorry, I forgot."

I looked at her thoughtfully wondering whether I missed eating or not. Certainly the thought of spaghetti bolognaise sounded good and made me want to eat it.

"Do you miss it, food that is?"

"I don't know. I don't feel hungry but I still remember my favourite things like chilli con carni, and egg'n chips." Melancholy started to swamp me as I thought about my life before.

"We'll sort this out," Ann-Marie stated matter of factly.

I broke from my thoughts. "I never knew those tunnels existed, they must have been sealed up for years."

"I've never been so scared in my life. I thought he'd see us. It's alright for you he can't see you." Ann-Marie sat on her bed stroking Mojo, trying to make amends for leaving him on his own for so long.

"Daniel, would you sit next to me and hold my hand? I have never seen Mojo."

I thought about her question for a second studying my hand as if by agreeing with her I was letting her invade my own privacy, yet it was so little to ask in exchange for the help she was giving me. I got up and sat next to her and Mojo. The tingling seemed to have lessened as I got used to it.

Mojo looked up at Ann-Marie as she looked at him through my eyes, he cocked an eye curiously, sensing that something was strange, but not sure what.

"He's got a lovely face." Mojo licked her face.

My mind was suddenly snagged by a thought. "The one thing that's been bugging me is I can't see who I am, when I… you know, go off into these visions or whatever you want to call them."

"What? Sorry. Oh yes," she said.

We both fell deep in thought. With this new discovery came more possibilities of how we could move forward but what was the next step? There were so many questions bombarding my mind that I thought it might explode. What was the point of the tunnels? Where did they all go? How did he know they existed? Why had the entrance in the theatre been sealed up?

"I think we need to see Aunt Rose again tomorrow, she should be able to help us. She might be able to explain a little more about these visions." Ann-Marie sounded positive. "And now I can see them too. Maybe that will help. Maybe she'll be able to see them as well if you hold her hand." I could hear the tenuous excitement in her voice and I wondered, maybe a little unfairly, whether this was just a big adventure to her as I had no idea what had occupied her time before I'd come along.

"So we'll go round tomorrow?"

"Yes, after breakfast, when mother's gone to work, we can head round to her house. It's not that far. Mojo knows the way don't you boy?" she kissed him on the nose and rubbed his ears. Ann-Marie had a bath and got ready for bed whilst I listened to the radio. It was strange sitting in the wicker chair not doing anything thinking that there must been something I should have been doing, a kind of limbo.

As Ann-Marie slept, the hours seemed to take forever to pass. Suddenly I felt what was becoming a familiar pain, ever increasing in intensity.

I was running. My chest was heaving with the pressure of breathing, my legs were beginning to feel like jelly. I was on the London Road heading away from the high street. I ran past a jewellers and ducked into an alley on my left. Sticking my head momentarily out, I glanced back the way I'd come, I couldn't see anyone chasing me and everything else seemed normal.

Back in the alley I headed further in to conceal myself from the light of the street lamps. Bending over I rested my hands on my knees and took in great gulps of air. Sweat was dripping from my face. I'd run for a while, but from what? The police? Someone else?

It was too dark to make out any detail on my clothing, although I could see I was wearing jeans, white trainers, and what looked like a leather jacket judging by the sleeves.

After gathering my breath I proceeded deeper into the alley. The alley was concreted over and ran to Burdett Avenue which was parallel to the London Road. I reached the exit, stopped and looked out to see if anyone was about.

The corner shop to the right and diagonally opposite was open. I heard the sound of a milk-float to my left and sharply turned my head. It was early morning. The shopkeeper placed an 'A' frame on the pavement with a local newspaper-heading emblazoned on it. 'Another victim – Residents warned to stay vigilant'. Underneath there was a photo-fit of a man but it was too small to see at this distance. I felt myself smile. Casually I walked from the alley.

Back in the bedroom all was still. I looked at the clock but couldn't make out the time.

I began to think long and hard about all the occurrences and what it was I needed to know.

It had started in the theatre. I was seeing visions through the eyes of a murderer. The underground tunnels, like rat runs. The murderer uses them. Why? How does he know about them? They didn't seem to have been used in years. The dream I saw the other night. So much information, so many pieces that were a part of a puzzle. How did they fit together? What was the key?

I needed answers. What was it that Aunt Rose had told me? 'That I was growing weaker. Soon I would fade away and become this person, losing my own identity.'

I was disturbed by the sound of Ann-Marie stirring from her sleep and, before she had time to gather her wits, I was entertaining her with my thoughts, trying to explain what I was thinking. It was as if by telling her it would organise them into some sort of proper order, a starting point.

She yawned stretching her arms. Mojo looked up from his position on the floor.

"The library might be a place to look," She said, halfway through a yawn.

"The library?"

"Yes. They've got a reference section, we can look up the history of Southend-on-Sea and the theatre. Maybe discover where all those tunnels lead and who made them. Might be a connection somewhere. What was that dream you saw?"

"A woman lying on the ground, lots of people standing around and there was a girl crying."

"Maybe it's not a dream. I told Aunt Rose about it and she said that maybe it's a personal memory."

"Yeah. But it doesn't tie up, the horse carriage, it was Southend alright but some distant past Southend. I recognised Ridley's hardware store, it was new but didn't look like it does today."

"Mmmm, I don't know then, but if we go to the library we can start by looking at the town maps."

"How? You can't see!"

"If you hold my hand I can."

12

After breakfast we headed to the library, leaving Mojo at home this time. Mojo fussed and whined a little and I could see the guilt on Ann-Marie's face as she closed the door behind us. He looked as if he was being punished yet he'd always been there for her. I held her hand as we walked in silence, the tingling in my fingers was less pronounced as I started to get used to the feeling. She felt a crackling sensation yet grew accustomed to it quickly as it gave her sight. A couple of times I lost the connection as our arms swung out of time with each other, it unnerved Ann-Marie as she became isolated without her companion.

"What's the library like?" I could hear the tension in Ann-Marie's voice.

I wanted to put her mind at ease but I didn't know what to expect myself.

"I can't remember exactly as it has been years since I've been. When we get into the library I'll direct you as I did in the theatre. I think I have a rough idea ofteh layout."

Ann-Marie nodded as her enthusiasm for this idea diminished. "Okay. I'm sure I'll be alright. Just remember if it's crowded I might lose your grip on my hand."

"It should be fine. There shouldn't be too many peop..."

A blur of images raced in front of my eyes. A woman's face, a young face, long mousy coloured hair, soft features and bright eyes full of life. She was talking in a loving way but I couldn't hear the words, her face was sweet and innocent. She leaned in to kiss me.

I heard a phone ringing. The woman's face faded. It was dark and the phone cried out again. I shut it out and went back to the image in my mind.

I was in the high street, a girl crying, a woman comforting her, people running around causing a commotion. I could hear voices even though the world was spinning around me.

Still the phone persisted and finally I was taken back to reality and my lounge where I was lying on the settee. My hand knocked over a glass but it was empty.

Back on the street, we were standing still.

"What was that about?" asked Ann-Marie curiously.

"I don't know." I looked at her.

"Don't look at me, it's weird."

"Sorry." I turned away from her.

"What happens if that occurs whilst we're inside?" Ann-Marie inquired.

I didn't know what to say. Depending on where it happened, the stairs, in a crowd of people, it could prove to be dangerous for her. Not life threatening, but if she fell she could easily hurt herself, especially without Mojo as back-up. I gripped her hand tighter, although she didn't notice.

"I really don't know," I said, barely audible. I wondered if maybe we should have brought Mojo, but knew it would cause her to stand out, especially if she was reading a normal book. We walked on in silence until we reached the library which was not open for another ten minutes.

There were some benches opposite the entrance near a small green area where, during the summer, I'd seen people sitting and reading. Ann-Marie sat down to wait.

"If you're alright here I'll go in and have a quick look around to get some idea of where to go once inside."

"Okay. Don't be long though." I sensed the vulnerability she felt without her friend and companion, Mojo.

"I won't." It was still very strange being able to walk into a closed building and not be noticed, a bit like a childhood fantasy, and it held a certain amount of excitement now that I had got used to its benefits. I had once wished that I could be invisible, although this wasn't quite what I'd envisaged at the time.

"Sorry dear," said the lady we hadn't noticed walking behind the bench.

"Oh, nothing, I was just talking to myself."

The lady smiled and walked on by.

I left Ann-Marie outside to catch some of the autumn sun which she had enjoyed seeing again as we walked to the library.

Wandering through the front doors I listened to the librarians discussing last night's Coronation Street whilst preparing themselves for the day's intellectual crowd to pass through the doors.

Mentally I ran through all the possible problem areas, looking for solutions before they arose.

The staircase spiralled up the centre of the building, each floor was open- plan like a large department store. The area we needed was on the third floor, tucked away in a corner, and consisted of a computer on a desk. There were shelves nearby stacked with reference material of the local area, books, maps, magazines, anything and everything you could think of. A coffee bar and canteen had been set up on the first floor.

I heard the doors below being unlocked and the first few people as they entered this glass walled building that was considered modern twenty-five years ago.

I could see Ann-Marie outside, her arms folded across her chest, her breath forming cloud-like shapes as she exhaled, and I went to join her. As I exited the building through the throng of people entering I began to feel uneasy. We were in a public place, we had to pass as one and I knew Ann-Marie was not feeling confident about it.

I connected with Ann-Marie's hand.

"Daniel?" she said, startled. "Oh yes."

"Are you ready?"

She breathed in deeply and stood up, temporarily breaking our connection.

"As ready as I'll ever be."

We headed for the doors and suddenly there was an explosion of people seemingly from nowhere bustling towards the entrance appearing as if by magic. Holding her hand proved difficult as she was jolted by people, students eager to find the reference books they needed, or to hire the latest CDs, OAPs with carrier bags of books they'd just read.

As I lost my grip on Ann-Marie's hand she found herself blind again buffeted around by the bodies surrounding her. I watched helplessly as she stumbled forwards trying to appear confident. I tried in vain to grab her hand again, but the attempts were lost in the array of people and coats.

"Watch it!" said a young male figure, wearing headphones.

"Sor..." Ann-Marie went to say, but was pushed in another direction. The guy just looked at her and then carried on walking.

"You alright love," enquired an older gentleman, as he steadied her.

"Yes," she stammered. "Thank you."

"It can be mayhem in here first thing in the morning, I normally try and get here a bit later but Beryl and I are going away later and I want a few books to take with us."

"I see. Thank you."

"You're welcome, my dear." With that the gentleman nodded and walked away.

The rush ceased and she stood just past the entrance, gathering her senses, not sure where to look, looking awkward but trying to appear relaxed. She unbuttoned her coat after getting quite warm in the commotion and I quickly rushed to take her hand to lead her to a quiet spot by the day's newspapers.

"Are you alright?" I asked.

In a low whisper she said, "I'm fine now. It's weird being

without Mojo. I didn't realise how much I'd miss him."

"I'm sorry. Sorry I got you involved."

I wanted to walk away but I couldn't leave her there. The silence between us was deafening.

"It's alright. I want to help. I'm just not used to not having Mojo with me."

"I'm sorry I don't know what's it's like for you. I just know that I want my life back, I want to see my parents again and have them see me." We both stood awkwardly.

"Come on let's go, just stay close to me and hold my hand."

"What?" said a young girl dressed in bright yellow tights and pink coat.

"Oh, nothing."

The girl slouched off.

Making our way up the staircase to the third floor Ann-Marie lost her balance a couple of times as her concentration lapsed as she got carried away taking in the details of the building. I felt so helpless. My efforts to try and catch her were futile although she managed to steady herself by tightening her grip on the chrome railing that ran up the stairs.

The section we needed was kept in good order as expected and contained maps and books upon books plotting the history of the town, true stories of the buildings. It was an Aladdin's cave of information. 'Where to start?' was the question that perplexed me.

"What shall we look for first?" No one was in this section so Ann-Marie could talk more freely.

"I don't know... how about the theatre? That's where it started, let's see what there is on that."

We scanned through the numerous book titles until one caught my eye. 'Theatre through the years in Southend-On-Sea' by Harvey Williamson.

Ann-Marie picked the book from the shelf letting it fall open in her hands. Moving behind Ann-Marie I rested my head on her right shoulder, causing her to shiver, whilst still keeping my hand on hers.

"That feels really weird." I went to move away, "No, no it's alright, just seems strange to be viewing a book from my shoulder." This proved to be most effective.

Her point of view was now as direct as it could be. This made it easier for her to turn the pages and know what I was looking at. The book mainly focussed on the performances that had taken place within the theatres in the town. There had been five theatres in the local area at one point, The Empire being third largest. We browsed further.

Book after book we took out and rejected.

A couple of times I found my attention distracted by her features, her button nose, her small ears and the way her hair was pushed over them, forgetting that she saw what I saw. Her response was to coyly tell me to stop.

Finally we found, 'How Southend Theatre came to life' by Alexander Partridge, published in 1963, which seemed to hold the information we were looking for.

We sat down at the table to our left to peruse its pages. The theatre was owned and built by the Hughes family, they owned half a dozen shops in the town, scattered about in various locations.

During the First World War they connected all these premises with secret tunnels enabling them to get from one shop to another without being seen. Mr Hughes was paranoid about protecting his family during the war, which he was sure would last for decades. He wanted to be sure that they could get together and escape using any one of the many external exits or at worst survive down there, hiding from the invaders. It took years to complete the passages and by the time they were finished the war had been over for four years. They still proved useful as it made it possible to collect all the takings from the shops and deposit them in the safe at the theatre. The access point to the theatre was via a ladder hidden behind a door in an upstairs corridor, which this author had not managed to locate and has only a letter, found in some old correspondence, when conducting his research, to confirm that one entrance.

Not many people outside the family knew about these passages, just trusted members of staff.

We scanned through various pictures, past pages and pages of irrelevant dialogue, although under normal circumstances it would have been of interest. About three quarters of a way through the book there was a chapter about the mystery of the remains found in a passageway near the bottom of a ladder. Even with the location of the ladder, the author still hadn't discovered where the entrance was because he couldn't gain access to the bottom of the ladder, it was a conundrum he would never solve before his death.

In 1957 when the theatre was to become a dance hall, the basement was being turned into a storage area with cloakroom facilities. According to the plans at the time there was another room hidden behind what was now the costume warehouse. When the builders knocked through the wrong wall by mistake they discovered the skeletal remains of someone in a hidden passageway. Although the remains were investigated thoroughly no formal identification could be made. There was no formal investigation of the passageway as the new owners wanted works completed as soon as possible. The wall was then rebuilt and the correct wall taken down. Before the Hughes family sold the theatre in 1921 they had blocked up the entrance to the ladder unaware that they were sealing the fate of the remains barely twenty feet from the foot of the ladder.

Mr Hughes was very generous to his loyal staff and gave a vast sum upon the sale of his businesses to each by way of compensation for losing their livelihoods, but also reflecting the dedication they had given to him over the years.

One employee, Mr Henry Highway was the only employee

not to receive a payment and only because he could not be found. He had worked for the Hughes family for more than twelve years, served them well with dedication to his job. The Hughes family were a good local family to work for and once accepted, you became part of their life. Henry got married to the young daughter of another wealthy businessman in the area, Mr Lansdowne. Unfortunately she was killed in an accident involving a horse and cart, six months after they were married.

The loss of his wife affected Henry greatly, he began to keep anti-social hours, drinking too much and being rude to customers and staff. One day he struck the only son of Mr Hughes, Albert, who was learning the business. Mr Hughes had to confront Henry. This incident was just one of many contributing factors that saw Mr Hughes thinking of selling up all his businesses and moving out into the country, ill health and the fact that Albert didn't have a head for business, being others. He already had an offer in hand and this was the straw that broke the camel's back.

Before he sold his businesses he had all the entrances to the tunnels, in each property, bricked up.

When Mr Hughes was unable to locate Henry to show him his gratitude with a tidy sum, to help rebuild his life, he filed a missing person report. Deep down he had thought of Henry as a son, which was why he took it so personally when Albert was struck, he didn't like fighting, even less when it was his own family.

Finally, after making enquiries and paying for newspaper advertisements Mr Hughes set up a trust account should Henry turn up. Even up until Mr Hughes death he hoped Henry would come forward, but he never did.

Stories started to spread amongst the gossip-mongers in the town that he got caught up in the occult, and the devil took him. There was a spate of murders around the same time which just fuelled the fire, especially as they stopped about the same time as he disappeared.

"Maybe there are some newspaper stories in the local papers of the time," I announced, sure that we were onto something.

"But surely when they had blocked up the entrances to the tunnels, they would have found his body?" Ann-Marie asked curiously.

"You would have thought so. Maybe there was a recess that he crawled into, out of sight."

"But the smell would give it away, surely?"

"Mmmm. They may have thought it was a dead rat or something."

"Come on Daniel, there's got to be quite a difference."

"I don't know. Maybe they had really bad BO or something so didn't notice."

"Err, that's a horrible thought."

We fired up the nearby microfiche scanner and sorted through the extensive library of data for the year and time we were looking for...

I was in a derelict building from the glimpses I caught. I was raining down blows on something, no someone.

Then with disgust I realised I was stabbing a body, the venom I felt was fuelled by anger. I could feel the tip of the blade making contact with the concrete floor underneath. Blood was pooling around me, everywhere. The victim's initial struggle quickly subsided but still I carried on. I was angry, hurting inside, revengeful. I could feel it yet didn't know why.

I could hear screaming but couldn't work out from where it came.

I finally stopped, my arm weary from the exertion, tears streaming from my eyes. Blood, thick like treacle on my hands and clothes. The pool seemed to be growing at an alarming rate as it drained from the body that now lay lifeless on the floor. I dropped the knife, the metal blade striking the floor sending echoes around the desolate place. I threw my head into my hands and cried...

Back in the library a few people had gathered around, talking to Ann-Marie.

'Are you okay?' 'You were screaming?' 'Can we help?'

Ann-Marie looked up at everyone like a rabbit caught in the headlights.

"I'm… sorry? Yeah. Fine… I… just"

"Excuse me, do you know where I might find 'Churches in Southend-on-Sea' by Cannon Thetford." A middle aged woman asked the librarian, who was staring at Ann-Marie, bewildered.

The focus of the librarian changed to address the question being asked.

"I need to get out of here," Ann-Marie whispered frantically. She stood up abruptly and I could see tears forming in her eyes. "Alright," I said begrudgingly, but deep down I knew she'd already helped more than was reasonable.

I glanced back at the screen as we left, an article caught my eye and I couldn't resist the urge to read on, briefly forgetting that Ann-Marie needed me. It was the missing person's article about Henry Highway but also on the same page was a report about recent murders that came to an abrupt end, the only connection being that all the victims were young girls, stabbed repeatedly, the brutal crimes started for no reason and ended just the same. No person had ever been charged with the murders.

Out of the corner of my eye I saw a figure stumble to my right, it was Ann-Marie, she wanted to leave, yet I wanted to stay and read on.

13

I couldn't help feeling annoyed with Ann-Marie for needing to leave. I knew it was selfish after all she was helping me and needed my eyes to get her out of the Library without hurting herself. Feeling cheated I reluctantly caught up, doing my best to hold her hand as she walked away, clearly agitated by what she had witnessed. Outside Ann-Marie sat down on the bench her breathing laboured, I knew she needed to be comforted but physically I couldn't, she could have done with Mojo here.

Her normally smooth rosy complexion looked pale and ill. Tears began to fall as the full horror of what she had witnessed became too much for her to bear. The previous visions she had witnessed had been harmless but this was the full gory picture.

In my mind I tried to shut out the horrors preferring to believe I was just watching a video nasty of real life proportions. It eased my mind. I wished she hadn't witnessed the vision but in order for her she had allowed herself to be part of my nightmare.

After a few minutes the colour came back to her face and she wiped the tears away with the back of her multi coloured woollen gloves that she put on as soon as got outside.

"Is that what you always see?" The words came out in between sniffs.

"No." I thought about them for a moment "What I've seen hasn't always been so disturbing. You know, you've seen some of them. They're strange, like watching short films. That's only the second time I've witnessed something so… horrific."

"I feel sick." She bent over, resting her elbows on her knees, forehead in her hands fighting the urge by taking deep breaths. I watched vaporous clouds of warm air rise in the air emphasizing the coldness.

"I'll hold your hand and we can go back to yours,"

"No," she snapped, the full fright of the image still fresh and ugly in her mind. "Sorry, I didn't mean it like that, I just not sure I want to see anything like that again"

I understood, but was concerned as to how we were going to get Ann-Marie home without Mojo or sight. "I don't know what to sa…"

I was still in the derelict building the sting of tears in my eyes. I felt the hatred I had for myself, for what I was doing, even though I was compelled to do it, an insane justice going on in my head.

I left the body on the floor and moved to a half-boarded upstairs window and stared back at the macabre scene in front of me. The body bloodied and motionless, vacant eyes staring up at the ceiling. I wanted to go over and take a closer look but my legs wouldn't move, I was frozen to the spot turning over thoughts in my head.

For the first time I sensed weakness, even confusion instead of strength and power.

Slowly I walked to the body. I studied the skin as it grew paler, the mouth frozen in mid scream, the tiny hands that laid palm up covered in blood, dirt and dust from the floor. Satisfaction came flooding back to me, followed by a sense of a duty achieved. Somehow I'd justified my actions within me and I set about dragging some loose broken pieces of wood and other dirty materials to cover the body, my work.

Once done I walked down an old wooden staircase turning right at the bottom to head across a large open space towards a doorway. I pulled back a piece of wood and viewed the overgrown alley outside. Looking both ways I checked the coast was clear before glancing down at my clothes. Thick red blood stained my light brown jumper and blue jeans. I knew I couldn't walk out like this it would only draw attention to myself. I pulled the jumper off and threw it to the floor picking up a lumberjack style blanket jacket that was lying on the

ground. Brushing it down, I put it on, it was torn but it would do.
Picking up handfuls of dust and dirt I rubbed them into my jeans to
disguise the blood as best I could.
  Leaving the building cautiously, I headed deeper into the alley.

I was standing by the bench, Ann-Marie was gone. Panic
raked me as I looked around for her, scouring every direction,
expecting to catch a glimpse of her. Nothing. 'Damn', I cursed.
  For a few minutes I stood dumbstruck before starting to run
in the direction of her house, it was the only possibility I wanted to think of. I ran as fast as I could, praying she'd be there,
wishing she'd be there.
  I was suddenly concerned that she'd been abducted but I tried
to push it away, fearing that if that was the case I was to blame.
  At her house I ran straight through the front door past Mojo
who was lying on the floor, waiting patiently. He lifted his head,
he knew I was there. I stopped suddenly. From this I knew Ann-
Marie was not.
  Fear gripped me. What had I done?
  I turned and left.
  At the front gate I stopped, looking left, then right. I didn't
know where to go. She could be anywhere, and with anyone.
  Guilt tore at me. If only I knew where Aunt Rose lived I
could talk to her.
  Helpless I went back inside and up to Ann-Marie's room with
Mojo following me, he sensed something was wrong. He was
watching me as I searched for an address book before realising
that she was blind.
  "Where is she Mojo? What have I done?" I asked rhetorically.
  Mojo stared at me blankly, cocking his head to one side
curiously. Like Ann-Marie, he could always tell where I was.
  I paced the room, wishing she would walk through the door.
I needed her to.

I was watching her. She was with Aunt Rose.

What was I doing?

I was spying on her. Not just her but generally watching people from a secluded place, crouching hidden behind some bushes viewing the scene waiting for my next victim, the next opportunity. I recognised the area, North Road. I had to be in the cemetery. That was the only place that had any sort of bushes. There was a school about one hundred yards along the road. The road seemed overcome by a relaxed silence, lesson time. Now I was watching Ann-Marie and Aunt Rose intently.

They walked slowly, reaching Cliff Avenue and turning into it. I looked up and down the road from where I was situated. All was clear. Dread filled my thoughts as I moved out of the bushes and started to cross the road. I reached the closed-down bakers on the corner of the street and observed the two figures walking in the distance.

A sudden colossus of noise started behind me, school was out.

I sprinted out of Ann-Marie's bedroom, down the stairs, and out through the front door. I felt fear, fear for her, Ann-Marie's life and Aunt Rose's. Now I knew where they were I made good progress, no longer limited by my mortal constraints of fitness.

Within minutes I was in North Road viewing the same scene I had witnessed, school children were scattered along the road chatting and playing. I stopped and watched, looking and hunting for a killer, someone that looked out of place.

I wanted to make sure all the kids got home safely, an impossible task I knew, I couldn't protect them all, but that didn't matter. I was looking for him, without the knowledge of what he looked like, so I was searching out any unusual characters in the hope of catching a glimpse of anyone acting strangely. I hoped he would stand out of the crowd.

I was wrong. The parents were littered amongst the young ones all dressed so differently, anyone of them could be him. A scream! I spun round on the spot. It was just a group of kids mucking about. Another scream! Again, just kids playing. My ears were acting like highly sensitive radars. I had to find Ann-Marie.

I headed along Cliff Avenue, past the closed-up baker's, picking up speed, running faster and faster. At the end of this street was Salisbury Avenue, I had to make a decision which way to go, left or right. I couldn't see them in either direction. I headed left, again at full speed, the road bent to the right, heading towards Balmoral Road. When I got to the 'T' junction I still couldn't see them. I called out, hoping Ann-Marie would hear me. There was no response. I turned right into Balmoral Road, still calling Ann-Marie.

Walking and calling like I was looking for a lost dog. Finally a familiar voice behind caught my attention.

"Daniel."

I turned and saw Aunt Rose. She wasn't looking in my direction she didn't seem to pick up my aura the way Ann-Marie did, but I was thankful to see her soft features and warm eyes. I walked towards her.

"Aunt Rose."

"Daniel, Ann-Marie is inside." I turned and faced the open door. Ann-Marie was standing there, one hand against the door frame.

"I thought I'd lost you. I came back but you weren't there. I went to your house. I didn't know where else to go. I had another vision. I saw you. I was watching you and Aunt Rose. I thought. I thought…"

"It's alright Daniel. I'm okay. You went again but this time I couldn't even sense you near me. It was as if you had gone completely. I was scared. Then I heard Aunt Rose's voice and…" She stopped suddenly, I turned, a mother with her two children was walking past staring in Ann-Marie's direction.

"Let's go inside," Aunt Rose announced.

I wanted to throw my arms around Ann-Marie and apologise

for everything I'd put her through, but there was no point. We sat down in Aunt Rose's living room whilst she made a pot of tea. It was a darkly decorated place, very oldie-worldly with flock wallpaper, dark-red heavily patterned carpet. The woodwork which looked as though it had started out as white was now very pale cream colour. The settee and armchairs had lacework covers on the arms, lightly decorating the corduroy fabric. The large coffee table was hidden amongst a collection of books and various trinkets, including a crystal ball, which sat on its stand on a purple swatch of velvet.

Aunt Rose came back with a tray in her hands, on it were two cups, a tea-pot hidden underneath a knitted tea cosy, and a plateful of bourbon cream biscuits. The sight of the biscuits reminded me of the taste and I wished I could have one. She poured out the tea and set a cup down in front of Ann-Marie, taking the other for herself.

"Daniel dear, Ann-Marie tells me she has seen what you see. When you touch hands she can see through your eyes. Now, I have never known a connection quite that strong. And it is very strange. However, she wonders whether it might work with me, if you would let me try, if you don't mind of course?"

How could I mind? This person was trying to help me. I knelt down in front of Aunt Rose and placed my hands in hers. Like before she fell into a trance-like state and I wondered what she was hoping to achieve.

I felt myself being tugged. My whole body jerked forward. "Dani…"

I was holding my right hand, it was hurting. There was blood coming from a wound. I was kneeling on the ground, the pain from the wound gripping me like a shock of electricity. I released my grip and viewed the damage. It was a bite mark - from what, I couldn't tell but it hurt like hell. Deep inside I was almost glad.

I was facing Aunt Rose her eyes showed that she had seen

it also.

"My hand, it hurts," I said lamely.

"What do you mean it hurts?" asked Ann-Marie

"My hand. It stings. I've been bitten, I think." I looked down at my hand, nothing, no marks.

Aunt Rose was still in her trance.

"Your aura doesn't feel as strong as it did Daniel," Ann-Marie said, concerned.

"Oh my, oh m…" Aunt Rose said alarmed before falling back onto the settee. This time I wasn't as concerned, knowing this to be normal.

"What do you mean my aura isn't as strong?"

"Daniel, Daniel are you there?"

"Yes. What do you mean my aura isn't as strong?"

"You were. Never mind. When I first felt your presence it was like nothing I'd ever felt before, powerful, almost over-whelming. Now you feel like a faint spirit. I can't really explain it. You just seem weaker."

"But nothing's changed…" I stopped mid-sentence. Things had changed. It had been a slow progression but now I was feeling more, hearing more. The first vision I had was silent. The dream. Now the pain in my hand, it had all become more and more real, every vision taking me one step closer. One step closer to what though?

"What is it Daniel? What are you thinking?"

"I was just thinking how things have changed, the visions that is. They're becoming more real. Like the pain in my hand, I can still feel it now, yet it was just a vision. Why?"

Aunt Rose started to come round.

"Oh, deary me."

"What is it Aunt Rose?" I said, panicking.

"It's worse dear. Much more than I first thought."

"What is it?" inquired Ann-Marie impatiently.

I awaited more bad news. Not that I believed it could get any worse. I was dead anyway. I believed that now.

Aunt Rose picked up her cup of tea with a shaking hand to take a sip, then replaced the cup on its saucer.

"What is it?" There was urgency in my words.

"I'm afraid it's as my friend said. I spoke with Heather, she's a white witch. I asked her for advice. And, and… you just confirmed it to me. Not only are you connected to this person, you are becoming this person."

"What?" Ann-Marie voiced with alarm.

"Heather said that sometimes when there is a connection such as this, one side is normally stronger than the other. There is a tug of war struggle, only one will win, the stronger of the two." She looked at me. "Unfortunately, my dear, you are losing. I could feel the strength of this other person, he is powerful. Evil now."

"What do you mean, 'NOW'?"

"I could feel that he wasn't always like this, there was a time when he was a good, caring person. Daniel, according to Froxidian beliefs you only have eight days before you'll fade out completely. He would have won."

"I don't understand, Aunt Rose, who are the Frostians?"

"Were! Froxidians, Daniel. According to Heather they were a cult quite strong in the local area around the nineteenth century. Outwardly they were fairly harmless in themselves, and no one could ever prove otherwise, although a lot of people were afraid of them, afraid of the unknown I suppose. I'm not quite sure of the exact facts, but, at the head of the cult were three Arcs, powerful Wizards or Witches, each representing a book of the Froxidian belief; Naga, Tisar, and mmmm…". Aunt Rose thought for a while "… and Degan, I think she said. As I say, there is some knowledge just not detailed. Well, apparently, together the power they could yield was phenomenal. She told me stories of people going insane after crossing them. One of the things I do remember Heather saying is that in order for an

Arc to be replaced he would be challenged by another follower, a challenge of strength, both physical and mystical. If the Arc lost physically he would try to possess the loser's body, throwing out their soul so it became a shadow. They had eight days to try and win it back before they dissipated. This also gave the Arc a new lease of physical life."

"A cult, you say?"

"What is it Daniel?"

"I'm not sure yet, Ann-Marie, something about what we found out in the library."

"What was dear?" Aunt Rose asked.

"We looked up the history of the theatre and…"

"Henry Highway?" I said curiously.

"Sorry?" Aunt Rose added

Of course, it was all starting to piece together. I explained my thoughts as quickly as I could get the words out. Why the name Henry Highway rang a bell, it was the name at the bottom of the poem, although I'd only seen part of it before blacking out, yet it had to be, it was too much of a coincidence, in the theatre the night this all started. Reports of him being involved in a cult, The Froxidian cult were around at the time, it was all starting to form a connection. The only part that I had trouble understanding was how he could take my physical body. That thought took the wind out of my sails and my heart sank.

14

The world spun round in front of me, no way out, no way to win with the end looming closer.

"Is there any way that Daniel can fight him?" Ann-Marie expressed. She really cared, I could hear it in her voice.

"I'm sorry dear, I don't. But maybe…" She thought for a second before speaking again. "Maybe Heather can help, being a white witch, she knows a lot more about this sort of thing."

"A what?" I said brought back from my own thoughts.

"A white witch, a good witch. She may be able to help you. I'll go and speak with her, she only lives two doors down." She glanced at the elegant silver watch on her wrist, "and she is normally in about now." With that she got up and started to walk out of the living room.

"Aunt Rose, why can I see through Daniel's eyes when he holds my hand?"

She stopped and turned to face Ann-Marie. "Well, my dear, you have a special gift. You can never tell how strong a gift is until the time when it is needed, you can go a whole lifetime never knowing. Daniel is not a spirit, he is a 'Soulshadow', a stronger, more physical entity than you have come in contact with before, and it seems you have found a new strength." She paused thoughtfully. "And now is the time when you need it."

I looked at Ann-Marie. She understood. Aunt Rose walked out of the house, leaving the front door ajar.

I had no idea how much difference it would make talking to Heather. A part of me felt all was lost, whilst another part of me still held out some hope, some sliver of a chance. What I expected to happen I didn't know, some strange phenomenon that would put everything straight, back the way it should have been. Put me back in that corridor on Sunday night.

That night appeared a distant memory yet it was only Wednesday now, three days had passed. How?

"Daniel, what's the time?"

"I don't know." I glanced around the room for a clock. "Three-twenty. Why?"

"I've got to get home before mum, otherwise she'll worry if she sees Mojo still there and I'm not and after yesterday." With that she started to fuss around gathering her things.

"Good point," I agreed. "Did you ever tell your mum about your gift?"

"No," she stated mockingly. "She'd freak out. She hates the supernatural and anything vaguely unfamiliar. I tried once to explain to her about dad, that I'd spoken to him. That he helped me through my transition to my 'dark world' as I used to call it. I think that's kinda what made her make up her mind about moving in the first place. She didn't say so but I could hear it in her voice. She seemed scared by it all.

When I first went blind, I started to pay more attention to the stresses in people's voices, noting intonations. Things I didn't think about when I could see, I didn't need to worry as I could see people's faces."

"S'ppose it would frea…

Blood was still dripping from my hand, the bite had been deep. I'd made it back to my flat and was in the bathroom washing my hand. I was shaking with the pain. I ran cold water over my hand washing the flow of blood exposing the two puncture wounds, round with clean edges.

The reflection of my shirt shone back at me from the shaving mirror that hung on the wall near the sink. It was one of the red polo shorts I used for work, it looked dirty. I stepped over to the toilet, the seat was down, bandages, lint, cream and scissors were resting on it.

Kneeling down I tried to put the dressing on, but found it awkward one-handed. Every time I got it tight enough it would come undone. Getting frustrated only managed to aggravate the pain, which was already intense.

After about ten frustrating minutes and endless attempts I managed to fasten the bandage loosely with a safety pin, flexing my hand slowly to make sure it would stay in place, ignoring the pain that ensued. I hoped the blood would stop flowing shortly as I had put enough wadding on it. Finally I went back downstairs to the lounge where, on the floor, I had placed the local evening papers from the last two nights. To the left of these were cuttings from them and a whole front page. Another paper to the right still lay folded in half where it had been thrown, covered in spots of blood.

I sat down on the settee before slipping on to the floor with my legs spread out in front of me.

Picking up a pair of kitchen scissors I glanced at the double glazed French doors, a pair of eyes were watching me, next door's cat, I growled and made as if I was going to lunge at it, the cat flinched, but stayed for a while longer until it got bored.

I read the lead story about the murders and laughed to myself. They had no leads to go on and were asking for witnesses to come forward.

The victim from the field who had had a lucky escape was still in shock and couldn't give a very good description as she never actually saw her attacker. What little she did know washed mentioned and along with a photofit formed part of the article, but the picture didn't look familiar. I smiled then winced at the pain of my hand which still stung. I was so smart.

Carefully I cut out the story and placed it with others on the floor, satisfaction was mine. I lay back against the sofa resting my head on a cushion and drifted into a sleep that was made uneasy by the throbbing from my hand.

Ann-Marie and a new face were staring at me.

"…derstand what you mean. Hello, I'm Heather,"

Like an object on show in a museum, I studied the new face that appeared to be studying me, even though she couldn't actually see me, just felt my presence, it was all very unnerving.

"Hi." was all I managed to get out.

Heather was a shortish lady in her mid forties with cropped hair, wearing a brown heavy jumper, jeans and trainers. She held a book under her arm but I couldn't see the title.

"Aye, you can certainly feel the power that takes him Rose, it's strong, very strong." She spoke with a northern accent I couldn't place.

"He is getting weaker. When I first met him I felt an almost overwhelming aura now it's not so strong," Ann-Marie stated matter of factly.

I was beginning to feel I wasn't there, talked about behind my back, but in front of me. "I am here you know," I said curtly, without meaning to sound rude.

"It's okay, Daniel, I'm here to help."

"Yes. I'm sorry. I realise that. Thank you." I didn't know why I was so annoyed. Maybe it was because I felt helpless. I was used to managing for myself, not having to rely on other people.

Heather sat down next to Rose on the settee, placing the book on the coffee table in front of her. We all watched as she flicked through the pages intently looking for something in particular, finally settling on a page. She opened a small bag she had brought with her and lifted out a carefully crafted wooden box which was hinged in such a way that it opened to form a flat 'T' shape, exposing a crystal ball wrapped in a silk handkerchief.

"Why don't you use that one?" I pointed to the crystal ball already on the coffee table, forgetting that they couldn't see my actions. They understood what I meant anyway.

"Because they are very…" Ann-Marie and Aunt Rose said together.

Aunt Rose continued, "because they are very personal to each user, tuned into our own psyche."

Gently Heather stroked it, her eyes transfixed by it. Normally I would have laughed as I didn't have much faith in this sort of thing, however, recently I had found my beliefs well and truly tested, and blown apart. She took it off its perch and held it in her lap. Flicking through more pages of her book, she muttered to herself, whilst we all watched with bated breath.

"What's she doin…" A familiar pain hit me.

I was awoken with a start. The doorbell. It took me a while to get my bearings. I looked at the cuttings on the floor and contemplated gathering them up.

In the end I left them where they were and walked into the hallway, leaving the light switched off so I could glance down the stairs through the glass panel above the door into the lobby, trying to avoid being seen by anyone who might be there.

The doorbell rang out again. In the dim street light which oozed into the lobby I could make out the shape of my parents, one of their surprise visits that they made to make sure I was looking after myself. I hesitated, wondering whether to answer, still looking on, watching them. With no lights on they could not be sure if I was in or not. Again the doorbell chimed.

I switched the light on. 'NO', I wanted to cry out but it was too late. I made my way down the stairs to the front door and slowly opened it…

"Nooooo."

"What is it, Daniel?" Ann-Marie enquired urgently.

"My parents. They're there. At my flat now." I got up, heading towards the door.

"Don't go, stay," Heather said firmly. "There won't be anything you can do."

I stopped in my tracks. "What?" I was astounded by her indifference, but before I could add anything, she continued.

"There's nothing you can do about it." The edge of firmness

in her voice compelled me to listen. I turned to face her, taking a step closer, still het-up inside.

"You know that you have eight days before you completely become one. At that stage it will be too late, your Soulshadow will be gone and your physical body and this spirit will be one, forever. If you want to put this right you have to locate the physical body of the spirit and perform a binding ritual that will tie his spirit to his remains, therefore enabling you to take back possession of your physical self."

"My physical self? I'm not sure I understand." My mind was a whirl.

Ann-Marie and Aunt Rose were listening as intently as I was, this must have been new to them as well, as their faces showed their curiosity.

"The spirit here present in this room is the Soulshadow of your physical entity, which has been taken over by the spirit of someone else."

"Henry," Ann-Marie interrupted.

"Unless you get possession of your body within the eight days, Henry Highway, if it is him, will take over your life...," Heather continued.

"You mean all this time he has been parading as me?!"

"Yes."

"So the murders have been committed by Daniel's physical side?"

"Yes Ann-Marie."

I was horrified. It was bad enough I was witness to the gruesome crimes, but now their blood was on my hands.

"My parents!" I exclaimed.

"Wait," Aunt Rose said.

"But I've got to go and see what I can do, they're in danger."

"They are okay," Heather added.

"What? How do you know?"

"They are not what he is after. The shadows show they are

sitting and talking, he is even at peace for a while." She spoke with such certainty that I found it hard to disbelieve.

"How are we going to find Henry's remains?"

"Ann-Marie, that, I cannot help you with, for that you will have to consult the town records should they have that information. Since this town was just a small parish it shouldn't be too hard or take too long, providing…" She broke off in thought. "… he is from around this area and died here too. There is too much mist… I can't give you anymore information."

"Providing that is the case, what do we have to do then?" I asked, wanting to get as much information as possible, still confused by the revelation that he was me.

"Then you have to find out where he performed the ritual that enabled his spirit to live on past the death of his earthly self. And destroy the very thing that made it possible for his spirit to take over another person."

"So we find the remains and perform this binding ritual. Then we have to find where the door is that opened this chain of events."

"That is correct Ann-Marie. The ritual is in this book and has to be performed on the grave of his remains, also you'll need something personal, something precious."

Heather passed the book into Ann-Marie's hands open at the page we required. I saw Ann-Marie's hands dip from the physical weight of it.

"But how am I going to do this?" Ann-Marie asked.

Heather leaned forward.

"Daniel will be with you, you need each other for this. He is your eyes." Heather said with a calming gentleness that gave Ann-Marie strength, or at least made her look more relaxed.

We were all silent for a few minutes, contemplating the future events with me still concerned for my parents' safety.

15

Ann-Marie and I left Aunt Rose and Heather talking whilst we headed back to her house with the book in a carrier bag. We hoped her mother had been held up on her way home. She was reluctant for me to take her hand because of the visions but logic told her it would be best, and quicker. I could see the anxiety riding her.

"I'm sorry I left you at the library," I said lamely.

"It's not your fault."

"I know but…" I let the words fade as we carried on in silence.

Time had run away with us and we had not left until gone four. Sometimes, Ann-Marie said, her mum got in early. Hopefully this was not one of those nights.

It was too late today to go to the town records office it would have to wait until the following day.

Walking in silence, we were lost deep in our own thoughts. We needed each other. That thought was so true. I couldn't complete this task without her and she needed me to make it possible for her to fulfil her side of the bargain. It was such a perfect pairing.

Yet another thought that hung around in the back of my mind like a nightmare waiting to pounce, was the dreaded thought that at anytime another vision could come and take me, inadvertently taking her as well, thus rendering Ann-Marie helpless in the street alone. I did my best to rush her along. It was dark and the side streets were badly lit, and we were too close to my own flat for my liking. The paradox of it all would be if he was watching us when I got another vision. Worse was the irony that she and I would see it all but not be able to do anything about it all the time she held my hand, a possible living nightmare.

I was still concerned for my parents, they had met this murderer. Heather said they were alright. Would they know any different, as far as they were concerned it was their son? I hated knowing that they were talking to him, that he was impersonating me and there was nothing I could do about it.

The journey seemed to be taking ages and I wished we'd taken up Heather's offer to come with us, at least I would know Ann-Marie would be safe if a vision did take us. But Ann-Marie was defiant and strong-willed, despite our earlier episode in the library. She wanted to face her demons, my demons. I broke our voluntary silent deadlock.

"Sorry, I shouldn't have got you involved in all this."

"You didn't make me do anything I didn't want to." She frowned. "Stop looking at me I can't see where I am going."

"Sorry." There was that word again.

"It's nice in some respects. The holidays between terms can be so boring. I've got a few friends but we don't really see each other during the holidays. I think that sometimes I'm a bit of a burden on my mum, although she rarely shouts or rushes me. It can't be easy for her having a blind daughter. I've been learning braille, but it's not easy. I find it hard to learn to read all over again." She paused reflectively. "It's been nice helping you, because I get to see again even if it is a double-edged sword."

"What do you mean?"

"Whatever the outcome of the next few days, I'll be back to being blind all the time." She paused for thought. "But I've got Mojo and he's great. I'd miss him if I could see again." I could sense the fondness she had for her friend and it was beguiling. "I often wonder how my life would have turned out if I could still see. Not that being blind is holding me back, I'm studying economics and business studies as I want to prove to the world that blindness isn't going to stop me making something of myself."

"I don't think there's much chance of that."

"Of what?"

"The world stopping you, or holding you back."

"What do you mean? And keep looking ahead. Besides it's weird, seeing myself outside of myself, if you know what I mean. I still need to see where we are going."

"Sorry. Well you certainly don't strike me as the sort of person to let the world put up barriers. Look how you've helped me. You didn't have to, and nothing seems to faze you, whatever I've asked of you. I'm not sure I would do the same if the situation were reversed." I caught her smile out of the corner of my eye as it effervesced across her face. "Thank you. Maybe after this is over we can…"

The lights were on in Ann-Marie's house, damn, her mother was in.

Ann-Marie slid her keys silently into the door, turning the key as to avoid the click of the lock unhooking itself; pushing the door inwards waiting for the inevitable squeak of the hinges that this time didn't happen. Carefully stepping forward over the threshold she closed the door, holding the lock in the open position until the door was firmly in place before releasing it gently.

We stood there for a minute and I wondered what Ann-Marie would do next.

"Hi mum," she shouted. The words caught me unawares.

"Hi honey, you feeling better now?" came the voice from the kitchen.

"Sorry?"

"You feeling better? How long have you been asleep?" Quickly catching on, Ann-Marie slipped off her coat felt for the stairs, placing it on the treads ready to pick it up again when she went up, before walking briskly into the kitchen.

"Yeah, I'm fine just felt a little tired. What's the time?" She stretched and yawned.

"About four-thirty. I got away from work a bit early today. Dinner will be ready in about half an hour. Hope you're hungry, I got a nice bit of lamb for tea."

"I'm famished. I'm going to put some music on." She left the kitchen, making her way upstairs to her bedroom, collecting her coat on the way. Mojo was waiting in her room to greet her.

"Sorry I had to leave you boy." Mojo licked her face. "I've got to do the same tomorrow," She gave him a big hug then sat on her bed. "Daniel? Daniel?"

"Yes."

"Oh you're there. Do you know exactly where we've got to go tomorrow?"

"Not exactly, I ju…"

I was in my lounge again. Three mugs sat on the floor, empty. My parents! There was no sign that there had been any sort of trouble. I was sitting staring at the TV set, puzzled.

Of course all this was new to him, Henry. A home improvement program was on and they were knocking down a wall. I was intrigued, captivated by it all, looking at the power tools being used. I sat there and watched the whole program without moving.

After it finished I got up and moved about my flat paying closer attention to the shelving units, full of videos. I took the odd one out and read the back cover, the CDs - opening the cases and viewing the silver discs inside.

In the hallway I took in the picture gallery I'd created up the stairway, pictures from shows I'd been in. Behind my bedroom door was a full length mirror and I took the time to look at the image, me.

Suddenly I didn't want to see it, see the reflection of myself looking back, it was too disturbing, but I had no choice. The events of the previous days came hurtling back into focus. I was disgusted with myself. It was my body that had committed those crimes. Those unspeakable actions I didn't want to believe it. I screamed.

"… aaarrghhh,"

"What is it, Daniel?"

I was back in Ann-Marie's room. "I just saw myself for the first time. I saw me. The me, that is me now. Not who I really am." I struggled to sound coherent. If I could have cried I would have done. I flumped into the wicker chair feeling like the wind had been sucked from me.

"Why me?" I muttered. "Why me?"

There was little Ann-Marie could do as we spent the evening going over the events until she finally went to sleep and left me to replay all the visions again and again. Sometime over the course of the night I started to understand the twisted sense of sobriety that kept him killing. Why he saw things the way he did, how he justified it. I found myself strangely torn between sympathy and hatred for this monster.

After Ann-Marie's mother had gone to work we walked to the Town Hall. A prestigious building, and the focal point of the high street, faced with large fifty-foot high columns of carved stone with ornate features top and bottom. There were steps running the full width of the building and they only helped to give it a majestic feel. It had rained during the night and puddles lay on some of the steps. A big revolving door led into the fancy lobby with its decorative plasterwork and wooden parquet flooring.

The reception desk was an add-on from the sixties and didn't sit right in amongst the grandeur, but no one cared enough to change it so it remained. It was unmanned with a sign that read, 'Please ring for attention'. Ann-Marie did so.

After a minute or two she rang it again. A guard wandered out from a room at the back.

"Can I help you miss?" His voiced boomed around the vast entrance lobby's hard surfaces.

"Yes. Can you tell me where I can find the records for all deaths in the area, I'm doing some research for my family tree and I know my Grandpa died locally but I'm not sure where he is buried."

I was taken aback, Ann-Marie had really thought her part through.

"Follow the stairs up to the second floor then take the second door on the right down the corridor." He moved his arm around, doing his best to visually point to where he meant. He looked quite silly when he did, this in turn made Ann-Marie smirk.

"What's so funny?"

"Sorry, nothing." The guard was bemused by her.

"If you speak to Vivienne who is up there she'll point you in the right direction."

"Thank you."

It was a long, winding marble staircase, the treads of which were about five foot wide with carpet just covering the centre three feet and stair-rods holding it in place.

Ann-Marie knocked at the door we required, not sure whether to enter or wait for an invitation. She gingerly pushed it open after minute's hesitation, revealing a big ominous room full of shelves upon shelves of books. In the corner was a lady sitting at a computer talking to a couple sitting in front of her. We waited until she had finished before marching over, looking around at the tomes, the sheer size of some gave the impression they weighed a ton.

"Thank god for computers," Ann-Marie whispered.

"Hello, can I help you?" the young lady, who had now finished with couple, in her mid-twenties enquired.

"Hi, I'm looking for a record of my Grandpa's death. You see I'm researching my family tree, and trying to trace where all my relatives are buried… and were born."

"Well let me see, what was his surname?"

"Highway."

"Do you know when he died, just the year will do,"

"No I don't." She bit her lower lip nervously. "His first name was Henry though, will that help?"

"Let's try and see what the computer brings up."

I was in my car. Driving out of town, a country lane, heading towards Woodsea, a little village about three miles north-east of Southend with a population of about fifty and the requisite pub and church, but not much else.

Within a few minutes I was in the main street. It ran fairly straight until near the end where it veered left to a dead-end. This was where the church stood.

A small quaint church with headstones all around it and a low crumbling dry stone wall marking the boundary. The entrance was through a gate that was in desperate need of repair.

I parked up and walked into the churchyard surveying the headstones. Studying the names written upon them I was looking for someone in particular. I knew they were here, but could not remember the exact location, it had all changed so much over the last, how many years? The trees were larger, bushes fuller, even the lay of the land looked different.

I searched through the headstones like pages in a book, trying to remember. Slowly it came back to me. With more haste I made my way behind the church.

There it was, a small oak tree. I'd planted that, when I was here.

Had it really been that long?

The gravestone I was looking for lay underneath the foliage, leaning to one side - not as I remembered it - the stone was discoloured with yellow moss, the inscription hard to read.

I knelt down in front and brushed away the dirt and moss with my bare hands revealing the name of 'Violet Rose Highway, 1887- 1915, My sweatheart'. I started to feel sadness well up inside.

"Are you alright?"

"Mmm... yeah. I'm fine, thank you. Sometimes I suffer from... from a form of epilepsy, where I just blank out. It's okay, honest. Sorry. You were saying,"

The lady looked inquisitively at Ann-Marie before continuing. "There is no record of a Henry Highway being buried anywhere around this area."

"No? He's got to be buried around here somewhere." She sighed, then thinking quickly about the vision. "How about his wife?" she said inquisitively not absolutely sure it was. "My Grandma, Violet Rose Highway, she was buried out in Woodsea, the little church out there, I can't remember its name,"

"You mean St Mary's." Vivienne tapped away on her keyboard. "Yes we have her records, 1915, but no husband I'm afraid. If you knew what year your grandfather, grandpa, died we might be able to narrow the search,"

"No, I don't I'm afraid,"

"Maybe he moved abroad, or died in the war. Was he in the services? We could do a nationwide search of the service databases."

"No, I don't believe he was."

"The only other place you can look is through the records over there." She got up from behind her desk and walked us over to an area of the room that had only a few books on a table. "If, for any reason when he died he couldn't be identified at the time, his records would be filed here. There might be a possibility he could be amongst these, but without knowing more of the circumstances it will be like looking for a needle in a haystack."

"Thank you. Is it alright if we..." Ann-Marie corrected herself. "I look through."

"Be my guest."

The search proved to be fruitless and after an hour and a half we gave up. There were too many pages, too many names, too many unknowns.

16

Avoiding the puddles, we sat on the steps outside the town hall.

"What do we do now?" Ann-Marie whispered, wary of people within our vicinity. Her shoulders slouched with her hands clasped between her legs to keep them warm.

"I don't know. He can't just have disappeared, he's got to be buried somewhere. But where?"

"Maybe we should go back to the …

"I'm Father Michael. I Hope you don't mind me asking. Was she a relative of yours?" The polite enquiring tone attracted my attention. As I turned round I saw a vicar with an old ragged face and white hair, a tall man in his fifties. Staring at him I didn't reply, letting the slow progress of a tear rolling down my cheek answer the question.

"Maybe I had best leave you alone," the vicar said calmly "If you n…"

"No I…" I said sharply and then stopped the rest of the words coming out.

There was a silent pause as he waited for me to continue but I didn't, preferring to stare forlornly in his direction.

"In your own time. Maybe you'd like to come inside?" He indicated towards the front entrance of the church.

"She was my wife… once," The words were like a stranger's and I faced the gravestone, caressing Violet's name affectionately. "I miss her so much. We only had a short time together. She meant everything to me. Why? Why was she taken from me?"

The vicar started to explain. "Everybody has their time. The reasoning is not always fathomable, Gods work…" he broke off staring at the headstone more closely. "Excuse me sir for saying, but this lady died in 1915," I looked sternly at him my eyes piercing his being.

"Are you calling me a liar?" My annoyance grew inside.

"No, no sir, but she can't have been. I mean you don't look…"

I stood up confronting this man of the cloth that questioned me. "You calling me a liar?" I spat out. "You think I don't know where my own wife is buried?" My menace grew as the emotional turmoil inside boiled over.

"I'm sorry sir." The Vicar tensed and stepped back from me, visibly shaken by the sudden outrage "I merely wished to point out that you can only be about your mid twenties, this la…" his voice trembled as he tried to maintain his decorum.

"She WAS my wife… a long time ago…" I turned back to the gravestone and knelt down resting my hand on the top. "My Violet Rose."

"Of course," he remarked apologetically, walking backwards. "Please accept my apologies I didn't mean to… err… doubt you." He looked bewildered, but didn't want to pursue the matter further.

"Why? We were going to have a family. Remember you wanted two girls and a boy first to look after them." I sat and talked to the gravestone. "Remember the house you always dreamed of, a little cottage for us all. Oh Vi, I miss you ever so. I know not what I am doing here. Without you I am lost." I stroked the ground.

"Will you forgive me for what I have done? I always blamed the little girl for your death. I know you would say she was only having fun, doing what children have to do, she didn't mean any harm. But after you were gone I could not see that. I had to blame someone. Please forgive me Violet Rose." I sat in silence, wishing I was with her.

"Now, I'm confused." I looked around at the churchyard and some of the fields beyond with the electricity pylons standing as sentries. "I do not know where I am. It all seems so worthless now. But I can't go back. Why could I have not just died?"

I felt a hand on my shoulder…

On the steps again, Ann-Marie was still sitting next to me.

"What happened this time?" she whispered hesitantly, she wanted to know but was also aware how horrific these visions could be.

"The dream. Of course! The dream is the reason for the killing," I snapped.

"What do you mean?"

I repeated the whole conversation to Ann-Marie. Suddenly the picture was becoming clear.

"I think we need to investigate the papers from 1915. He mentioned 'The killings'. This is just a continuation from then. If he had been caught and sent to prison, maybe his death was never recorded, or the records are held somewhere else."

"So we've got to go back to the library?"

"Yes," I said, pausing at the discomfort I saw on Ann-Marie's face. "I'm sorry, I know you probably don't want…"

"No, it's fine," she interrupted with a deep sigh. "One thing life has taught me is that you can't let anything hold you back. Besides I can't see them. Can I?" She shrugged dismissively.

"Only if I hold your hand." As soon as I said it I realised it was the wrong thing to say as her shoulders sunk. Quickly I added. "Maybe they won't recognise you," trying to make the previous visit sound less memorable than it was.

"I think I made a big enough fool of myself for them to re-member alright,"

"It probably wasn't as bad as you imagine."

"Yeah, right. It's okay Daniel I have to face my demons. I'll go. Might just wear a disguise this time though. Although I suppose we ought to go now as we're almost there."

"Thank you," I muttered humbly.

We made our way across the main road directly behind the Town Hall towards the library. It only took a few minutes.

"Are you ready then?" I looked at Ann-Marie and saw the apprehension on her face, she took a deep breath.

"As ready as I'll ever be, if I didn't have to see it, it would be easier. How's that for irony?" She smiled.

Walking through the doors we made our way straight to the stairwell past the returns desk. I noticed she was a lot more comfortable walking with me holding her hand, how much more naturally she was starting to move.

"They're staring at me," she whispered.

"It's probably just the toilet paper hanging from the back of your jeans."

"What?" she gasped, putting her free hand behind her back in automatic reflex, before realizing I was joking, she smiled.

"Only kidding, made you smile though."

"Yeah, now they think I'm completely insane talking to myself."

"Well be quiet then."

"I'm trying to but you keep talking to me."

For the first time since we'd met I found myself relaxed enough to allow a smile and a bit of friendly banter, it broke the tension.

At the top we turned left and headed to the first computer we came to. Ann-Marie sat down and punched in all the details of what we were looking for.

Various headlines flashed up, we didn't exactly know what we were looking for except that, from what I'd heard, I had to assume that there had been more than one death at the time, a spate of deaths.

Ann-Marie typed in various parameters to narrow our search. By now she was getting accustomed to seeing via a different perspective. The computer raced away in the background, highlighting stories, and then storing them to one side whilst it searched for some more.

Finally grinding to a halt with the search completed, some two hundred and fifty-seven records had been found. From this, and assuming that they had to have all been young girls, another one hundred and sixty-three records were eliminated, just ninety-four to view and draw our own conclusions from.

Slowly we started sifting through them, closing any we thought inappropriate, gradually shutting out whatever was going on in our own surroundings, consumed by our task.

I was in my car driving back towards town, I was at ease, calmness like a warm soft blanket, no hint of anger possessed me. I still felt guilt. Guilt for what I had done. It confused me as there was nothing I could do to change what I had already done.

The demeanour of the person I was feeling had changed, the brutality and rage gone. This was a human being and not some monster I'd made him up to be. It had been so easy to hate him at first as the horrific images haunted my visions. I was beginning to feel compassion and an understanding of what he must have gone through. The tragic loss of a loved one, the injustice of it providing a strange kind of reasoning for doing the things he had. There was a reason. Albeit, a twisted one.

Even so I, he, had still done wrong, both here and now, and way back then.

A police siren broke my thoughts. It cruised by and suddenly a deep rooted evil rose within me again, I flexed my right hand contorting it into a ball. I was remembering a murder nearby. All my sense of reasoning ran from me like wild horses. I smiled, the pleasure had returned. I'd enjoyed it. Wrong or right didn't matter any more, I enjoyed what I did. It had taken a hold of me like an animal I couldn't subdue, when I tried it fought back...

The picture in front of us was of a girl aged eleven, with long blonde hair. She wore a pretty little summer bonnet. She had been murdered and her body dumped in an alley off Warrior Square, there were no witnesses. She had been brutally stabbed without motive.

We found a local map of the area from the reference section and then photocopied the Southend-on-Sea part of it before bringing it back to the desk. On it we plotted this first murder, we had no idea how many we were looking for.

The next couple of articles, a nineteen year girl old raped and murdered, a six year old girl attacked by a dog. We closed them down. Next was a murder that took place in Lucy Road near the seafront, again a young girl, no motive. Ann-Marie marked the photocopied map.

Time was passing and I forgot that I didn't need to eat, but I could hear Ann-Marie's stomach rumbling, so we folded up the map and headed to the canteen on the first floor where she sat and had a coke and a sandwich, whilst perusing the map.

In total Ann-Marie had marked seventeen murder scenes on our map, not all relevant, as proved by a little further research. As we sifted through the newspaper articles it had become clear that we were following the trail of a serial killer which we believed to be Henry.

We now had a series of dates and places starting in March 1916. March 13th being the first one discovered. Next, March 29th, then April 17th, April 27th, April 31st, May 4th, May 17th. There was no regularity. Local residents were scared to let their children out to play alone.

A rumour had bandied about, according to newspaper reports at the time, that it was a religious thing, a devil worshipper or witch stealing the children's souls and using their blood for spells. There was no evidence to substantiate this, but the people felt happy, believing something out of the ordinary was to blame.

There was such a group in the area at the time, The Froxidians which we knew about but nothing could ever be proved. The members, whilst being considered outcasts, always pleaded their innocence, and nothing could ever be proved.

No one had been seen at, or leaving any of the crime scenes. He was good. He had audacity with some of the crimes committed during daylight hours. Some of the headlines that we had read called 'him' - they believed these crimes could only have been done by a man, 'The Slippery Slasher'. Police were baffled by the whole affair.

In August 1916 they stopped. The streets settled into peace again. No crime with such ferocity was reported again for another two years and then the murderer was apprehended and, despite attempts to pin these murders on that culprit, no connection could be made and no murder weapon was ever recovered.

The locations were all over the town and, as we studied them, an idea occurred to me.

"The tunnels," I said.

"Mmmm," was Ann-Marie's reply. "Look at some of the locations Lucy Road, Warrior Square, Clarence Road, Weston Road, Hotel Road. What about them?" she whispered, conscious that the canteen was filling up with people.

"I wonder if they are close to some of the exits of the tunnels?" I reflected.

"You're thinking he used the tunnels as escape routes."

"Well, no one saw anyone leaving the scenes or hanging around. If the entrances were concealed enough behind shrubs and the like, would anyone know they were there?"

"Surely the police would have checked the areas out thoroughly though."

"Only if they knew the tunnels were there and where to look. If you think about it, when you had your sight how often did you not notice something that was in front of your eyes? The crime scenes weren't necessarily in front of the entrances, just close by, enabling…"

"Enabling him to be in a completely different part of town quickly, with a change of clothes, if prepared."

"Seems a bit contrived though. Sounds like he thought it out. I thought you said it was revenge for killing his wife."

"Excuse me?" a member of staff asked.

"Sorry? Oh sorry I was just…" Ann-Marie started to explain and decided better of it.

"Have you finished with…?" The staff member pointed to the remnants of Ann-Marie's lunch, and she nodded.

I continued. "The bag, the canvas bag that I saw him take out of that hiding place in the wall must have contained a change of clothes. Maybe even the weapon."

"How?" Ann-Marie said loudly, before remembering no one could see me. "How does this help us find his remains?" she continued, whispering.

"I don't know."

We again sat in silence, sorting through our own thoughts.

"Let's go back to the computer and see what else we can find out," Ann-Marie commanded, totally taken by this mystery.

After finding the computer we were using occupied by someone else, we searched out another on the second floor. Ann-Marie sat down and started typing furiously.

"What are you doing?" I asked.

"I'm looking for missing persons reports."

"Why?"

"The killing stopped abruptly. Why did it stop? There is no death record for him, according to the records, assuming that he stayed local, and we have to for now."

"Right!" I agreed.

"Well there must have been a reason why he stopped killing, maybe if we follow the papers through in date order for missing persons we might be able to establish a location where he was last seen."

I thought for a second while Ann-Marie carried on typing on the computer.

"That's not going help though is it?!"

"Why not?"

"The missing persons report will only acknowledge that he was missing, not where or when he died. And we already know there were missing person reports filed by the Hughes family." Ann-Marie stopped what she was doing resting her hands on the edge on the desk. "Damn."

"I've got it. We are trying to establish where he went missing, when we should be locating where he was found."

"I don't get it."

"There is no record of his death and we have to assume that he died somewhere. Now, through the natural course of time, one would like to think that a body would've been discovered, maybe badly decomposed, or a pile of bones, some way, shape or form that because of bad medical records, that he couldn't be identified."

I looked at her, expecting a note of coherence to what I was saying, nothing. I tried a different tack.

"What are the chances of a body's remains laying undiscovered somewhere to this very day?"

"Unlikely. Depending on where they are."

"Exactly. But, if we make the assumption that they have been found, then we go through the newspapers looking for stories about remains being found."

"I think I get it." Her hands leapt uncertainly to the keys of the computer, and I almost lost my connection with her. Then as she understood my train of thought her fingers rapidly punched keys as if possessed, setting the search criteria to cover the period from 1915 to present day. "Then we can cross-reference the locations with possible locations where Henry could have been."

"Exactly."

Fortunately there were only three unidentified remains found in the local area. One in London Road, one in Bridge Road, one actually discovered at the bottom of a shaft in the Empire Theatre in 1957, which we knew about, when it was being renovated and converted into a Dance Hall.

"We knew about that already."

"Of course." Ann-Marie smiled. "We've been looking at this the wrong way around, we've known all along where he died we just didn't know how important it was or that it was him."

An air of satisfaction came over both of us as we read on.

The grizzly discovery was made by builders as they hammered their way through the wrong wall in the basement. They were trying to connect two adjacent chambers to create a large storage area and, getting their bearings wrong, found themselves in another chamber. On the ground lay a skeleton, now known to be male, approximately thirty years old. The few rags that were still attached gave no clue as to the identity of the person.

Police were called in to investigate. There seemed to be nothing suspicious. The broken leg bones could have been caused at any time, although forensics dated the breaks as occurring thirty-five to fifty-five years previously, there was no evidence of anything sinister. The investigation was short, the remains removed for burial in a local church.

"It doesn't say what church?" I stated. Ann-Marie smiled. "What are you looking so happy about?" I added gruffly.

"We know the year and location of where he was found." She stated eagerly.

"Is it definitely him though?"

"It has to be, the theatre connection, the tunnels, it can't be anyone else."

I didn't share her enthusiasm, but had no better ideas.

17

After discovering the date the bones were buried we headed back to the Town Hall, knowing we could narrow our search through the books listing the burials of anonymous remains.

The grey sky made it feel like it was night-time again but couldn't dampen Ann-Marie's spirits as she enjoyed the sight of it once more.

By the time we got to the records room we only had half an hour to spare before they closed. Vivienne pointed us to the correct set of books and left us to get on with our search. The large record books held all the information we wanted, not just for the local area, but for the county of Essex. The books were in chronological order, which made it easy to find the relevant year. There were one hundred and twenty-seven books to view covering all the church constituents in the county, narrowing our search to the immediate area left only seven books to look through. We knew the remains were anonymously buried so that made the search easier as we scanned through the pages, relying heavily on luck. In the fourth book we found what we were looking for, the remains from the theatre, buried in a graveyard, in Hockley. Now we knew where we had to go.

With this information we headed back to Ann-Marie's house with one question playing on our minds. 'How are we going to get to the remains?' We couldn't exactly go into the cemetery and simply start digging them up.

"Do we have to dig up the remains?" Ann-Marie asked hesitantly

"I don't know." I looked at Ann-Marie and she almost lost her balance.

"There has to be another way. I'm sure Heather and Aunt Rose wouldn't have wanted us to dig up his remains."

"Maybe you can give her a ring tonight and ask her. See if there is another way."

"Okay. But what if we do?"

I thought about that for a moment. The process of digging up someone's remains filled me with dread and I wasn't even sure how we would accomplish such a task.

"I don't know. I guess we'll figure something out." Ann-Marie didn't answer and I sensed her unease at the prospect.

Getting in before Ann-Marie's mum gave us time to make a call to Aunt Rose with Ann-Marie relaying the conversation to me as it progressed.

"Hello… Aunt Rose? Fine, thank you. We've discovered where the remains of Henry are. But when you said we needed to find them. Did you mean we had to dig them up as well. She says 'no'. Thank god for that. We just need the location because that's where we need to perform the binding ritual. And we need something personal of his to tie his soul with his physical presence. Right. Thanks. Yes I will." she put the receiver down. "Did you follow that, Daniel?"

"Yeah, I think so. So how are we going to find something personal of his?"

"The tunnels," we both said simultaneously, smiling.

"The canvas bag that he got out of the little hiding hole that must have contained some personal stuff in it," I said, knowing that was our only hope.

"Yes, but is it still going to be there? If you remember he removed it and you didn't see him put it back. So if he took it with him we won't know where it is now."

Ann-Marie had a good point, a point we couldn't ignore. The tunnels seemed the only obvious starting place to look and at least we now had knowledge of other entrances, so we didn't need to go through the theatre. This eased Ann-Marie's mind.

"Look. I'll go and search tonight while you sleep, at least that way it will

speed things up, especially as I don't need sleep,"

"Alright. Wait, you won't be able to see in the dark?"

"Shit!" Every time we found a solution a problem presented itself. "No, wait. He'd take the bag back to my flat, wouldn't he?"

"Because that is where he is staying." Ann-Marie agreed.

"It would make sense. So we know whe…"

Suddenly I was holding someone in my arms, holding them against their will. They were struggling, fighting to break free. Their hair was loose and shaggy, strands straying into my mouth, I spat them out, cursing the fury of the struggle. I pulled them slowly into a nearby alley. It was overgrown with vegetation; hampering my progress.

Gradually the struggling subsided as my strength overpowered them. I couldn't make out the person, although I guessed female from the length of hair. I had one hand over their mouth to keep them from screaming and it was covered in saliva from the effort of their struggling.

Strangely I had tears in my eyes and I sensed a hint of regret, even though it didn't stop me from the course of action.

What was I doing?

We reached a junction down the alley and I turned right dragging the body with me. Suddenly I knew where we were heading. Towards my flat. Why? This seemed ludicrous. All the other crimes had taken place in various sites around the area, but now I was heading home. Taking a victim with me. I couldn't see the logic.

As the back garden to my flat loomed into view a lump got stuck in my throat. I hesitated, just out of sight, behind a low fence, the body I held no longer struggled all fight long since gone, just saliva and snot ran over my hand, which still covered their mouth. I wanted to be sure no one was watching. When I felt the coast was clear I made my way to the stairs that led up to the balcony and my back door, lifting the body almost effortlessly now the struggle had subsided. I had a key hidden underneath a flowerpot. The security light popped on. I always believed in having a back-up plan if I got locked out.

I laid her down on the decking and saw the young girl was about seven or eight, I had one hand on her throat ready to squeeze in case she tried to scream. She looked terrified, her eyes red raw from crying, laying quite still as I opened the door to my flat and what I thought was her certain death.

I wanted to shout 'run' but knew it was pointless.

I lifted her small body through the door before closing and locking it behind me, drawing the curtains for privacy. I placed her on the floor.

"Do not say anything or I will kill you. You hear?" The voice, my voice was commanding. She slinked up against the wall tears still running down her cheeks. I quickly taped her hands and feet together with a roll of insulation tape I had left on the floor, as if I had planned this all along, then tied a gag over her mouth to make sure she didn't scream.

I stood up and looked at her. Stared at her red puffy eyes, her features seemed to have aged in a matter of minutes. Her knotted blonde hair hung lifelessly, sticking to her face, her burgundy school uniform was dirty and torn in places, green stains littered the arms of her shirt like an abstract painting.

She looked so helpless, so innocent. A victim of something from another time. I couldn't do anything. Mixed emotions ran through my mind.

Ann-Marie had gone when I returned from my vision. Panic ran through me like lightning. But as quickly as I decided what to do she re-appeared in the doorway.

"You're back. Hope you didn't mind, I went and had my dinner."

"No, no, that's fine," I spluttered out.

Ann-Marie yawned. "Sorry. I'm so tired. These active days are wearing me out. You don't mind if I go to bed do you?"

"No, of course not. Sorry I don't mean to…" She didn't let me finish.

"It's alright, I'm enjoying the distraction." She stopped. "Sort of. It's nice to be able to help." Silence filled the gulf between us.

"I'll go and check the flat and come back in the morning." The prospect filled me with dread knowing what I would find there.

With that she yawned again and left the room with her pyjamas in her hand whilst Mojo stayed sitting on the floor. He looked dejected and I sympathised. For the last year or so he had been Ann-Marie's eyes, now I had taken that away from him.

Ann-Marie had become a good friend to me in the few days I had known her.

When Ann-Marie re-entered the room and sat on the bed, Mojo didn't even raise his head.

"Mojo, come here boy." He reacted slowly, barely lifting his head. "Come on Mojo," she re-iterated in playful tones. "Ann-Marie does love you, she doesn't mean to leave you on your own. Come on boy, give me a hug," Finally Mojo jumped on the bed and lay beside her, she cupped his head in her hands and he licked her face enthusiastically, they were friends again.

"Are you alright Ann-Marie? It's a bit early to go to bed isn't it?" came a voice from the door.

"I just feel really tired, spent longer than usual going through the braille books. It's getting easier though. Anyway I want to start the Harry Potter series, it will be nice to know what everyone else is talking about."

"Well don't overdo it. Your teacher said she was pleased with your progress, especially as you started so far behind the others in your class."

I listened to mother and daughter and remembered my own parents and the thoughts stung like a million bee stings.

"I know."

"Oh, by the way, Tracey at work has two extra tickets for Robbie Williams at Knebworth next year. I said I would se…"

Ann-Marie's face lit up like a Christmas tree. "Really."

"I take it that is a yes you would like to go then?"

"Definitely."

"What have I let myself in for?" Her mum shook her head I mock disapproval.

"You like him too. You know you do."

"He's alright… I s'ppose," she conceded.

"Thanks mum, that's brilliant. Daniel did you hear that?" The question had escaped her lips before she had time to stop it.

"Sorry dear?"

"I mean, Daniel at College will be so jealous," Ann-Marie quickly added.

"Anyway, I thought you were tired."

"I was. Oh I'm so excited. Thanks Mum." She got out of bed and hugged her mum, Mojo tried to join in.

"You're welcome. Now night dear, sleep tight…"

"… and don't let the bed bugs bite. Mum, I am a bit old for that."

"I know, but you'll always be my little girl."

"I know. Night."

Her mother turned and pulled the door closed behind her and after a few moments when she knew her mother would be out of earshot she said, "Did you hear that? She is going to take me to see Robbie Williams. I have never been to a concert. Wow. That's brilliant." She sat stroking Mojo, a smile beaming across her face lighting up the room, despite the fact that the light was off. Suddenly the smile faded. "Sorry. Your vision what did you see this time?"

"It's alright." Suddenly I had a question I wanted to ask Ann-Marie, but it almost seemed rude to ask it, yet I knew she had been so open with me. "Ann-Marie, I hope you don't think I'm being rude, but why would you want to go to a concert, you can't see anything?"

"There is more to being at a concert than just watching you know. I can still pick up on the atmosphere, the excitement, just being there. Okay it may not be quite the same as if I could see, but it will be nice to at least experience it. Have you been to a concert before?"

"Yes, Madness."

"Who?"

"What do you mean who? Madness, you know, Our House, Baggy Trousers."

"Oh, I think I've heard of them, can't say I really know them that well. Was it good?"

"Brilliant, absolutely brilliant, it was the last but one concert before they split up, the 'Mad not Mad' tour. Me and my friend had these two guys in the seats in front of us, although everyone was jumping about having a good time, they just stood still the whole time when Madness came on, it was as if they had gone to the wrong show, they were right in our way as…" I stopped talking as Ann-Marie appeared to be watching me and smiling. "What?"

"You just sounded so happy then, I hope I feel like that after the concert."

"Thinking about it, I think you will, you're right, the atmosphere is everything."

"Oh, you were going to tell me about the vision."

The concert seemed a lifetime away, a lifetime I missed. Saddened again, I told her what I'd seen and her face turned from joy to disgust, I hated spoiling her jubilation at her good fortune, it made me feel guilty. I wondered if she felt obliged to listen despite the friendship she had shown.

"So he's there now, this minute, with another one?"

"Yes."

"What are we waiting for? Let's call the police. We've got

to help her."

It hadn't even occurred to me. That such a simple thing like that could save her life and put an end to all these crimes.

I was back in my flat the girl was conscious, fear still in her eyes.

"I guess you're wondering what I am going to do with you." I detected a sick note in my voice, toying with my victim.

She nodded nervously.

"I have got to do it. You understand?" I drew my face close to hers. I could see the tears of despair rolling down her cheeks. "I do not want to, but I have to. It's the only way. I loved my wife. It's not fair. IT'S NOT FAIR." I shouted at her. "You understand." My voice pitched from calm to agitated.

The girl shook her head. Her skirt was wet from urine. Fear driven right to her core.

I got up and walked around the room thumping the walls with my fist, the bandage round the bite wound slowly turning red as the wound opened up underneath.

"You are all to blame, you took her life. Caused her death. If you hadn't been playing in the street she would still be alive today."
I saw the canvas bag behind the lounge door.

I turned and picked the girl up so she was standing on her feet. Tears filled my eyes.

"It is your fault the horse reared," my voice broke, "… and killed my wife. She never did anyone any harm. She loved everybody. So much love. But no. Now she is gone and it is your fault. Do you hear me? Your fault." I shook her as she tried to cry out, but only a muted sob came from her, the gag doing its job. "You are all the same. Never think about the consequences, just do whatever you want. Well what about me?" I could feel the raw energy of anger welling up inside. "I had to live with your mistake. Do you know what that was like?" I picked up the little girl and thrust her like a rag doll back against the wall banging her head. "DO YOU? Do you?" And with that I thrust the knife, that I was unaware of holding in my hand, straight into

her belly, tears streaming down my cheeks. Her eyes widened as shock took hold.

I thrust the knife a second time, followed by a sob from myself. "I'm sorry."

The girl started to go pale as blood oozed from the wound. I stabbed her again and again and, as her life ebbed away, her eyelids gradually grew heavy and closed for the last time in her life, her head lolling forward.

As I let go the body fell in a heap on the floor, blood pooling on the carpet.

I stood with one hand against the wall, supporting my weight, the other still holding the knife. Slowly I let the knife fall to the floor.

I was back in Ann-Marie's bedroom.

"What's happened? I wanted to call the police but I couldn't tell them where you lived."

"Shakespeare Drive," I said automatically, my voice cold and emotionless, my mind still picturing the little girl's face.

Ann-Marie reached onto her bedside table and grabbed the phone. "What number?"

It suddenly became clear.

The canvas bag.

"Wait, we need the canvas bag."

"We've got to help the girl," she retorted, panic rising in her voice.

"It's too late for her," I said quickly, my mind a swirl of irrational complacency, yet still saddened by my own inability to prevent the crime from happening.

She paused. I could see she felt sickened as the full consequence of what I had said hit her.

"We need to retrieve the canvas bag, it's our only possibility," I pleaded, half sobbing myself.

"What about…" Ann-Marie's voice was empty.

"I…"

I wanted to put my arm round her for comfort. Mojo edged his way up the bed and licked Ann-Marie's face, she put her arms round him and hugged him like never before.

I kept quiet, knowing she had to deal with this the only way she knew how, with the one that was closest to her, Mojo.

I watched her in silence, until she fell uneasily into sleep, as if I was some sort of guardian angel. Although I felt more like a traitor.

18

Morning seemed to take an eternity to come round, and with it came a feeling of trepidation, entering my flat was a must but we also knew the atrocity that would greet us. Ann-Marie couldn't face breakfast as she tried to come to terms with the images her mind conjured up. I could see her reluctance to go through with what we needed to do and, inside guilt racked me and I would not have blamed her if she had decided enough was enough. We both knew the police needed to be alerted yet it was double edged sword. My physical self would lose its freedom and with it my only chance to correct the situation if that was at all possible.

As soon as her mum left for work we left. Ann-Marie was more distant and, once again without her faithful companion. I knew what we were about to do was dangerous and I had to make sure that Henry was out.

I'd had no more visions during the night, so could not even guess where Henry would be and in a strange way found that disconcerting.

Walking down the road I kept a watch out for my car, praying that it wouldn't be there. I didn't see it. I sighed with relief. I guided Ann-Marie to the alleyway that would lead us to the back garden, the balcony and my back door. I hoped that the key had been put back under the flower pot as this was going to be our only way in.

The alleyway proved difficult for Ann-Marie as she had to fight the undergrowth and discarded rubbish; twice she almost fell over. Near my back garden I left her briefly so I could search my flat and check it was clear.

Inside I was met with the only evidence of a murder taking place, a large blood stain on the carpet. It amazed me that it was so large, it brought back the memory of the vision from the night before and the girl's face, how her life ebbed away like a turning tide as the blood pool grew around her. It shocked me as I had somehow managed to save the image as if it was just a shot from a gory horror film. Now faced with evidence, I knew it was real. Very real! That frightened me; all the visions frightened me, the gruesome nature of the killer and this, the first real evidence I had witnessed close up and personal.

I would give Ann-Marie the choice of whether she wanted to see via my eyes, or have me verbally guide her. Hopefully, she would choose the latter, therefore not having to see the dried blood pool. She was braver than I thought as I held her hand whilst she retrieved the key and unlocked the door. Opening it she temporarily baulked letting go of my hand, her bravery suffering an initial set back, it was as if she sensed the residual energy of the dead girl.

"You ready? Do you still want me to hold your hand?" I asked.

"Yes." She uttered. "Yes, to both. I need to." I didn't think she did, she had nothing to prove to me.

Ann-Marie quickly found the canvas bag behind the door steering clear of looking at the blood stain, which was difficult as it took up such a large portion of the carpet. The bag wasn't light, but she managed to hoist it onto her shoulder, and we hastened our exit leaving the macabre scene behind. In silence we walked back to Ann-Marie's, mission accomplished.

"Daniel, we didn't lock the door!"

"Shit! Well it's too late now." That was the least of my worries.

Safely back in Ann-Marie's room she opened the canvas bag and quickly laid everything out on the floor. I did my best to hold her hand whilst she did this but it became quite difficult as she moved so deftly.

Mojo observed the proceedings from his place on the bed. Some of the packages were small, whilst others large and heavy. In particular there was a huge weighty book shaped one, bigger than A4 and as thick as a jumbo file. The array of shapes and sizes made it feel like Christmas, all the presents in order, deciding which to open first. Somehow I didn't think we were going to find any pleasant surprises.

"What shall we open first?" Ann-Marie enquired.

"Don't know, s'pose it doesn't really matter. Might as well start with the nearest." I absently pointed to an oblong package. "The oblong one?"

Ann-Marie gulped in trepidation and I watched as she opened each bundle blind, describing the feel of each one, more for her benefit than mine, constructing a picture in her mind.

"It's quite long," She ran her fingers along the length of a parcel. "… and it is thicker at one end." I wanted to urge Ann-Marie on as it was taking so long. "It's got a cross-section sticking out about a third of the way down." She turned the package over in her hands, each time another layer coming free. I watched, frustrated that she did everything so methodically. As each layer came off, I watched in horror as I realised what the shape was. Ann-Marie's eagerness to unwrap the parcel slowed as she also realised what the package was. Finally a knife fell out onto the floor.

I held Ann-Marie's hand as we looked at it. A dark, rusty, jagged blade, approximately seven inches in length, black blotches of dried blood covered it. The handle was made of carved bone. Ann-Marie physically shook as she tentatively picked it up to place it on its own wrapping. We sat in silent contemplation of what this knife represented. His murder weapon.

I studied the other packages on the floor and knew that we needed to proceed and turned to Ann-Marie.

"Are you alright?"

"I think so. Please stop looking at me."

"Sorry."

"I think I feel sick." Her face look pale and I saw her eyes start to roll. "I'm going to be sick." She started to get up and as we lost our connection she stumbled. I reached out instinctively to steady her, but it was useless, she fell against the door, banging her shoulder. Mojo jumped of the bed to be by her side. She put her hand to her mouth as she headed into the hallway towards the bathroom, with Mojo doing his best to guide her. A few seconds later I heard her retching. I looked back at the knife wondering how someone could actually want to hurt another person with this weapon. The concept was alien to me. Even in times of anger when I wished ill of someone whom I thought I hated, I would never have done anything so savage. How could he have crossed that line?

As I waited for Ann-Marie I tried to feel the unopened parcels, concentrating as hard as I could, but it was useless, so I tried to guess what they were from the shapes. Most were square or rectangular, but there was an odd one which was small and nondescript. Eventually I heard the toilet flush and the taps being turned on and Ann-Marie returned with her cheeks flushed.

"Are you alright?"

"I think so. It's just." She stopped. "It's just... I don't know, that knife makes me..." Suddenly her demeanor changed. "What makes a man do such a thing to someone else?" It was a question that came more like an accusation as if I was the guilty party. "Well."

I sat chided, not sure what to say.

"I'm sorry," Ann-Marie finally added. "It's not your fault. I just can't understand what can make someone like that."

"Neither do I, but we can't change the way he thinks, however, we can put a stop to this. I know I am asking a lot but we need to carry on. If we can find something personal then we can..."

"I know, I know." She patted Mojo's head as he sat beside her before kneeling down again feeling her way to the parcels. As her hand touched the knife she flinched, taking a moment to build the emotional strength to touch it.

She opened the rest of the parcels in silence placing each on their respective wrappings, then studying them.

There was the knife, a couple of lockets, a wooden jewellery box, a pair of worn out gloves, some letters, a large book entitled 'Frodixan Book of Incantations', two pairs of men's shoes, and one bundle was just men's clothes.

The photo I had seen earlier was not there.

Ann-Marie opened the wooden box, it contained a collection of jewellery; a pocket watch, five rings - silver and gold, a silver hand-held mirror (broken) and a pendent which Ann-Marie picked up to look at through my eyes, she tried to read the inscription engraved on the back.

"My true one, always, H XX. I wonder," an idea started to form. "Can you pick up the pocket-watch and see if it has got anything inscribed on it, something that proves it belonged to him." Exploring it in her hand, she flicked open the case. "You are my one, forever V XX. That's it. Something that has to be his."

"Can we be sure?" Ann-Marie questioned.

"As near as damn it. It's got to be. It has to be." I looked at the objects in front of us. "It's our best choice. We've got to at least try before…" I left the sentence unfinished. "Come on let's go to his grave at least we can try that ritual and, hopefully, put things right." I let a sense of premature relief wash over me as I saw the end nearing.

Ann-Marie clasped the watch tightly in her hand and looked towards me.

"Will you ever speak to me again?"

"What?" I replied, taken aback by her question.

"When we've done the ritual, will you visit me again?" Her voice was edged with sadness.

"Yes," I responded, wondering what it would be like when things were back the way they should be. Would I still speak to her? I wanted to think I would, she had done more for me than I could ever have hoped. "Yes, yes I will. I will make sure I do." Realising that sounded more like a chore than a pleasure, added, "Look you've done more for me than I could ever have wished. I could never not see you again, I owe you so much. And I like you."

She smiled half-heartedly and for a moment I was sure I saw doubt in her expression.

"I want to and I promise, I will." I let the words settle before adding. "Your Mum will probably wonder who the hell I am though."

Ann-Marie smiled and I noticed her thin lips curl up at each end showing a perfect set of white teeth. "I think I'm going to miss my eyesight all over again when you've gone. It's been weird, but nice to see again. I know we don't have time but it would be nice to look around the house whilst I can see."

Without thinking, I replied, "I'm sure we can do that." As soon as I said the words, fear shot through me that any delay left Henry out there killing more girls.

There was an awkward silence, the sort of silence when no one needs to speak, but often people spend time thinking of something to say anyway.

"Are you sure?"

"Come on, but we'd better be quick before we have to head off to get to the cemetery and get this finished. I think Mojo better come with us this time so you can get back on your own," I stated matter of factly.

Mojo almost sensed that he would be needed full time again and barked.

"Okay Mojo. Just let Ann-Marie see her home first," she said, stroking him.

Ann-Marie gathered everything we needed to complete the

ritual, the book Heather had lent to us, candles, the pocket watch, and another small box stored in the bottom draw of her bedside cabinet, placing them all in a rucksack ready for when we left. Then we explored her home.

Just outside her bedroom we hovered at the pictures of her father, studying them for a short time as she told me stories behind the photos, detailing what sort of a man her father was. I sensed that she wanted to stand there forever drinking in the happy memories but she knew we had a task to fulfil and, reluctantly, we continued; exploring her mum's bedroom, the bathroom, even the cupboard on the landing. I forgot it was new to her.

Downstairs in the kitchen we looked out to the garden.

"A-ha," she stated. "I need something to mark out the 'Sign of Olizan', just in case the grave is grassed, the stones from the path should do the trick." She pointed to the garden path which was made of shingle. "I just thought, I don't like the colour of my room much, it's a bit bland. I always imagined a nice shade of green." I looked at her bemused.

"Well you can't exactly tell your Mum that, can you?"

"No, not really." There was the briefest pause for reflection. "She might think I have had a miracle cure or something."

"Have you got any small bags we can put the stones in?"

"I think she keeps carrier bags in the understairs cupboard." We found a plastic Ikea holder stuffed with plastic bags. Ann-Marie took two and put one inside the other for strength before we went into the garden to gather some stones.

She marvelled at the lovely courtyard-style garden, with its raised beds and shingle pathways. There was a stone star-shaped patio in one corner with a table and two chairs.

"It has always smelt nice out here in the summer. It's nice to finally see it."

I didn't respond as I felt it she was just sharing her thoughts. I could sense a desire to spend more time studying the rich scented flowers but she knew time was against us.

After we had the stones we went back upstairs and collected her rucksack.

Leaving the house, an ominous air enveloped us and our thoughts turned to what we were about to do. We let silence prevail for most of our walk to the bus stop, Mojo proudly taking the lead for his friend.

Hockley was five miles north of the town, a pretty village, although it had grown over the years into a bustling community. It was still very picturesque as all the new buildings had been forced to keep to the architectural nature of the existing buildings, using similar materials.

"How are you going to get back? Maybe we should see if Aunt Rose can come too," I suddenly interjected into the silence.

"I'll be fine. I think I'm quite capable of catching a bus, Mojo and I have been getting about quite well for the last year or so without too much of a problem, thank you." Her reply was slightly sarcastic and I realised how much I underestimated her.

"Sorry, I only mea…"

"Daniel, where are you?"

"What do you mean? I'm here."

She had not wanted me to hold her hand, her eyes today was Mojo's task, she felt she had hurt his feelings more than enough. I was walking beside her although I hadn't realised how much farther away I had drifted. I took a sideways step closer to her.

"Ah, that's better, I can feel you again."

"I was only a few feet away, no more than usual."

"That means you're getting weaker then."

"I don't feel any different."

"You won't but your Soulshadow is growing weaker, it's been how many days? Five? Six?"

"Something like that."

"Come on we need to get this sorted," she stated, with a renewed urgency in her voice.

After just the short couple of days, I had observed how quickly she had got used to seeing things through my eyes and a skewed perspective. Now back to her normal way of life she had been clumsy initially and I realised why she didn't want me to take her hand this time. Also, I thought she was proving to me that she didn't need my help, which deep down I knew, it was always the other way round.

Catching the bus wasn't a problem, Mojo was a highly trained dog. Then it was a case of asking someone if she was at the right bus stop. As I was there this was easy.

"Aren't you ever worried about someone guiding you in the wrong direction? I would be," I asked, knowing how I would feel.

"You're very pessimistic aren't you."

I hadn't thought about it before but now she had said it I guessed that that was how it appeared. I tried to justify myself.

"No… not really, I just think that some people might… you know."

"You can hear a lot in someone's voice, you have to listen. People are a lot more trustworthy than you think." It was all second nature to her.

I began to ponder whether her blindness was a disability or not, she was more in tune with her surroundings than I was.

We didn't have to wait long for the bus, and the driver was helpful saying he would let her know when we reached Hockley village green. Ann-Marie took a seat at the front so she would hear the driver. This gave us no opportunity to talk, I could, but she wouldn't reply.

It was one of those times when I wanted to say something really touching but didn't know what, just something to let her know how much I appreciated her help, her friendship. Everything I thought felt honest, but too contrived, I kept quiet.

By the time we reached our stop the sun was shining, breaking the initial grey sombreness of earlier.

The church and graveyard stood just the other side of the green set amongst a backwash of trees and fields. It stood proudly at the head of the village. The houses and other buildings ran away from it like a carpet stretching out for miles, widening into a wedge shape.

The church was huge for a village, with the cemetery surrounding it like a barrier. It had a well kept hedge forming the boundary, and an ornate carved archway framing the way in. There was no gate. We walked through...

I was sitting in my car. My jeans and jumper were covered in dirt, I was slightly out of breath as if I had been running. I started the engine and pulled away, calmly.

A dirt track stretched out in front of me, two channels in the grass the only evidence that vehicles travelled this way with some regularity. Either side of the track was nestled thick with trees. It didn't look familiar to me.

A revelation hit, I knew what we, I, had just done. I'd just dumped the girl's body from last night. Things were becoming clearer. I was beginning to feel the consciousness of my possessor, his thoughts. I'd left early in the morning to avoid being noticed. I'd parked my car in the block of garages down the road out of sight, using the alleyway to hide me from prying eyes. That's how I'd got the body out and now I was heading home again.

"Daniel? Daniel?"

"I'm here," I said, alarmed.

"I wasn't sure if you'd gone completely or ju..."

I turned right, off the stretch of track onto a more prominent pot-holed track. I knew where I was going, I was gathering speed, looking round to make sure I wasn't being watched. This was a long track lined with trees.

"Ann-Marie? What's happening?"

"I don't know. Help me locate the grave, quick before it's too late,"

"What are we looking for? Do we have any idea at all?"

"No, I guess something discreet, it won't be very…"

A horse and rider came into view as I rounded a bend. I swerved. The horse reared.

"Don't go, Daniel, Don't go. Please don't go. Not yet, I can't do this without you," Desperation rang in Ann-Marie's voice, and fear ran through me that we may not be able to complete our task.

"It's alright I'm here. I crashed. I think."

"How are we going to find the grave?"

"You wait here, I'll have a quick search, maybe there'll be something obvious, anything."

"Daniel, don't leave me on my own."

"But it will be the quickest way." I didn't wait for an answer instead darting off, knowing I had to find the grave quickly before it was too late.

I could see blood on the steering wheel. I could hear a horse thrashing about somewhere in the vicinity. I looked around. Steam rose from the bonnet and I wearily opened the driver's door to get out. I stumbled as my feet didn't seem to belong to me, holding onto the car for stability.

The horse was on its side with its rider underneath, not moving.

I watched but did nothing.

I turned about disorientated expecting to see trees and a horse. In the distance I saw Ann-Marie talking to an old lady. I knew she'd be safe now and resumed my search, randomly checking grave after grave, trying to locate Henry's anonymous burial site, something that would have been placed as a mark of respect, anything.

Nothing!

I went back to Ann-Marie as I didn't know how long I'd been away.

I was limping along the dirt track. Numb from any real pain although my left leg was dragging a little. I heard a human voice calling out.

"Ann-Marie." She was still talking with the lady. I ran to her. "I can't find anything." I listened to the conversation knowing Ann-Marie couldn't speak to me without appearing mad.

"… 66 or was it 63, I can't remember. My Albert would know. Always particular he was. Took great care in his duties you know. They found the remains in the theatre behind a wall. Shame. They gave whoever it was a decent reading though, Father Grace was very good, believed everyone deserved a proper send off, whether he knew who they were or not. He called them the lost souls. He laid a special area for them all so they wouldn't get lonely or lost amongst the others. Just to the right of the church, by that chestnut tree." She pointed to a tree about forty feet tall. "Silly me you're blind, I'll lead you there. This way dear," She gripped Ann-Marie's arm gently and led her towards some small plaques in the grass, each marked with a date and where the remains were found, apparently with the foresight that if they ever got identified they could be reunited with their correct families.

"Here you go dear."

"Thank you very much."

"Irene, my name's Irene. You're welcome dear. I'll leave you now."

"Thank you Irene."

Irene walked off leaving us to do what we had to do, the binding ritual. Ann-Marie laid her rucksack on the ground.

19

Each copper plaque, twelve by six inches, sat on an individual square stone and looked jaded after years of being out in all weathers, perfect placed in a neat cluster in the shade of the chestnut tree. In my mind I had expected to see graves, suddenly I was unsure Henry's remains were buried here at all, even though the date and location were correct.

"Ann-Marie, are we sure these are his remains, there is no way there is a coffin down there?"

"They probably cremated the remains. It was probably cheaper. You know what the council are like."

"But we've got to be sure otherwise this might not work."

Ann-Marie's face sank as doubt settled in. "Is that woman, Irene, around she might know?"

"I'll go and check." I started off but stopped as Ann-Marie spoke.

"But I need you to help me set up."

"We need to be sure. Look, I'll be quick." I started to walk away.

"Daniel! Daniel!"

"What?" I said, rather too sharply, stopping in my tracks, torn between looking for Irene and staying. "Sorry. I'm here."

"Daniel!"

"I'm here Ann-Marie," I said urgently, all too aware that time was against us.

"Great Mojo, looks like we are on our own."

"Ann-Marie, I'm here. Can you hear me?" I stepped in closer to her, concerned that we were losing our connection and that

I had grown too weak for her to detect.

"Daniel, is that you?"

"Yes, you know it is." I had to find Irene. We had to be sure Henry's remains were buried beneath the plaque. I didn't want to think of the consequences if they weren't. "Look if you can hear me I won't be long." And with that I ran off to search the graveyard and church for Irene.

I found her in a pew staring at the pulpit as if studying it looking for inspiration. Dashing back out to Ann-Marie I saw her kneeling on the ground in front of what we believed was Henry's resting place, unloading the contents of her bag onto the grass in front.

"Ann-Marie! She's inside the church." There was no reaction. "Ann-Marie?" I shouted as if that would make a difference. As I got close enough I placed a hand on her shoulder.

"Daniel?" she said, shocked by my sudden touch.

"Yes. Can you hear me?"

"Just. You're getting faint."

"She's inside the church." Ann-Marie looked concerned.

"Come on Mojo. We need to be quick. Daniel…"

"I know, but if his remains are not there then…" I let the sentence remain unfinished, we both knew it could be the end for me.

Ann-Marie got up and instructed Mojo to take her into the church. I walked with her and tried to hold her hand so she could see where she was going but our connection was growing weak, creating a blurry mess, and I wondered if it was already too late.

As she went inside the church I stopped at the door. How would she read the book? I began to lose hope. My anxiety faded as I started to wallow in self pity conceding the end was near. I turned and stared out across the graveyard looking at the stones scattered throughout the ground, wondering what would happen to me in the end.

A couple of minutes later I felt an electric shock as Ann-Marie walked straight through me.

"Daniel?"

"Yes. Is it?"

"They cremated the remains and yes they are buried there." We headed back to the plaques. "It was what they did, back when he was discovered, they put the ashes in a china urn and buried it in the ground until such a time as the identity was discovered."

Relief surged through me.

Back at the plaque Ann-Marie continued to empty her rucksack. I tried to keep hold of her hand but it became difficult as she efficiently identified each object by touch, the pebbles, the book, the candles, now all neatly laid out on the grass. The last object to be taken out was a plain brown cardboard box. I was intrigued, but frustrated at how slow she was being. She opened the lid and started to unwrap the contents, which were enveloped in tissue paper. As she unravelled them it became obvious what they were.

"My father gave them to me when I was eight. I used to like sleeping in a tent in the garden at night in the summer. But I was scared of the dark, so my father bought me these glass holders. They rest over the candle to stop the wind blowing them out. I used to put them outside the entrance to the tent, weighted down with small stones in the glass bases. I'd watch them for ages before I fell asleep. In the morning the candles were all but gone…

I was still stumbling along the dirt track. The horse's distressed neighing was barely audible now. But the pain in my leg was stifling, cutting me like acid, I had a pain in my head, behind my eyes, it was a throbbing pounding pain. My focus blurred.

A few more steps and I fell to the ground crying out in pain as I rolled over onto my back clasping my leg.

I tried to get up again but felt the strength drain from my body. My eyelids became heavy and suddenly the pain faded.

Darkness.

"... up and come back Daniel. I need you. I can't do this without you."

"I'm here," I interrupted, all too aware that I was fading in and out all too frequently.

"Daniel, I'm scared, my vision is going, you're too weak for me to hold on to. When you go I don't see what you see anymore. It just goes dark."

"Did you not see any of it?"

"Only a slight blurred vision."

Fear started to ooze into me. What if I become too weak for Ann-Marie to use for her vision. How will she read the incantation from the book.

"Aargh."

"What is it?"

"I can feel the pain in my leg. The same as in the vision."

Ann-Marie visibly shuddered as she picked up the book. Post-it notes protruded from the various pages she needed. As I wasn't holding her hand at the time I watched as she felt for them, this was the first time I'd seen her struggle, as she deciphered which one was first and which was second. Rather than helping, I just watched almost traumatised. She eventually opened the book at the first marker and I rested my hand on hers as I knelt down opposite her. There was a diagram, a symbol; an octagon with a square inside touching alternate angles, a triangle within that drawn up from the bottom two corners, bisecting the top horizontal line in the middle.

The instructions detailed the positioning of the candles. One, on the upper-most point of the octagon, with two either side, on the next points down. A fourth candle was to be placed just inside the bottom-most point of the octagon.

Ann-Marie untied the bag of pebbles, picking a handful out.

As I opened my eyes I had to shield them from the glare of the daylight dazzling them. I was still lying on the ground, all pain seemed to have gone but I was cold. I felt moisture soaking my clothes. Suddenly an intense lightning bolt of pain shot through me and I rolled around, again clutching my leg.

Struggling, I got to my feet, although my weight rested only on my good leg. Dazed, I leaned up against a tree and took a closer look, my focus kept blurring in and out.

Dirt or blood, I couldn't tell. I ran my hand gently down my bad leg, I felt the rip in my jeans, and an open gash that was causing so much pain. I winced again as my fingers gently eased over it. Then I became warm, the pain abated.

I took a few deep breaths, composing myself, then forced myself onwards, not sure where I was going, aimlessly stumbling forward.

Sirens. I could hear sirens in the distance. I was void of any emotion as I limped on.

Re-orienting myself.

"Ann-Marie, what's happening?"

"You're getting weak. Hold my hand." I did as requested. "Come on hold my hand."

"I am." 'Oh no' I thought.

"Concentrate Daniel, please focus I need your sight." I tried to focus all my strength through my hand and into Ann-Marie in the hope it would make a difference.

"Is that better?" I asked, finding it hard to stay calm.

"How does it look?" Ann-Marie showed me the picture in the book and I compared it with what she had done. "Not bad for a blind person." She tried to lighten the mood but it didn't work.

She lit the candles, covering each in turn with one of the shades, then turned to the next marker in the book. A page with the heading, 'Spiritual Binding'.

I had never believed in witchcraft before. Now, here I was, my existence depending on it.

Ann-Marie retrieved the pocket-watch from her bag, carefully unwrapping it and placing it in the centre of the triangle.

"I think we are ready now."

"Are you sure you can do this?"

"Heather said it is easy to do, providing you have the power and belief. She seems to think that I can do it, but I must believe." She paused, taking a breath and with more confidence, continued. "Yes, I'm sure I can do this. Scared to death though, in case something goes wrong."

"It won't, you'll be fine…"

I was strapped on a stretcher with a red blanket covering me, keeping me warm. A surgical collar round my neck meant I couldn't move my head and I could feel them cutting away my jeans to get a better look at the wound.

"Aargh, that hurts."

"Can you tell us what happened?" The paramedic was ripping open a dressing.

"I don't remember. I…" I tried to point to the edge of the track but my fuddled brain couldn't think straight, words were like strangers.

"Do you remember ringing for the ambulance?"

"No." I felt the dressing being laid on the open wound.

"We are going to take you to Southend Hospital. There doesn't seem to be any broken bones so it looks as though you've been lucky. You seem to have hit your head pretty badly and we need to get that checked out." She spoke confidently and I just let her words wash over me as silence enveloped me and I faded into unconsciousness.

"Ann-Marie we've got to get this done quick, I'm in an ambulance."

"I can't do this without you, Daniel. Where are you? Please come back quickly, I'm scared."

"I'm here, next to you. Holding your hand."

"That is you isn't it? I can't feel you." She sounded panicky.

"I'm here."

I covered her hand with both of mine and concentrated hard, hoping it would make the connection stronger. Mojo watched the events unfold from his seated position a few feet away behind Ann-Marie.

"You're back. I'm ready."

She started to read the incantation

> Abyssium, Contortium
> Tresyteria
> Crytada
>
> Power of the Octagon
> Take back the force
> That set itself free
>
> Power of the square
> Give back life
> To the Soulshadow
>
> Power of the triangle
> Restore the three levels of life
> Heaven, Earth, Hell
>
> Entortius, Cryssedius
> Attoria
> Implata

As Ann-Marie said the incantation we felt the ground jolt. The pocket watch started spinning fast on the spot, stopped, then the lid flicked open and shut, in quick succession. Heat began to radiate from it, intense heat.

I felt less and less as I watched the events unfold and it became more difficult to see things, my vision blurred then cleared again.

The candles went out, one by one in sequence, middle top, bottom, right top, left top. Then they re-lit in the same sequence. This occurred three times.

I didn't know what I was expecting to happen, but I began to feel this was useless, and we were just observing some special effects show.

The ambulance was moving and I felt the gentle rocking. The world seemed to be spinning in a blur making me feel sick. The paramedic said something but I couldn't make it out as a warmth engulfed me.

The pebbles were glowing, candles burning brighter than I'd ever seen before.

The watch began to hover a few inches above the gravestone.

Mojo barked but Ann-Marie didn't react.

"What's going on there? Excuse me. What do you think you are doing? This is a church not," a Vicar came rushing towards us voicing his concern. He stopped in his tracks as Ann-Marie turned to face him, her eyes wild, as though she had seen some terrible event. The Vicar hesitated a while, before turning and walking away, without uttering another word, then at the corner of the church I saw him make the sign of the cross on his chest with his finger, his lips moved in silent prayer.

I looked at Ann-Marie. Her hands were hovering over the two bottom corners of the triangle and there was a channel of light running from her palms to the corners.

"Ann-Marie, what's happening?"

She didn't answer.

Repeatedly she said the last line of the spell.

"Entortius, Cryssedius, Attoria, Implata," her voice growing stronger.

The back doors of the ambulance flew open and I felt the bed move although I was not fully aware of what was going on around me. I tried to take it all in. I was confused and couldn't place where, or who, I was. People were talking around me as if I wasn't there.

"Ann-Marie, what's happening?"

Dread filled me and I still doubted it would work.

The watch still hovered above the centre of the triangle. The lid opened, spinning faster and faster, then in an instant vanished in a burst of busy red light, leaving only a scorched patch on the brass plaque.

I could see a policeman walking behind me, he was explaining something to the paramedic. I didn't know what.

I wanted to move but my body didn't seem capable. A nurse on my right was speaking to me, her words were just a jumble of noise. I was pushed into a cubicle with a curtain running around it on a track and there I was lifted onto another bed.

The policeman stood outside whilst they closed the curtain around me.

In the graveyard Ann-Marie was flat out on the ground, Mojo whimpering beside her, licking her face, pawing at her shoulder, trying to wake her up.

I hadn't got a clue what had happened. I didn't feel any different. I turned to the symbol on the grave, the individual pebbles were vibrating. Suddenly they shot up into the air about two feet before crashing to the ground and shattering where everything became still. All the candles shades had melted into a molten mess on the plaque.

I stared at the scene, not comprehending what had occurred. Not sure what to make of any of it. Ann-Marie was still flat out on the ground. Had it all gone wrong?

Ann-Marie started to come round.

"Daniel, what are you still doing here? Didn't it work?

"I don't," I stuttered. "I... I guess... not."

"But I did everything right, I'm sure I did... I don't remember much but I'm..."

I felt every particle in my body contort, every muscle cramp at once as if I was going to implode. Then a flash of blue light pierced my eyes.

"AARRGGHH."

I was in the hospital bed with nurses around.

"It's okay You're in Southend Hospital sir. You've been in an accident, we are just making you comfortable, then we'll take a few X-Ray's just to be sure there is nothing more serious before transferring you onto a ward,"

"NO, it can't be."

20

I tried to sit up.

"Please just lie back down and rest sir. A doctor will be with you shortly."

The nurse gently, but firmly, pushed me back, all the time reassuring me that I was in safe hands.

As I laid there confusion started to parade around my head. I could see images of Ann-Marie in my mind, kneeling by the grave, I wanted to get back there and see that she was alright, but that soon faded as I relished the feeling of being real.

I flexed all the muscles in my aching body, savouring the feeling of being alive despite any discomfort from my injuries, pinching myself to confirm it was happening. The crisp white sheets felt so fresh and good. I enjoyed the solidity of the bed beneath me which overwhelmed my senses and made me realise how bland everything had seemed when I had been a Soulshadow, and not able to feel the world. I revelled in the fact that I was part of the real world again, and letting my head rest back on the pillow relaxing for a few moments allowing sleep to consume me.

The nightmare was over. I only hoped that Ann-Marie got back alright.

Then like a sting a thought pounded itself into my brain and I was awake again. Something was wrong. I'd hoped to find myself back at the beginning of this whole nightmare.

Suddenly I became more aware of the commotion going on around my cubicle and began to feel that I had been thrown further into the breech and that all was not over.

The course of events was still blurry in my mind, but slowly tiny details flashed back into my head, teasers, none of which made any sense. I could remember my time with Ann-Marie well, the visions all clear in my memory.

Henry's time when I couldn't see what he was doing, this was not deleted, as I expected it to be. It was there. I could sense it there in my head, yet not make it out with any clarity. Over the next couple of hours I experienced images flashing at me, titbits, like the visions, except this time, it was of past events.

Finally, when the doctors were happy with my condition, I was transferred onto a ward, which was all but empty save one other patient, who was asleep.

I rested uneasily as the afternoon turned into night. My thoughts scattered with images from the previous Sunday to now. I was concerned for Ann-Marie and desperately wanted to contact her. After lights out, the dark took me into a restless sleep littered with fresh images, replaying new memories.

Breakfast came round early the next day. I had forgotten how nice it was to eat again, I liked my food but I hadn't needed to eat. I wolfed it down almost without a breath, before I noticed that I was now the only one on the six bed ward, sometime during the night my co-habitee had been taken away.

There was a TV at one end of the ward. Pushing my breakfast table to one side, I struggled out of bed, my aching muscles screaming at me. My hurt leg resounding a dull pain. I switched the T.V on, easing down into the not-so-comfortable easy chair. The news was on and, even though I wasn't a fan of the news, it was nice to be part of the real world again and have the choices, and after the last few days it was a welcome relief. I relaxed deeper into the chair, placing my feet up on the magazine-filled coffee table.

'NOW THE LOCAL NEWS', said the presenter, followed by the jingle and title sequence.

'Police, who have been hunting a killer in Southend-On-Sea

responsible for a spate of murders of young girls, are now holding a suspect who is helping them with their enquiries. The man, believed to be in his early thirties, was arrested following various tip-offs from the public after the release of a photo-fit picture in the local press.

The vague description given by one of the victims, lucky enough to survive, after the attacker was disturbed by a vigilant farmer, led to a number of calls, with one name repeatedly turning up on the list.

His arrest followed a dawn raid this morning. He has been remanded in custody at an undisclosed police station for further questioning.'

The door to the ward opened and I turned sharply to see two police officers. A cold sweat gripped me and I realised I must have looked guilty. They walked confidently towards my bed before turning to face the chair where I was sitting.

"Daniel Stephens?"

"Yes," I acknowledged, crooking my neck to watch them as they approached me.

"We'd like to ask you a few questions about yesterday." The first officer was huge and stood nearly six foot four with intense dark eyes and black bushy eyebrows that met above the nose.

"A-ha." I tried to act calm, but my voice caught.

"I'm WPC Woodcote. This is PC Hamble." The other officer, who looked short in comparison, her blonde hair just showing beneath the hat that made her face look round emphasizing her button nose, all belied her svelt figure disguised underneath her stab jacket.

PC Hamble stood directly behind me whilst WPC Woodcote took up position to my right, notebook at the ready. I craned my neck to look at PC Hamble and his intimidating towering frame. Slowly I turned to WPC Woodcote as she spoke.

"Mr Stephens, in your own words can you explain the events of yesterday, leading up to when your car crashed into the tree?"

I gulped, a thousand thoughts rushed through my head. 'Guilty' flashed like a neon sign, even though I knew I wasn't. I cleared my throat and my voice trembled as I began to speak. "I can't really remember exactly what happened. I remember swerving and then hitting the tree... next thing... was... coming round." I thought back to the visions I had seen and used these to piece together my own version of events. "There was steam rising from the bonnet. I could feel a pain in my leg, I don't remember getting out. Just a little while later walking, well hobbling along the path, then it sort of goes blurry after that."

Both officers watched me intently. I could make out PC Hamble's reflection in the TV screen as he stood behind me, I'd switched off the TV when they had introduced themselves and his reflection became more intimidating on the blank screen.

WPC Woodcote continued the questioning. "Can you explain what you were doing in Belfairs woods yesterday?"

That's where I was, I thought. "Err... mm... I think I was just going for a drive, I was looking for a spot I know, but took a wrong turn. I think. I'm not too sure," It was all coming back to me now, a flood of pictures, a film sequence developing before me. The events that I had no control over, but was there. "No, I'm not sure, I know I left my house about seven am,"

"159a Shakespeare Drive?" said PC Hamble.

I twisted my body to face him "Yes."

"It's a bit early to go out for a drive isn't it?" said WPC Woodcote as I faced her again, she paused for effect. "Carry on, please."

I wondered how much they knew and if they were letting me dig a hole for myself. "Well, I couldn't sleep and didn't feel like staying indoors. I just fancied going out somewhere quiet, away from the world, my own little space. Yes, I think my neighbours downstairs were being quite noisy. I couldn't get back to sleep. I thought I'd do some writing. Thought I'd look for somewhere inspirational, there is this place I found once by mistake and I thought I'd try and find it again. I couldn't remember the exact location though." Now I had found the thread to my story I let it develop. "I knew it was there somewhere in that general direction. I sometimes do things like that if I'm not in a hurry, just chuck my guitar in the car and find somewhere to write."

"What sort of writing?" asked WPC Woodcote.

"Not exactly ideal weather at the moment for outside writing," PC Hamble interjected.

"Just songs, ideas. Different places, different inspirations. I do my writing all over the place really, depends on what I feel like. Sometimes I just sit in the car." I was beginning to convince myself that this is what had happened. It struck me that if they had checked my car they would not find a guitar! I was playing a dangerous game of bluff, relying on the fact that they hadn't.

"So you didn't know where the track, actually led?" WPC Woodcote walked round to the other side of the chair. PC Hamble took up WPC Woodcote's position. I now had one on either side. The pressure was mounting, but my belief in me, that I was convincing them, that this was just an innocent jaunt, was growing with each lie.

"No, I got to the end of the track and it was just a dead end so I turned round. I was on my way back. I knew it was one of the tracks off the main road. I wasn't in a hurry that day so I thought I'd try that one, you know, see where it went."

"Right." WPC Woodcote carried on writing in her pad.

"Do you know what made you hit the tree?" asked PC Hamble.

"I don't remember. As I say I remember coming round."

"And your leg hurt," PC Hamble finished.

"Yes," I uttered.

"You have no recollection of the events immediately prior to the crash?" finished WPC Woodcote.

"As I said, no, it's just a blur. You've already asked me this."

I was becoming more and more conscious that my body language was probably telling a different story. "Just a blur." I was repeating things. I sounded guilty to me.

"Sometimes you have to ask these questions twice because it can help trigger a memory. We just want to make sure we've got the facts as clear as they can be." WPC Woodcote paused and threw a glance at her colleague. It had a purpose that was hidden from me. "So, from your statement, you are not aware that you narrowly missed a horse and its rider?"

I swallowed hard. "Are they okay?" The words almost got stuck in my throat.

"The rider was lucky, just sustained a bump to the head and a badly bruised leg. However, the horse was not so lucky and had to be put down. Landed on a tree stump." WPC Woodcote fixed a stare at me, her eyes piercing the masquerade I was trying to create. I could tell she was questioning everything I had said. The only witness was the rider, so as long as I played it cool I thought I'd be okay, my word against theirs.

There was silence while both officers eyed me, and it put me on edge, they seemed to suspect something but had no proof.

"Well, Mr Stephens," PC Hamble said. "Thank you, for your time. If we have any further questions for you we know where you live," he stated, with an air of certainty that they would be seeing me again. WPC Woodcote flipped her notebook closed and placed it back in her pocket.

"Thank you, sir." Then both officers turned and walk to the door.

As she opened the door WPC Woodcote spoke once more.

"Your clothes were covered in mud when you were brought in."

An odd sentence I thought to throw in so late.

"Nothing else you want to add is there Mr Stephens?"

"No," I said nervously, trying to fathom what they were insinuating, then remembering the purpose of my visit to the woods.

"If you think of anything else, don't hesitate to give PC Hamble or myself a call. Thank you again for your time,"

They left, leaving me to sweat it out as the door closed behind them.

After a few seconds I got up and headed for the door to listen to the conversation as they wandered down the corridor.

It was a waste of time as I couldn't make out their voices. I limped back over to the bed and stood with my hands resting on the mattress, pondering the events of the last few days. Questions rattled round my head making me feel uneasy. I had my body back but that seemed to be it. Who did they have in custody? What had happened to Henry?

The murders came cascading back in a flourish of vivid pictures, my stomach cramped as I wanted to retch, as if indeed I had actually committed the crimes myself. Whilst in body, I had, in spirit it was not me. How was anyone else to know that? How could I convince others? I could hardly start to describe the events from my perspective. They'd have me locked up and committed. Maybe that would be my only way out, plead insanity, tell the truth. They'd believe it then.

"Wait," I said to myself. "They can't prove anything, can they?"

My real problem was I hadn't been witness to every second of every crime so I didn't know if I had been reckless and left any clues. If I had been careful I could just play ignorant if ever questioned about a possible link between me and the murders? In some instances that would be easy, but others I would have to lie through my teeth.

Then a thought struck me like a sledgehammer to the head.

My flat.

That was the one murder scene that connected directly to me, the carpet, the blood soaked carpet. Had it been investigated yet? No it can't have otherwise they would've arrested me, surely?

Where was the dawn raid?

I was dealing with a killer with no sense of covering his tracks. Was he stupid?

I started pacing the ward. My leg still hurt but I could walk on it with a limp.

My fingerprints or DNA in the abandoned warehouse, forensics were so clever these days. Talk about making it easy for the police, I've framed myself, whichever way I looked at it, I was guilty.

Sooner or later they would locate the body I buried near the car accident, probably sooner the way things were panning out. There is no way on earth I'm getting out of this without going to prison for the rest of my life.

A lifetime in prison for crimes I didn't actually commit, knowing that someone else did this using my identity. I felt even more useless than I did before as a Soulshadow, at least if I'd stayed like that I would have faded into non-existence. I wouldn't have known any difference then. So intent was I to get my body back I didn't think of the consequences.

I stopped pacing and stood still in the middle of the ward.

My only conclusion was to run. Now! Go and hide somewhere, until I can figure out what to do.

Who was the bloke they had in custody?

21

With my mind racing I looked around the ward for my clothes, hoping they had come up with me, there was only a bedside cupboard - it was empty.

A middle aged lady in an apron entered pushing a metal trolley piled high with trays.

"Excuse me, Do you know where my clothes might be?"

"No, I just do the meal runs," she replied sternly.

"Oh. Will the nurses know?"

She sighed. "The Sister might know," she slid my tray into one of the rack slots.

"Thanks."

With that I followed her out of the ward, the pain in my leg started to issue it's anger and I guessed whatever painkillers I'd been given were wearing off. I headed towards a desk that sat in a recess of the corridor, it was piled high with files and papers, behind it sat a woman in a dark blue uniform looking a little haggered and stressed.

"Excuse me, I'm Daniel Stephens, I was wondering where my clothes were." I rubbed my leg to ease the pain, and felt the large bandage that had been tightly wrapped around my thigh, I could feel the heat the wound emitted.

Without looking up she sharply stated, "they should be in your bedside cupboard."

Stunned by her reply I didn't want to pursue the matter but I needed my clothes.

"I checked and they're not." I tried to sound pleasant.

She took a deep intake of breath. "If they're not then they

might not have come up from…" she finally looked up. "You came in yesterday didn't you?" she stated distracted but politely. "In which case they might still be in A & E. I'll see if I can locate them for you, if you give me a few minutes."

"Okay." I limped back to the ward still trying to think through my next course of action, wondering how badly I'd hurt my leg as the pain started to intensify.

I was finding it difficult to sit still, uneasy at the way the course of events were unravelling. I wanted, I needed to speak to Ann-Marie find out what had happened. Pacing the ward I hoped the movement would ease the pain, but it didn't. Occasionally I stopped and stared out of the window, not looking for anything in particular, just staring as though it would provide me with all the answers. There was something I was not getting and I just couldn't put my finger on it.

Looking up at the clock, an hour had passed. I didn't even recall anyone saying how long I was to stay in for. I thought it strange that I was in a ward by myself as there was a shortage of hospital beds.

Finally the nurse returned carrying my clothes in a clear plastic bag, all neatly folded, although they still looked dirty.

The nurse's mood seemed to have brightened and her voice had a lighter tone to it as she joked. "Here you go. They were a bit dirty so we stored them offsite." She smiled, showing a line of perfect teeth. "One of the nurses was going to bring them up last night at the end of her shift, but things got a little hectic."

"Thank you," I said smiling, relieved knowing that I had my own clothes to hand.

"Sorry to ask, but do you know when I can leave?"

"Leave, sir, why would you want to leave such a fine establishment?" the sarcasm in her voice showed her distaste of the run down ward. "I think the doctors just want to keep you in for observation, probably just another night. Why have you got an important date?" She smiled warmly, her eyes teasing.

"No, no. I just…"

"Its alright, you don't need to explain. Look I'll check with the doctors and find out for you. That may take some time though. Is there anyone you want us to ring, Family? Girlfriend?" For a moment I thought she was hitting on me and felt flattered, she was older than me by about ten years with a raunchy sort of charm about her. Under normal circumstances I would have welcomed it but more important issues plagued my mind.

"Yes, my…" I caught myself as I was about to say my parents, but a part of me didn't want them to see me, not until I knew what was going on. "No, on second thoughts, it's alright thanks."

"You sure?"

"Yeah, positive."

"Well, if you need anything I will be around, swamped by paperwork but around. I'm sure you'll be joined later by a few more patients." With that she left.

I needed to leave the hospital. I couldn't wait around knowing that the police would return anytime and arrest me. However, I didn't want to cause a fuss or draw unnecessary attention, just slip out unnoticed. I needed a plan.

Casually roaming out of the ward into the corridor I paid close attention to the layout. The more I walked the more accustomed I became to the pain although the muscles appear to ease somewhat. I was still limping badly though. Looking in the direction of the desk I smiled at the nurse but, as she lifted her head, I saw it was a different nurse. I quickly averted my gaze and walked in the opposite direction to see where it went. The corridor had more wards scattered off it, each with six occupied beds, with nurses and orderlies, who didn't give me a second glance. Eventually, after turning a corner, the corridor came to a dead end.

I turned and started back to my ward and as I did I felt the gravity of the situation flood over me, making me feel sick. The murders, the innocent children, in my mind I made it feel as though it had been me and not Henry, even though I knew the truth. I wondered if it would ever be put right, if anything could be done to correct it. It would only be a matter of time before the police arrived to question me further, this time about the murders.

Back at my ward I knew I couldn't wait and also that I couldn't walk past the nurse dressed normally or she'd ask me where I was going. She couldn't stop me from checking myself out but she may insist on calling the doctor, which would draw unwanted attention.

Finally, I decided it would be best to wander out to the toilet with the gown on over my dirty clothes, my blood-soaked jeans rolled up above my knees. Although my clothes were dark maybe, from a quick glance, she wouldn't notice underneath the green gown. Next problem was to conceal my shoes and socks, I puzzled this issue further.

Getting dressed quickly, I noticed the right leg of my jeans had been cut vertically from the thigh down, obviously to allow access to my wound. 'Damn'. It would look silly walking along the street but I didn't have a choice. Carefully I rolled up my trouser legs, but immediately the cut one unravelled. I looked around the ward for something to tie it up with. The gown I'd been wearing lay on the bed and I saw the tie round the middle that would do just the trick, however I needed the gown to cover my clothes. Damn. Maybe it would just be easier to check myself out. 'No, that could take hours'. I ripped the material tie off and tied it round the rolled-up trouser leg, then put the gown on deciding that it would be alright without being tied. I undid my shirt buttons, allowing my shirt to freely hang below the gown, just under the neck line with the collar folded back under itself. Picking up a magazine and holding it in my left hand - which would be furthest away from the nurse as I passed her and slightly hidden by my own body - I collected my shoes positioning them in my grip so that they couldn't be seen behind it, praying it would work.

Checking my pockets to make sure I had everything, especially keys, I took a couple of deep breaths before stealing my moment and trying to look as casual as possible.

The nurse was on the phone and looking through a file. I thought this was going to be easy.

"Everything alright Mr Stephens?" she said, barely glancing up replacing the receiver.

"Yes," I shot back at her, then easing. "Fine, thank you, just going to the toilet."

"Just straight down the corridor fourth door on the right."

"Thanks."

It didn't quite take me through the double doors but if she kept her head down then it wouldn't be a problem. As I drew level with the door I glanced back, she wasn't at her desk. I couldn't see her anywhere, so, without hesitation, I slipped through the doors. The stairwell was not far from the doors.

For a busy hospital there were not many people about and I wasn't sure if that was a good thing or a bad thing. It was easy to get lost in a crowd but there was less chance of being approached if no one was about.

I headed down the stairs as quickly as possible without looking back, and soon found myself on ground level of the stairwell, which culminated in an enclosed lobby, unlike the other floors. Before I went through the final double doors into the corridor beyond I ducked behind the stairwell out of sight and rolled down my jeans, doing my best to tie the seam of the right leg together so it didn't flap about. Then put my shoes and socks on and threw the gown into the deepest recess under the bottom step, finally stepping out innocently and through the double doors.

I looked for a sign showing which way to the nearest exit,

but there was one for everything else except. I turned right and followed the corridor in the hope that it would lead me out. I felt more relaxed now I was in normal day clothes, even though they were dirty. The corridor turned left and then right and seemed to go on forever. I wondered if I was going in the right direction. It was like walking around a maze. The corridor took two steps down and I came to a 'T' junction. I turned right again and followed the passage then turned left and then right. I passed door after door before finally arriving at a waiting area with outside doors.

It was cold out and I didn't have a coat but it felt good to feel the real weather again on my face. I was curious how long it would be before they noticed I had left, an hour, two, half a day. Ultimately I didn't care I was free – for the time being anyway.

I glanced back quickly as I headed on to Prittlewell Chase, just to make sure I wasn't being followed. The dual carriageway was tree-lined with a grass divide separating the two carriageways.

Heading left, my first thought was to go home and get a change of clothes. Then to see Ann-Marie, make sure she got home alright yesterday. I hoped it was only yesterday. Yes, the police officers had referred to it as yesterday.

I only lived a ten minute walk from the hospital although I was limping and, as if on cue my injury elicited another reminder, I knew it would take longer. At one point I had to stop and rest it, rubbing my leg carefully, wishing the pain away. Thirty-five minutes later I neared my flat.

Stopping a little way along the street I watched it cautiously, making sure it was safe. Suddenly anxiety gripped me and even though it was my flat a chill ran down my spine.

A nagging thought made me decide that it was better if I entered via the back door. Maybe I was being overcautious, after all they had a man in custody, they weren't looking for me, yet I was sure they suspected I was hiding something. Once inside I knew I would feel safe again, maybe I could relax a little, have a drink and bite to eat as I was starting to feel peckish again.

A feeling of unease washed over me as I reached the back door. I pulled the keys slowly from my pocket but paused. It all seemed too perfect. Something sat uneasily on my shoulders.

Out of the corner of my eye I caught a movement inside my flat. I darted away from the glass back door, flinging myself tightly against the outside wall adjacent to it. 'Shit', I thought to myself.

The curtains twitched and I heard the key turn in the lock. Looking round I tried to decide my best option, fear pushing the adrenalin around my body, forcing it to forget about my injured leg.

I put my hands on the railings that separated my balcony from my neighbour's and jumped over, stifling the cry of pain as I landed on my injured leg, clamping a hand over my mouth, biting down hard. I half fell, half crouched down behind the brick-built shed that was there, the same as on all the balconies in this run of flats. Tears streamed down my cheeks as inside my head I let out a stream of obscenities.

The door opened then abruptly closed. No explanation. No voices. Someone apparently changing their mind.

I waited a few minutes before I dared look, but took the time to study my leg and re-tie the flaps of material. The bandage had also worked itself loose and I could see the start of an angry zig-zag of stitches that ran down my thigh. I peered carefully round the corner of the shed. The balcony was clear and I knew I couldn't go in now. I didn't know who it was but I had to leave.

I made my way down to the garden below using my neighbour's stairs, heading once again into the alleyways that threaded their way behind the gardens. I didn't want to leave the way I'd come, in case it was being watched, so I took the alley further along that lead out into the road behind, Gainsborough Road, running parallel to mine. All the time I was paying attention to what was going on around me and aware of the throbbing pain in my leg.

At the edge of the alley I checked the coast was clear. It was.

I had to get to Ann-Marie's house. That was the only place I could go now. No one knew about her, I was sure her house would be safe.

I limped along unsuccessfully shutting out the pain, which my recent exertion had exacerbated, the odd tear making its way gently down my cheek as I grimaced. A warm sensation engulfed the area around the wound and without checking I guessed that it was bleeding again. I hoped the stitches would hold up under the strain.

I took the most direct route to Ann-Marie's and found I needed to rest my leg along West Road. A car pulled up curtly by the curb, tyres screeching to a halt. I jumped, almost ready to run. It was a false alarm as a boy racer got out and went into the house he was in front of.

I proceeded along the road, all the time aware that my limping was getting more pronounced hampering my progress. I wished the pain would subside.

An eternity seemed to pass before I made it to Tickfield Road. I could see the yellow door of Ann-Marie's house. The pain numbed briefly replaced by a feeling of security.

I rang the door bell. Again. And again.

Finally the door opened and I saw Ann-Marie. I wanted to hug her, not sure whether it was relief she was safe and in, or just the fact that I was pleased to see her.

"Thank god you're in, I was beginning to wonder what I was going to do, I wasn't sure if you'd got home alright yesterday or anything."

"Daniel? Is that you?" she inquired, with an inflection of doubt.

"Yes," I said, with resignation.

"You sound different."

"Do I?"

We stood there poised, like two friends meeting for the first time in twenty years.

"Come in. Sorry, I didn't think I would meet you again." She closed the door behind us. "It worked. I can't believe it worked," she said jubilantly.

"It worked alright. But now I think I'm the murderer. For real! The one the police are hunting."

"No, the police have a man in custody. I heard it on the news this morning."

"That may have been this morning. But someone was just at my flat, I didn't get a proper look, but I think it was them. As soon as they see the bloodstain on the carpet, then find the body buried near the car accident, yesterday, my days are numbered for sure."

"Oh," she gasped.

"Exactly. I thought the ritual would put everything right, but it hasn't, this is worse. If…" I corrected myself. "… when they catch me I'll go to prison for the rest of my life."

Silence blanketed the hallway as we stood contemplating the situation.

"Aunt Rose, we need to speak to Aunt Rose she might be able to help," I said, finally breaking the silence. I saw Mojo behind Ann-Marie his head slightly cocked to one side.

"I'm sorry. I thought it would put everything right," she said, her face showing guilt at her failure.

"So did I." I looked at her, then embraced her. "I'm sorry, it's not your fault. You've helped me so much and I'm just throwing it back in your face,"

I felt her reciprocate the embrace. A warm feeling penetrated every fibre of my body.

"I'm sure Aunt Rose, or even Heather, will be able to help. They must be able to do something."

"Is there any chance they could come round here, I'm not

sure how wise it would be for me to go out on the streets? Especially during daylight. Not anymore."

"I'll give her a ring."

She released her grip from me and picked up the phone, dialling the number she knew by heart.

22

Ann-Marie explained the situation as best she could to Aunt Rose and I took the opportunity to make myself at home, first making us both a cup of tea, before settling down in the lounge. It felt good to be able to do things that I'd taken for granted.

I half listened to the one-sided conversation taking place in the hallway, savouring the aroma of my tea. I switched on the TV, the time and channel flicked up in the top right-hand corner. It was 11.38am. Flicking through the channels I couldn't find anything of any interest to watch, although I hadn't really thought I would, I just wanted to experience the normality of my physical being. I heard the phone being put down and lowered the volume.

"Aunt Rose said she'd be round shortly, she is going to speak to Heather, to try and find out what went wrong," Ann-Marie announced as she entered the room, Mojo at her side. Settling in her favourite armchair, she continued. "The ritual should have returned you to the moment of the original transfer of power. That's why I wasn't worried about going to the cemetery, I didn't expect to still be there afterwards. Everything should have been as if it never happened. I don't know what went wrong. I did everything as I was supposed to. Heather said I had enough power, and…" She stopped mid flow.

"And what?"

"And it had to be done by someone who… had the power… and strength enough to see it through." She looked almost embarrassed about blowing her own trumpet.

"I'm certainly glad you do. But why didn't it work?" It was a rhetorical question on my part. "I hope you didn't mind I made a cup of tea, it's just on the table where you normally have it." She smiled.

"No, of course not. Thanks." She picked it up and drank slowly. "Yuk!"

"What?"

"No sugar."

"Sorry, I didn't know you took any."

"Two normally."

"Two! Sweet tooth eh?"

"A girl's got to have some vices you know, I like my sugar."

"I'll go and get some."

"Thanks."

I left the room and headed for the kitchen, returning a few minutes later carrying the sugar bowl and a spoon, adding two sugars and stirring noisily.

"There you go m'lady," I joked, in my best Parker from Thunderbirds impression.

She smiled.

"I guess you got back okay yesterday without any problems."

"Sort of. Thanks." I sat back on the sofa. "A little while after I'd done the ritual I was gathering up my things when I heard someone behind me. He was saying something but I wasn't really listening, I just wanted to get away from there. As I said I wasn't expecting to still be there although I wasn't absolutely sure. I think it was the vicar, he must have been uttering some sort of protection. Called me 'the child of the devil'. Never been called that before. Well, not since I found my mum's wedding dress in a box at the bottom of the wardrobe when I was five and drew crayon all over it. He probably thought I was trying to conjure up the devil or something. As I walked by him he tried to grab me, luckily Mojo was there." At the mention of his name he cocked one eye. "He snarled and he let go. Good, brave, Mojo." Ann-Marie stroked his head and he sat up appreciatively. "We just left as quickly as possible after that."

"Can't say I'm surprised, you looked really wired and wild at one point."

"What do you mean?"

"You looked as though you were possessed when the vicar first came out and saw you."

"Oh. It wasn't until I got home that I registered that the glass shades my dad gave me had melted." Her head dipped slightly and I could sense the fond memories she was picturing.

"I'm sorry." It sounded useless. These were precious objects which she treasured and she had sacrificed them for me. Even if I could replace them, it wouldn't be the same, it was the person who gave them, that made them special.

"Anyway." Her face brightened. "I did chant some gibberish at him as we left, gawd knows what he thought."

"Did you catch the bus home?"

"No, we walked. It was quite nice as it wasn't raining. It gave me time to wonder whether it had worked, I knew I couldn't sense you near me but you had been growing weaker."

"It must have taken you... that's Belfairs Woods," I exclaimed, as I saw pictures flash up on the lunchtime news. "Quick turn up the volume."

"Where's the remote?" she said feeling the around the coffee table.

"Sorry. I've got it."

POLICE HAVE DISCOVERED BODIES OF TWO MORE YOUNG GIRLS THOUGHT TO BE THE VICTIMS OF A KNIFEMAN WHO HAS BEEN TERRORIZING THE LOCAL AREA OVER THE LAST FEW DAYS.

THE FIRST DISCOVERY WAS MADE IN BELFAIRS WOODS IN THE EARLY HOURS OF THE MORNING WHEN POLICE AND A RECOVERY TEAM WERE INVESTIGATING THE SCENE OF AN ACCIDENT FROM THE PREVIOUS DAY. TYRE TRACKS WERE

TRACED TO A SECLUDED SPOT WHERE A SHALLOW GRAVE HAD BEEN DUG.

POLICE ARE NOW HUNTING THE DRIVER OF THE VEHICLE WHO WAS TAKEN TO HOSPITAL BUT LATER DISAPPEARED. POLICE HAVE TAKEN THE UNUSUAL STEPS OF RELEASING THE NAME OF THE SUSPECT THEY WANT TO QUESTION, 'DANIEL STEPHENS', AND ARE APPEALING TO ANYONE WHO KNOWS HIS WHEREABOUTS TO CONTACT THEM. DO NOT APPROACH HIM AS HE COULD BE ARMED AND DANGEROUS. IN ANOTHER TWIST TO THIS STORY, EVIDENCE OF A MURDER HAS BEEN FOUND IN A FLAT OWNED BY MR STEPHENS. POLICE FORENSIC TEAMS ARE TAKING DNA SAMPLES.

THEY ARE TYRING TO FIND A MAN SEEN RUNNING FROM THE SCENE.

A SECOND BODY WAS DISCOVERED IN AN ABANDONED WAREHOUSE IN GORDON STREET.

POLICE THINK THE MURDERS ARE CONNECTED.

"It was the police at the flat his morning," I stated, confirming it in my mind.

"What? How did you get away?"

"I jumped onto my neighbours' balcony. And hid, well waited. Then, when I thought the coast was clear, used the back alleys to get away. I wasn't exactly running though, more like limping."

"Limping?"

"Yeah." I told Ann-Marie about the accident in Belfairs Woods and the fact that I had found myself in the hospital after the binding ritual. "That reminds me, don't suppose you've got any jeans or something I could change into? The nurses cut the ones I'm wearing and they are quite dirty. Also some pain killers would be good, if you have some?"

"You'll be okay here for now, you'll have to be gone by the time mum gets in though. If she sees you she'll call the police for sure, especially if she has seen the news. I don't have any jeans that would fit you. I'm guessing, as I haven't seen how tall you are. There might be some Nurofen in the kitchen cupboard, I'll check in a minute."

I was just an average build for my age, pretty non-descript but Ann-Marie had narrow hips and was a good four or five inches shorter than me.

"It's okay I didn't think you would, but had to ask. I was hoping to get a change of clothes from my flat this morning, but I don't think that will be possible now," I said, as I thought of my options.

Ann-Marie got up and turned the TV off. "I'll get the Nurofen. Do you have any idea where you can hide?"

"Nope." I called as she left the room. I waited until she returned and the added, "I can't exactly go to any friends. Not if they've seen the news. Hold on, wait a minute…"

"What? Hear you go. They are the Nurofen aren't they? Mum does mark the boxes so I can tell." Ann-Marie interrupted.

"Yes, thanks." I took two tablets and swallowed some tea. "The tunnels, I can hide out in the tunnels, if they were good enough for Henry they are good enough for me. Not exactly the Ritz but they'll do."

"Be a bit cold won't they? And dark?"

"Haven't really got much choice, have I? Have you got any candles that I could borrow and matches or a lighter?"

"I don't think so. I'll check if my mum has got any in the kitchen." I settled back into the chair letting my body relax completely. I still ached all over. My injured leg was no longer throbbing and I placed my hand gently on it as if testing it, the wound was warm, I pulled back the material of my jeans and saw some dried blood soaked through the loose bandage. I would have to ask Ann-Marie for a clean dressing.

All energy suddenly seemed to drain from me and I started to feel tired, tired like I hadn't slept in weeks. My eyelids became too heavy and slowly they closed letting sleep take me.

"… got any candles,"

"Pardon? What? Sorry." I jolted awake.

"Oh. No, we haven't got any candles."

"I'll have to get some on my way to the tunnels." Then I realised I didn't have any cash. "Damn, I haven't got any money. Look I don't like to ask…,"

"Can you borrow some money?" she finished.

"I promise I'll pay it back." I hated asking, she had done so much, so freely for me and all I seemed to do was keep asking for more.

"I'll go check." She left the room for a second time and I felt sleep close in on me.

The doorbell rang, breaking my drowsiness. I went to the window and discreetly peered through the net curtains. It was Aunt Rose. I breathed a sigh of relief and answered the door.

"Hello."

"Daniel, I presume?" Aunt Rose chimed.

"Yes, in the flesh this time," I joked, as Aunt Rose walked past me and went into the lounge. I closed the door and followed her.

"Where's Ann-Marie?" she inquired. This could easily have been an accusation if she hadn't known the full story.

"Just gone upstairs. Be down in a minute."

I didn't know what to say at this point. Although she'd helped us to get this far, it was still a meeting between two strangers.

"You're quite different to what I'd imagined. Quite a handsome fellow really."

I felt my cheeks blush.

"Thanks, I think," I replied, feeling awkward.

"Have you seen the news this morning?"

"Yes."

"So do you know who the other person is then?"

"Other person! What other person? Oh the one they've got in custody."

"No, they let him go but they have discovered two sets of fingerprints at your flat, so the police believe they are looking for two people now."

"They are probably my parent's fingerprints, they have got a key."

"They have already been eliminated," she said curtly.

"Then I don't understand."

"This is all the money I've got." Ann-Marie burst into the room with Mojo padding alongside. "There's about £23 and some small change. Aunt Rose?"

I took the money and put it in my pocket, thanking Ann-Marie.

"Hello dear."

"There is... two of us, now," I stuttered.

"How can that be? I thought you were the murderer." As soon as she spoke she seemed to pick up on my shame. "Sorry. How can there be two?" Ann-Marie was just as perplexed as I was.

The whole situation seemed to have changed in an instant. Not only had my life been turned upside down by the events of the last few days, but now there was someone else involved, whose identity we didn't know. I started to think that maybe it wasn't the police at my flat. It could have been the other person. 'I should have looked to see who it was'. That must have been who ran from the police after I'd already gone. Thoughts cascaded round my head in freefall with one question top of the list. Who was this other person?

"Aunt Rose, is there any way we can track this other person?" I sat down on the sofa.

"I could use my crystal ball." It sounded so alien to me, almost lame, like something out of a horror movie that I had to fight my 'scoff' back. "But that will only tell us what it wants to. I will give it a...," she paused, looking first at Ann-Marie and then to me. "There is something else you should know which might tell us who exactly this second person is."

"What's that?" we both said in unison.

"First, Ann-Marie have you got the book of incantations that Heather lent you?"

"Yes, it's upstairs. Why?"

"Would you mind getting it, dear?"

"Sure."

"Heather said one of the reasons the ritual might not have worked the way it should, is that you might have not followed the instructions accurately and possibly not set up the DoxTrident Octagon correctly."

"But I followed the directions and the diagram," she said adamantly.

"It's alright dear, I'm just trying to establish a few facts."

"Sorry." She lowered her head abashed. "I'll go and get it."

"Thank you." Ann-Marie started to leave, but hesitated as Aunt Rose continued.

"It would appear that if the candles are placed at the wrong points it gives life back to the spirit in its own form. That's why I need to know what exactly you did."

I looked at Ann-Marie with disbelief, she gulped.

"So we could have brought back a murderer from the grave?" she said, finding it hard to comprehend.

"Yes, I'm afraid that might be the case."

"And that's why everything is still carrying on, rather than reverting back to the beginning?" I asked rhetorically.

"Yes," Aunt Rose confirmed.

"I did my best. It was difficult Daniel, you kept fading and…" Ann-Marie didn't finish her sentence as tears formed in her eyes.

23

Ann-Marie's face turned pale as she consumed by her thoughts. "Excuse me," she suddenly announced fleeing the room. I listened as I heard her hands sliding up the wall, closely followed by Mojo, padding behind her. A door slammed shut and was followed by heavy sobs.

I eyed Aunt Rose, my mind full of questions I found difficult to ask. Dread was pulsing through my veins like liquid nitrogen, sending shivers along my spine. Aunt Rose sat on the sofa as if spinning a thought around in her head.

Silence, broken only by a faint sob coming from upstairs, echoed through the house.

At first I didn't know what to do then I followed the sound upstairs to the bathroom where I rapped lightly on the door.

"Are you alright?" I knew it sounded stupid but it was my way of letting her know I was there.

"I'll be fine in a second," came the choked reply amidst the sounds of sniffs, and nose blowing. I listened further as I heard a tap being turned on, followed by the flushing of the toilet. A few seconds later the door opened and I saw Ann-Marie's red eyes and puffy cheeks which only managed to instil guilt in me for getting her involved. I placed a hand on Ann-Marie's shoulder as a sign of comfort. Mojo eyed it with caution.

"Are you ok?" I said softly.

"I feel sick."

I wanted to give her a hug but held back unit finally I conceded. She rested her head on my shoulder and reciprocated. "I'm sure there is something we can do." I was not convinced.

"Come on, let's go down stairs and see if Aunt Rose has any ideas." I wanted my words to sound confident but I had too much doubt in my own mind.

I released her from my hold and took her hand, leading her slowly down the stairs, with Mojo following dutifully behind.

Aunt Rose was busy with her crystal ball, gently caressing it, muttering away to herself. It was as if she were polishing it, staring into its effervescent shine, her eyes glued in place. I led Ann-Marie to her usual armchair where Mojo joined her.

"I can see a man," Aunt Rose announced unexpectedly. "Rugged face, slim build, dark eyes with neatly kept hair. He is wearing a red shirt, blue jeans and black anorak. Cold, he is very cold. Sitting in some gardens, watching the people go about their business. He appears to be waiting, waiting for someone." She paused, the concentration on her face intent. "No, it's gone."

"Is that him?" I asked, joining her on the sofa.

"Yes, I believe it is." Aunt Rose replaced the crystal ball on its stand on the coffee table.

"Do you know where he is?" Before she could answer me my mind surged with anger. "How can he sit there so calmly? Waiting. This is ridiculous. I've got to hide." I stood up as the anger boiled inside me. "He openly goes about his business like he hasn't got a care in the world. Whilst I, whilst I…"

"Daniel!" Aunt Rose stated curtly breaking my train of thought. "You must remember that he has been living your life for the last few days. He knows the police are looking for you. They thought it was you running from the flat this morning. He has the advantage. His face has not been seen for nearly eighty years. No one knows him."

"So I can end up in prison for the rest of my life while he walks away scot-free," I clenched my fists, trying to control my anger. "Can you tell where he was?"

"No, I'm sorry, it was just a garden, I couldn't see too much clear detail, although there was a fountain behind where he was sitting."

"A fountain? I can't recall any fountains in the area."

"Aunt Rose is there anything that can be done to put everything right? Correct my mistake," Ann-Marie interjected, her voice still showing signs of distress.

"It's not your fault Ann-Marie. You've done everything you can with me fading in and out. You can't blame yourself. It's my fault for getting us here in the first place."

"What's happened has happened and there is nothing we can do to change that now. But we need to focus on what we can do now," Aunt Rose implored.

Chagrined, I stepped towards Ann-Marie. "I'm just glad that you have been there to help me. Thank you."

"Thanks." She found my hand and held it in hers.

"We need to locate Henry." But I knew it was me who had to find him. "But I can't exactly go out during the day. I still don't recall seeing a fountain in any of the gardens in the area. Would your mum have a map of the area Ann-Marie? Do you know?"

"I don't, sorry." I realised it was a stupid question as it would have been no use to her.

"I have one at home Daniel. I could go and get it. It may take a while though."

Aunt Rose had a motherly way about her, always helpful, always having a solution to a problem.

"Hold on." I put my hands up to my face, palms together, forefingers touching my nose as a memory worked itself free. "Now I think about it, there is a fountain. If I recall, in a newspaper article about a year ago, one of the local freebies. There was a fountain being erected in memory of some local person, but the name escapes me. A politician I think." I let my hands animate my thought process. "Can't think of the name of the gardens though!" I closed my eyes trying to picture the article in my head, believing it would help me remember. "Oh, come on, what was it?" I could have kicked myself. I could picture it but not see the name clearly. "Parry, Parly, Farley... Falley... Farry," I said reaching out for the answer.

"Farndon Gardens, near the town hall?" asked Aunt Rose.

"That's them. Yes." I stood excited as the information flooded my brain. "The fountain was erected as the final piece to the gardens which were in memory of Ex Mayor, Charles Farndon, who served Southend-On-Sea in 197... 2, I think, until 1988, when he retired because of ill health. He died in 199..."

"... 9, and they decided to commemorate all the good work that he'd done. I remember him. He was a good Mayor. Shame. He always cared about the local community, not like the ones nowadays, who just want to make a name for themselves. He didn't, just wanted to do the best he could." Aunt Rose obviously felt very passionately about his accomplishments.

I seem to recall they also discovered an entrance to a tunnel or storage space, no one seemed to know exactly. It was only about ten to fifteen feet long with debris piled up at the back. No one could explain its presence and, as nothing untoward was ever discovered they sealed it up again. That's why I remember, I thought it was weird and interesting. I wonder if he realises yet that that entrance has gone?" I smiled, thinking how different the world must be to him now, after all these years.

Beep, beep!

I looked at Aunt Rose who, in turn, looked at me before realising that it was her mobile phone. She reached into her bag and pulled it out, squinting at the tiny screen.

"Ooh, I've got a message. Oh, bother, I can never remember how to work these things."

I went over and showed her, it was a message from Heather. Aunt Rose struggled to read the little screen.

HAVE FOUND WAY. WILL CALL LATER. Hx.

"What does that mean?" I asked.

"Before I came over I explained the situation to her and asked if she knew of any way we could correct what had happened. I suspected straightaway, as soon as I got the phone call from Ann-Marie, what had occurred and the possible consequences…"

I went and watched the world outside the window, letting Aunt Rose's voice fade into the background. It was starting to get dark, the fact that it had remained overcast all day just helped the night sky form its shadow over the town sooner.

"I'm going to try and find him," I said resolutely. "I can't stay here and do nothing. It should be dark enough now. If you've got a coat or top with a hood on it that I can borrow, Ann-Marie? That's big enough of course. I should be able to get by without being recognised."

She walked over to where I stood and put her hands to my chest, then slowly feeling her way to my shoulders. Luckily I had quiet narrow shoulders. "I think I might have. But what are you going to do?"

"Honestly? I don't know, but I've got to do something. At least if I find him then we will be one step closer."

"But there's no point if you can't do anything. You might get caught, and that won't help at all," Ann-Marie reasoned.

"Ann-Marie, I've got to go," I stated, rather more sharply than I intended. "I'll simply have to be careful, that's all, and not get caught."

"Yes. I'll get that top. Oh, What about your jeans? Didn't you say that you needed some…" Before she had time to finish Aunt Rose interrupted her.

"Ooh yes, of course. Daniel here you go." Aunt Rose handed me a carrier bag.

I looked at her astounded. "What's this?" I asked hesitantly.

"Trousers."

"But?"

"Something made me think you might need some. So I

popped into the secondhand shop on the way," I was astounded by her psychic ability.

"Thank you. I don't know what to say."

"Never mind that, I just hope they fit. I've never bought men's trousers before and they didn't have a great selection. But somehow they seemed right."

I opened the bag, and inside with a tag still attached were a pair of beige chino-style trousers made from a light denim fabric. Ann-Marie fetched me a new bandage and some lint so I could redress my wound. From the exertion the wound had bled and two of the stitches had broken free, tearing the skin, but it had stopped bleeding. So carefully I secured my clean dressing pulling it tighter which caused me to wince at the pain. Ann-Marie headed to her room to find me a coat. Ann-Marie was a bit of a tomboy and the coat she had was a three quarter length Blue Parker, with a fake fur lining on the cuffs, and rim of the hood. It was a tight fit but it had to do.

"Thank you." I noted the clock on the mantle. "Your mum will be back soon, so I'd better go. I'll see you tomorrow okay?" I hesitated for no real reason. "Bye. Bye, Aunt Rose, and thank you."

"It's alright dear. Be careful."

"I will."

With that I headed out into the dark night, immediately putting the hood up as I heard the door close behind me. It was cold so I didn't look out of place with the hood wrapped tightly round my head and my hands thrust deep into my pockets. I knew my destination and I walked there briskly, mindful of my stitches and limp.

Fifteen minutes later the entrance to Farndon Gardens came into view. I stopped outside and took a deep breath, as if confirming my fate. I had no great description to go on so wasn't absolutely sure who to look for. In the depths of my mind I hoped I would recognise him by the clothes he was wearing.

A lot of people were milling around. The new town clock, which sat at the head of the high street towering over the small trees, showed it was half-past four. I watched people already heading home from work to snuggle up in their warm houses in front of the TV.

I thought about what night it was and realised that I should have been going bowling with some friends, a few drinks, and a bit of fun. Instead I was playing the 'Game of my Life', tails I lose, heads I lose - that's how I felt.

Searching even a small crowd of people wasn't an easy task, every male face I imagined to be him. I just didn't know what to look for. Walking into the gardens I scanned the area which was barely two hundred feet long and sixty feet wide. There were plenty of thick bushes and small trees which could conceal someone easily, even during daylight. But it was dark and the shadows just added to the secrecy.

After ten or so minutes I decided the gardens were deserted except for me. I stood deflated, watching my breath vapour form clouds in the air in front of me, before dissipating. I didn't know what I expected to find, but it wasn't here.

Before leaving I glanced round once more.

Over in the furthest corner there was movement, a shadow in the darkness of the bushes. My heart jumped into my mouth. I gulped down another mouthful of air then slowly walked in the direction of the movement.

My nerves were rattling on edge, fists clenched in preparation. I was ready for a fight. It was what I wanted, for everything that had happened, to let out my frustration. The closer I got to the bushes the more the adrenalin was pumping through my body, fuelling my actions, making me forget rational thought.

I took a step off the path and into the bushes, pushing the branches aside, careful of any sudden movement.

A force like a wrecking ball struck me across the back of the shoulder blades, forcing me to the ground. Winded and confused I laid there trying to fathom what was going on. My arm started to go numb where I'd banged my elbow as I hit the ground. I turned over to see where the force that had hit me had gone, expecting a further blow. There was no one. I struggled to my knees and peered through the branches of the bushes to a figure running through the gates of the gardens.

I stood up sharply in readiness to run. Pain issued a reminder of my injured leg. "Aaarggh, damn, shit," I said, falling to the ground again. I didn't know what to grab first, my elbow, my leg, or my shoulders as they all smarted at the same time.

I fought the pain and fumbled to my feet, stumbling to the entrance of the gardens as fast as my leg allowed looking like drunk. When I got there whoever it was, was gone. Standing, I looked back to the corner where I had been knocked over and limped back hoping to find something, a clue, anything. I found nothing. It was dark and I wasn't sure if I was expecting to find a body or an entrance to some tunnels. That was a thought - maybe he was looking for the entrance, which had once been here. My shoulders started to feel stiff so I rolled them around to loosen the aching muscles.

That thought firmly planted in my head I left the gardens to the night. I was hungry and needed food as well as candles. There was a chip shop not far from the gardens.

One problem was I had to avoid being recognised. All the shops were well lit and I needed to conceal my face. If I left my hood up it might just draw the shopkeepers gaze to my face, especially in a well-lit shop. I couldn't risk it. I would have to find a shop where I felt I could get away with it.

I made my way along the high street, keeping in the shadows, passed a side road where one of the pubs was full to bursting with people. Suddenly I noticed a kebab van further down the street waiting for the early evening crowd. I didn't like kebabs but I was hungry and I needed to keep my strength up. It was cold already and was set to get even colder during the night, so I was left with little choice.

When I reached the van I found they did quite a selection of food, so I bought a burger and chips. There were no crowds and it proved easy to conceal my identity. Walking away, I ate quickly, my leg loosening up again, making the limp less pronounced.

Warrior Square was where I was heading, there was an entrance to the tunnels and I knew the place would be deserted about now. On the way I passed a corner shop closing up for the day. Half the lights were already extinguished and I decided to take my chances. I persuaded the owner to sell me my requirements just before he closed for the night, some candles, matches, and a few snacks for my overnight stay.

In the gardens I looked around to make sure I was not being watched, before disappearing into the trees and bushes to locate the entrance which I had seen a couple of days previously, through the eyes of an exiting murderer. With a lot of effort I pulled the door open, it was not easy, the growth of vines on the walls held it tight. I squeezed through the tiniest gap then closed it behind me, finding myself thrown into complete blackness.

24

I opened the box of candles and lit one so I could see where I was. Beyond the realm of the light the darkness seemed like an abyss of nothingness and, for the first time since this had begun, I felt really scared and alone, the fact that I was real again only managed to cement it deep in my core. Knowing it would not be long before the cold started to bite only made me feel more vulnerable and my ears became like radars listening to every unusual sound, the occasional whistling which I hoped was a breeze somewhere, the scraping sound which I eventually worked out was the bushes outside the door. There was also a stale odour that whilst not repulsive emphasized my desolation.

I moved the candle in a slow arc, letting it light the narrow tunnel, which was barely three feet wide, its brightness seemed inadequate. The blackness ran from me as I held out the candle in front of me and I considered staying near to the entrance as for some inexplicable reason, the tunnels appeared even more sinister than they did during the day, even though the daylight had no effect in here. A draught penetrated the door emphasizing how cold it was, and reminding me that it would only get colder as night drew in.

I would also have less warning if someone else entered, so reluctantly I moved along the tunnel. The scraping of my feet on gravel punctuated the darkness, firing my imagination, creating all sorts of images of sinister things lurking in the shadows.

The small flicker of the candle was useless in the vast void of black but it was the best I could do. It was better than the torch in that it provided a little heat, but the flickering flame made my own shadow dance on the walls, making me more than a little edgy.

I was looking for somewhere to settle down for the long night. I was looking for somewhere clean and cosy, I laughed to myself, I expected the Ritz in a damp horrible tunnel. Lowering the candle I surveyed the ground conditions, dusty and hard but dry. I looked back the way I had come but it was just blackness beyond the realms of the candlelight. This was the best I was going to get.

I emptied the carrier bag that I'd holding the few snacks, shoving them into the pockets of the coat and, taking three more candles out of the box, lit them, after building up little piles of dust around the bases to keep them upright. I then split the bag as carefully as I could down one side and along the seam at the bottom, spreading it out on the ground. That was the best I could do to keep myself clean.

Settling down I tried to get comfortable, resting my back against the hard brick wall. After a while I moved the four candles closer to me, trying to make the most of the little heat they gave off, lighting a couple more from the pack. Then, closing my eyes I tried to sleep in the uncomfortable sitting position, but sleep wouldn't take me. I tried taking deep breaths, expelling the air slowly, attempting to relax. Every time I was near to falling asleep a noise from the darkness would stir me, making me alert, ready to defend myself if necessary.

Without a watch I didn't know how much time was passing. I was relieved in a way, as I would have constantly been looking at it, getting more and more frustrated, thinking the hands probably would not have moved, wondering if the battery had stopped.

After what seemed an eternity of restlessness the cold started to nip at my toes and fingers. I thrust my hands deep into my pockets, making my hands into fists but this felt uncomfortable because of the way I was sitting, although I had to concede that at least they were warmish. I wiggled my toes about to get the blood flowing again. The heat this generated only lasted for a few seconds before dissipating quickly, leaving the cold biting back with a vengeance.

With backache starting to set in I sat bolt upright, stretching every tense muscle, lowering and raising each shoulder in turn to ease the muscles.

As I moved, it reminded me how cold it had become, every movement emphasizing the warm patch of my body that I had uncovered. Clenching my knees to my chest, I rocked on my backside, hands buried in the alternate sleeves of the coat. 'Is this night ever going end?' was the thought that rallied round my head as I sat there wishing time away.

After a while sleep finally consumed me.

It was full of visions, replaying scenes in my head, the past few days echoing in silence. Unfamiliar faces started to haunt my dreams even though I felt they should be familiar to me, I didn't know them, strange situations. Men in long red hooded cloaks were kneeling on a floor, a dozen or so. Two were standing at the front before a table with a naked man on it. The ones kneeling were chanting the same thing over and over again. Candles burned, lighting the whole room. There were no windows in the concrete bland walls. The floor looked like bricks laid in a herringbone fashion.

Symbols had been drawn upon the walls behind the table, an upside down cross in the middle. On the right of this was what looked like a cutlass with an eye in the top of the handle. The image on the left was a moon or sun – could have been either. The two men standing at either end of the table held the hands and feet of the man lying down.

A priest-type figure dressed in the same style red cloak, and holding a staff in one hand that was at least six foot in length with an upside down cross at the top, stood behind the table. In the other hand he carried a silver chalice with what looked like the handle of a pestle in it.

He spoke in a language I didn't recognise and the room fell silent. Then, resting the chalice on the table, he lifted the pestle out and drew a shape on the chest of the man, all the time chanting. The man was conscious, seemingly relaxed, as the candles burned brighter.

All fell silent and the pestle was replaced in the chalice. The priest's left hand hovered above the man's chest. The man began convulsing, his whole body writhing around in spasms, the two men holding his feet and hands struggled to keep them still. Steam rose from the marks on the man's chest. Then all went still. Every single pair of eyes in the place suddenly focussed on me.

I stood up and began to run, but I felt hands grabbing at my shoulders, my ankles, my waist. I was being hoisted into the air before being placed on the floor, held down by four men, one on each limb. The priest towered over me, standing just at my head; he said something, tapping the staff rhythmically on the ground first to the right of my head, then to the left, then directly above it, finally raising it to about two feet above my face. I saw it move towards me in a sudden sharp movement.

I screamed.

I was awake. A cold sweat ran down my face and I was shivering. It was pitch black, the candles had long since extinguished. My breathing was heavy and laboured. Shaking, I glanced in every direction but blackness was all I could see. Cramp caused my left leg to spasm and I rubbed it with both hands, massaging the calf muscle. As the cramp eased I stood up and started to pace around in a circle to get the blood flowing, my hand out in front of me feeling for the walls.

I tried to make sense of the dream, but in the end wondered if it was just an image from a horror film I had seen. That was my best prognosis and it made me feel better.

In my rush to go to the gardens I hadn't brought a phone to contact Ann-Marie.

Feeling around on the ground for the boxes of candles, I lit two more, one for each hand. I couldn't wait where I was, it was uncomfortable and cold, I needed to keep moving. I decided to investigate the tunnel further so headed away from the door, walking slowly but steadily. Within a hundred yards the tunnel took a sharp right turn. Every now and then I stopped and looked carefully at the walls to see if there were any markings, or even anymore cupboards like the one before, nothing, just bricks with the odd patch of green slime, where a small trickle of ground water had found its way through.

The passageway narrowed to about two feet wide until I came to a step ladder fixed to the wall. Raising one of the candles above my head I tried to see where it went. The ladder disappeared into the dark. Debating whether to climb up or not was easy. I had the whole night to while away.

I placed one candle at the bottom of the ladder and climbed carefully, holding the other with my free hand. From the entrance where I'd entered the tunnels, I wasn't aware that I had travelled down further underground but the ladder seemed endless. Only briefly did I hesitate, when I banged my injured leg against a rung, making it smart, the cold had up to then numbed it fairly well. I pondered whether to continue and, hooked my left arm round a couple of rungs of the ladder, holding the candle up above my head. It didn't appear to be far from the top where something blocked the ladder.

I continued. I could feel something sharp on the rungs and, on closer examination, they looked like barnacles, similar in colour and texture. The top of the ladder had been cut, and in place directly above my head was a concrete slab. I tried to push it but knew it was hopeless. I didn't waste anymore energy and descended the ladder.

Continuing the passageway widened again to approximately five feet, and a spur tunnel ran off to my left, up ahead the tunnel appeared to turn right. In the dim light I could make out another entrance on the left. My eyes were starting to adjust to the shallow light of the candles.

In my head I tried to work out approximately where I'd be in relation to the streets above, calculating distance as best I could in strides. I concluded that I was either under the high street or under the shops on the other side of it, not far from the railway station. The town hall would be to my right, theatre to my left. I went left.

Something in my subconscious made this seem the appropriate way to go.

This tunnel went on for an age, without any further junctions. Dust started to fall from the roof of the tunnel as a low rumbling sound reverberated round the brick walls, quickly the vibrations became more severe, the light flickered in my hand as dust fell on my head. The noise suddenly became horrendous. The tremors seemed to reach their climax before settling, until all was still. It took me a while to realise it was a train, and then I knew I was definitely near Southend-on-sea Central Station.

Moving on, the passage narrowed again, barely eighteen inches wide this time, and I was forced to go through sideways. There was a recess on both sides. One side of the wall was smooth, no signs of anything. The other had bolts sticking out of it, evenly spaced, two parallel lines of them running upwards disappearing out of sight. I could barely see the entrance to another chamber, but it was about five feet above me, and I had no way to get up there to investigate.

Further along, another tunnel ran off to my left. I followed it. Within twenty paces my progress was barred due to a tunnel collapse, whether that was intentional or not, I couldn't tell.

I turned around continuing on towards the general direction of the theatre.

I passed a cavernous chamber on my right and glanced in, letting the candlelight envelope it. A small bundle of rags lay on the floor in one corner. I studied them from a distance before walking over to investigate further.

A couple of blankets had been laid down to make a makeshift bed, a small bundle of clothes at one end to form a pillow. A knife stood upright, point thrust into the ground. Bending down to unwrap the small bundle of clothes I heard a noise behind me. I froze before blowing out the candles instinctively. A slight glow of light became visible in the entrance to the chamber, gulping, I slowly stood up, doing my best to be as quiet as I could, feeling round for somewhere to hide. Panic starting to sweep through me.

The light grew brighter until the source finally came into view. It was an old style oil lamp in a four-sided glass housing.

"I know you are there. So hide from me not," was the rather well spoken voice.

I stood quiet, not moving, hoping this person was just bluffing, knowing he probably wasn't, all the time trying to look for some means of escape.

"Hard or easy? The choice is yours,"

"Who are you?" I said, finding my voice.

"Aah, you have a voice. Well, sir, first may I enquire the name of your good self?"

"Daniel, Daniel Stephens." I heard him laugh heartily, letting it fill the chamber with its mocking sneer.

A figure stepped into the chamber, the lantern at his side. No longer was I hidden and I became scared. Slowly the figure walked towards me raising the lantern up to chest height, stopping just short of where I was.

"Who am I? A question with an answer that might vex some." He smirked. "I think you know the answer." He raised the lantern upwards to just above head height and leaned in towards me, illuminating both my face and his. His eyes were dark and intimidating, his hair black and parted on one side, stubble only managed to make his face look more brutal. "I am Henry."

25

I stared at Henry in silent contemplation. My emotions raging from anger to intrigue, frustration to curiosity, spinning through my mind like tiny whirlwinds. Henry stood confidently as if he didn't have a care in the world and the reality was that he didn't. He was a free man, his crimes took place in history, and his new atrocities had taken place in my guise.

As I gained control over my emotions I realised that he didn't look like the man that I'd pictured, a distorted twisted being, rough features, dirty, angry eyes. Instead he was a well spoken gentleman, clever-sounding, sharp looking, wearing ill fitting clothes which looked as though they had been taken from the nearest available washing line. It didn't seem possible that he could be responsible for the crimes that I had witnessed. There was no malicious or brutal air about him, a model of self control, calm and collected.

A million questions raced into my thoughts. I wanted answers, but I struggled to connect the person to the crimes. Finally a weak-sounding question left my lips.

"Why?"

Henry looked at me and then walked over to his bedded area turning his back on me, confident in his manner. He picked up another lantern and lit it.

"Well, why?" I repeated, this time with more force and I heard the tension in my own voice echoing around the chamber. I continued unabated "Why did you kill those girls?" I tried to hide the anger that was rising inside. "What was that dream about? The horse? The carriage? The little girl crying? How did all this happen?" Questions ran from me like shots from a gun.

Henry turned to face me. His eyes like onyx hidden in the shadows of his face. He looked as though he was composing his thoughts. "Where would you like me to begin?" he said rhetorically, a hint of accomplishment in his voice, pausing as if expecting me to answer. "I suppose the beginning would seem the best place." He continued calmly, his voice emitting innocence, not showing the slightest hint of hatred for anything or anyone.

I stood, feeling inadequate, knowing this man had set my life on a course I couldn't change, a course that would see me go to prison for crimes I didn't commit. How could I just stand there? Deep down I had wanted to meet the man, now it had happened, I did nothing.

"I should start by showing my gratitude for what you enabled me to achieve."

I clenched my fists and stepped forward, but something stopped me attacking him. "What I've enabled you to achieve!" I stated defiantly. He stood his ground without flinching.

Oblivious to my emotional state, he continued. "Yes, if not for you, I would not be standing here at all. Things have certainly come about better than I could ever have planned. I will admit, I had my doubts. It is really quite remarkable what one can achieve." He smirked, obviously pleased with himself. Pacing the chamber he circled me. I stood like a statue looking at the bed and the knife which now lay upon it.

"What one can achieve! What sick plan did you have in mind then?" I felt repulsed being there with him. This was a game, a sick game to him.

"I did not have one, merely revenge... at first. Yet that is the astonishing thing. In the beginning after each killing the guilt racked me. To hide that, I started to drink and it worked. So quickly do the edges become blurred. In the end I started to enjoy what I did. It gave me a genuine thrill, it gave me life, a sense of right. Surprised me a little, in hindsight. A twisted morality takes over, the drink helps, of course, although at the time you do not realise it,"

I could feel every fibre of my being asking myself 'Why was I listening to him?' but, deep inside, I wanted to know.

"I was down on every person and everything I had ever known. I believe that is what brought me to the attention of the 'Froxidian Fellowship'," He smiled snidely at me as he walked back over to the bed, again showing me his back. "They were a local group with high hopes, quite feared by many. The truth is little was actually known about what they did and that is what scared people. People are always scared by ignorance. One supposes ignorance can be a blessing sometimes," he continued ironically. "I was the kind of person they liked to recruit. They thought I could be easily turned to their advantage. Yet I played them at their own game. I knew that it probably would not be long before I was caught so I wanted to make sure I had a back-up plan.

"It is… was rumoured at the time that judges filled the ranks amongst them and I thought I could curry favour if I was one of their order. They were a strange group, their rituals, their secrecy."

I wondered where this was going. "What the hell has this got to do with killing those innocent children?" I interrupted the recap of his life.

"Careful my friend," he stated firmly. "There are many things that you do not know." The words rested uneasily as he stared intently into my eyes, as though anticipating my next move, as our shadows flickered in the light of the lamps.

"One day I caught a glimpse of their sacred book. It was not something they wanted me, or the mere minions to see. I had heard whisperings that Froxidian magic was powerful. And if you have the power to wield it of course." He strolled casually until he stood behind me. "Guess I do. Looks like I was right as well. They suspected what I was up to. I do not know how. There I was enjoying my nice little killing spree when they set me up." He paced around me until we were face to face. "You have heard of the Froxidian Fellowship?"

I shook my head, then recalled the book, and nodded.

"Believed they could cure the world of all evil, the lowlife, scum of the earth, beggars and rich alike, they had their ideals. They met in secret in the basement of a warehouse.

"One night they cornered me, held me captive. They did not like people going about 'business' on their own. They had ways, formalities shall we say. Escaping, I stole one of only three copies of the 'Froxidian Book of Incantations' that they had spoken about. You should read it sometime. I guess you have." he walked back to the bed.

"What?" I said perplexed trying to take in every detail of what I was being told and still formulate a plan to hold him captive.

"You… have got my things?" He turned and looked at me confidently, he knew, but waited for my agreement, which I duly gave. "The book proved to be quite interesting. As I had not been a member that long and they had only told me what they thought I ought to know. I read the book with some excitement.

The Arcs are the powerful ones, not many people posses their power. Well, that is what they would have you believe. By the results I would say I do." Henry sat down on the bedding, placing the lantern next to him. "I guess I probably would have become an Arc if I stayed around long enough and followed their rules.

It was not a case of magic, more a case of connecting two ends together, connecting your spirit with the belief, a key, something to unlock the spirit, returning it to a physical being. I had nothing to lose. I feared it would not be long before the law caught up with me and my life would be over. So I set up my own little magic. I am so very pleased it worked. All I needed to do was write an incantation, there were certain words I needed to use and particular rituals to perform in order to invoke it, but the rest was up to me.

I did have one problem. I had to be sure the incantation would be visible to someone, yet in a place where obscurity and curiosity would gain invocation. I had no idea of how long it would be. I needed time for the dust to settle. The theatre seemed an ideal place as it was always being used, and the people were normally quite curious, often I had heard people discussing the writings on the walls in various places. I did not expect it to be this long, although it has served me rather better than expected.

I am intrigued by how much things have changed."

"So, why carry on killing? You've got the chance to start again, put the past behind you." Distaste was like salt in my mouth.

"Well." He got up and started to pace around me again. "At first I did not know where I was, the world had changed so much. Whereas to me it was one instant from the moment death touches you. Disorientated, the anger was still fresh inside me from all those years ago, still fresh in my head."

I looked around still confused about how I should react. The knife was just a few feet away. I could end it all now. Something was stopping me - morbid curiosity.

"So. Why did you start killing?!" I asked rhetorically. "By all accounts you were an upstanding citizen of the local community in a well established family." I was being brash now and mimicking him. "You had a good job, boss and family. They treated you well by all accounts. Oh that's it! Your wife died!" I didn't hide the sarcasm and I saw the anger boil in his eyes. "'cos you're the only one to ever have experienced that aren't you?" I paced the chamber, toying with him, trying inconspicuously to get close to the knife. No registration of pain in my leg as adrenalin kicked in. "No one else has ever had to go through

226

what you went through, HAVE THEY?" I shouted to make the point clearer. "No, it's just you," I had turned physically on him, facing him, staring into his eyes. "POOR OLD YOU!" I punctuated.

The anger drained from his face, he laughed at me. "You have done your research. BUT YOU DO NOT KNOW WHY SHE DIED DO YOU?" His voice was like controlled thunder, a tear pricked the corner of his right eye, glistening in the lamplight.

"Actually I do," I said cockily, taking a couple of steps away from him, turning my back on him. I was being brave. "She was run over. By a horse, trampled underfoot,"

"IT WAS HER FAULT!" I could almost feel the lunge that he made towards me, and I turned in time to counter it. "IT WAS THE GIRL'S FAULT" His hands had found my shoulders and I struggled to stand my ground. He was powerful. I thrust my hands to his throat only managing a loose chokehold, almost causing him to laugh at my feeble attempt. "She made the horse rear up and lash out AT MY WIFE, my wife, My Violet. My true one…" As quickly as he had raised his voice, it broke, trembling. His grip loosened before he grabbed fistfuls of my shirt, then I felt it loosen as he let go.

I backed off, half sympathising with the man that stood before me, and the other half seeing him for what he really was, a murderer, a cold blooded murderer. "Is that how you justified what you were doing? It was an accident, nothing but an unfortunate accident. Can't you… Couldn't you see that?"

"She killed my wife!"

"She didn't do it on purpose." I started to defend the innocent girl, like a father might.

"You do not understand. You were not there. You did not hold her in your arms and watch the life drain from her." Kneeling on the ground, he replayed the actions in front of me like a scene from a play. "I was so helpless, there was nothing I could do. I loved her so much. I held my Violet so tight in my arms. Never wanted to let her go. They made me let her go. They took her away. I watched as they took her away." His voice was broken by quiet sobs. "I couldn't stand it. My heart just wanted to stop. The pain did not go away." He paused. Finally I was seeing the loving man that he was before the accident.

Composing himself, he stood up. "I wanted to make someone suffer the way I was suffering. Feel the pain I was feeling. I saw the little girl." His face contorted, and sarcastically, sadistically he continued, "SHE was crying, as though she was the one in pain. But what did she know? She did not know what it felt like. She had no idea what it was going to be like without the one she loved! There she was crying, being hugged by her mother. Poor little girl!" He stopped and stepped away from me, then, turned to face me again. "I knew what I had to do. I would make her suffer." He laughed heartily.

I had heard enough, I went for the knife but he anticipated my move as my leg issued a sting of pain from the effort, beating me to it. We both fell to the ground in a heap, but he managed to roll away from me, the knife held tight in his grasp.

"Were you going to try and be the brave one, the hero?" He held the knife about waist height with three feet between us.

"No, I don't want to be a hero. Just put things right."

"Right? You have no idea what is right."

We paced around in circles, my leg still smarting forcing me to limp.

"And do you know Mr and Mrs Hughes never knew it was me? Yes, I started to drink more. I still turned up for work, played the dutiful little worker. We discussed the murders openly, the stories in the paper, trying to work out who the murderer was. They did not have a clue. The best part was that the tunnels provided me with the means to get round this town without being seen. He was an eccentric, rich, old fool, but you have got to love it. Part of me wanted to tell them."

"So what happened?"

He rested the point of the knife on the middle finger of his left hand and twisted it with his right.

"What happened? The Police were hopeless, they did not have a clue. The Froxidian's? They knew who was to blame. They were clever, they set up a trap. Good it was too. You have to admire them. They used one of their own daughters, merciless lot really. Who is sicker? Using your own daughter to catch a murderer. They were watching, and I was drunker than usual. It was so stupid. They were watching as I went to grab her."

"They jumped you."

"Yes. Kicked and punched me like a bag, they had no mercy, they had their own brand of punishment, which I was about to experience back at the sacred room, the meeting place."

"How did you escape?" I was desperately looking for a way to retake control of the knife but he was quicker and stronger than me.

"I sobered up quickly, not surprisingly, when I was being kicked and punched and managed to keep a clear head. I waited for the right time. It did not take long. They sent in one of the younger members to collect me from the room that I had been locked in, they must have thought I was too drunk to try anything, but I landed him one, he went out like a light. I put his gown on and even had the audacity to go and stand amongst them during one of their ceremonies,"

My dream came back to me. "They saw you, didn't they?"

"Yes," he said, surprised by my statement.

"They pinned you to the floor."

Perplexed, he carried on. "I thought they were going to thrust the staff straight through my head and then, would you believe it, the police of all people burst in. I could not believe my luck. In the pandemonium that followed I ran. Not before taking one of their precious books. I headed straight to the only safe place I knew. These tunnels."

He was lost in his own thoughts so I took the opportunity

to lunge at him, catching him off guard and wrestling him to the ground. We struggled, neither seeming to gain the advantage. Suddenly Henry regained his footing and hauled me unceremoniously to my knees, before dragging me with all his force against the wall, pinning me there like a rag doll with the knife held at my stomach and his forearm across my throat. My leg issued a sharp piercing pain which I tried to shut out. I looked around as best I could for something to use as leverage, to aid in my fight. Then, on impulse, I grabbed a handful of dust from the floor and rubbed it in his face. He released his grip and I coughed as the pressure was taken off my windpipe. As he brushed the dust from his eyes I stepped behind him and swung my arm round his throat, gripping him in a choke hold using my weight to get him face down on the ground. I cut out the pain issuing from my leg and reached to his right hand where I thought the knife still was. It was gone, lost in the fight. Frantically I felt around for it.

He let out a strangled laugh due to my tight grip and continued, "What are you going to do now?"

I had no weapon. No means to restrain him. I knew as soon as I let go he would be on me again, faster than I could get to my feet, my leg was letting me know how much I had just abused it.

"Even if you kill me, it won't matter, as I had done all the killing in your guise. All the evidence points to you. So go ahead, kill me. It does not matter anymore."

He was right. No matter what I did I was still a murderer in the eyes of the world. Only four people knew the truth. It was not a truth that anyone was going to believe easily, if at all. To put this right I needed him. As much as I hated that, it was the truth.

26

After a few brief moments I released my grip and rolled over on the ground, sitting upright on the floor. My mind was a haze of thoughts, darting round like ants searching for food. I rubbed my leg as the pain grew and for a moment I wondered whether I had ruptured more of my stitches.

I looked over at Henry who had got to his feet and was rubbing his neck.

"You have to hate life sometimes," he said, grimacing. In the dimness his eyes looked, for the briefest moment, regretful that the magic had worked.

I didn't answer. I didn't want to speak to him anymore. A silent question came forth. Did I need him?

Truth was - I wasn't sure. I hadn't given Ann-Marie or Aunt Rose a chance to explain, so caught up with being a hero, trying to protect the next victim, when I should have been looking at the overall picture.

Now!

Now I was here, no communication with my new friends. Only the one I'd allowed myself to get consumed by.

I remembered the fact that the police were looking for two people now, not just one. I smiled and, in the dim light, Henry noticed.

"What are you so jubilant about? I can walk out of here a free man. Back from the dead, finish my life. No retribution for my crimes." An air of cockiness hung in the air.

I smiled even wider as his curiosity for my sudden delight showed in his eyes. The evidence I needed to help convict him was here in this chamber, although confirming his identity might be a problem, they'd know they had the right man. In my mind I fixed it that if I went down, so would Henry.

"Go on then. Why don't you?" I said confidently, to his surprise.

He thought for a second before replying. "You have made it obvious that I have a few loose ends to tie up." With that, he smiled, and stared into my eyes.

It dawned on me, I hadn't even thought about the consequences for Ann-Marie. Did he know of her? Was he bluffing? I needed to know how much he knew. Was she one of those loose ends?

"So did you know that I could see the events through my... your eyes?" I corrected myself.

"Really," he said, not totally surprised. He carried on brushing the dust from his clothes. "Well, looks like we both got more than we bargained for." Then he glared at me and I could see every morsel of hate in his eyes. "What was it like watching them die? Seeing them helpless." He sounded deranged.

"What! Seeing what an evil person you really are."

The hatred disappeared as fast at it had manifested. "I used to think that at first." He came in close to me. "Yet I justified my actions. Then after a time it fades into insignificance and you do not care about it anymore. The odd tot helps numb the pain. Then, you can justify anything." My eyes followed him as he walked around the chamber.

"So what was it like coming back, back into a strange world after so long?" My questions were just a way of delaying him leaving, but also a part of me was curious. What was it like?

Suddenly he appeared pleased that I was taking an interest and that he could explain it to someone. "Like a blink of an eye. Last thing I remember is dragging myself along the ground after losing my footing on the steps of the ladder." He looked to the chamber ceiling reflectively. "It still sits fresh in my mind, the pain was immense. I became disorientated. I knew I had to get away." He stopped mid-flow. "I could not remember which way to go, it was dark, I had dropped my lantern."

"Oh poor you," I said, sardonically.

Henry ignored the comment. "I had just written the incantation on the wall." He paced like a man on a stroll. "Tied in the relevant loose ends, as you are supposed to, then bam." He clapped his hands together. "I fell thirty feet or so." He paused. "I remember knowing I had broken my leg. Quiet suddenly, the pain went and I felt nothing. For a moment I thought I was going to be alright. The next thing I knew I was back in the corridor. I did not know what had happened at first. The entrance to the ladder was gone. I felt around in the dark. Everything was not as I remembered it.

I bolted for the door. There were people milling around on the stairs, people I did not recognise. Everything was different from what I remembered. People were calling 'Daniel'. I ran out the front door into the street. I was not lost exactly but did not know where I was, nothing looked the same." He stopped and looked at me questioningly.

I felt uneasy, as if the next few breaths might be my last.

"I ran along the street for a while until I slowed to a saunter. I found myself in a familiar place, Prittlewell Square and the gardens there. It had changed, the trees and shrubs were more mature, yet it was familiar ground. I sat down. I remember sitting there a long time.

"I remember getting cold. I got up to go and I knew where, yet I did not know why.

"Then I saw a girl, on her own." He seemed to be savouring the gory details. "The familiar stirrings vexed me. The anger. The pain. I became compelled to act." Once again he smiled curtly.

"You just had to!"

I tried to get up using the wall behind as means of support, the pain stung like a million bee stings.

"The urge. The anger. Came flooding back. Felt right. Made me feel alive to kill her." He savoured the thought, as I staggered to my feet. "As I walked back to your flat my head became full of information, things that should have been unfamiliar to me, yet I knew were not. It was your life." He looked at me with his penetrating eyes. "Every single experience you have ever had, every private thought."

I wanted to hit him, shut him up. I lunged, but my leg buckled from the pain, sending me crashing to the ground. He was using my life against me. He had access to all areas.

"It was a strange feeling, walking back to the flat, everything familiar, but everything new. A thrill. My surprise that the magic had worked so well. I almost forgot about the blood on my clothes. Luckily it was dark and I managed to avoid being seen at close quarters. Once I had the correct key and had entered your residence I found a mirror and studied the reflection that came back at me.

"You have no idea what it is like to see a different face staring back at you from the one you once knew." He came in close to me, face to face with me on the ground. "I stared at it for ages, pulling it this way and that. I did not know what to make of it."

I turned away from him, disgusted at being so close.

"Why didn't you just get on with your life you had my body, my life? Surely it would have been easy just to carry on, start again, a free man?" I said sourly, cringing from the pain in my leg.

He saw me rub it. "Pain." He muttered thoughtfully reminding him of his broken leg, then, reaching full height continued, "The magic worked better than I thought." He put his hands in his pockets and strolled over to the knife. Retrieving it, he smiled as he placed the point of the blade in the palm of one hand and twisted.

"What do you mean?" then before he answered I remembered how the skeleton had been found with broken leg bones.

He let that thought fall to one side. "Well, there's the thing. I could have done just that. Leave my life behind me. I was already going to do that before I died. I had only really gone back to the tunnels to gather my possessions as I had decided it was time to leave, decided it was a little uncomfortable here. People knew too much. I needed a back-up plan, just in case. I did not expect to meet my demise quite in the way I did. Some might say 'Poetic Justice'." He looked at me expecting my agreement. I made no gesture.

"Once here though, something pulled at the back of my 'new' mind, it was me again. I was safe. Yet I still had a score to settle." An evil grin spread across his face, his eyes lighting up like that of a madman.

"One child causes an accident that unfortunately kills your wife and suddenly it's everyone's fault," I said incredulously. "Then you get the chance to put all that behind you and you throw it away, you're insane."

"Yes, maybe I am." He scoffed. "Everyone has their own way of dealing with life, this is mine," he said, with a dignified shrug of the shoulders.

"Most people manage to deal with it, without harming others in the process."

What was I doing? I was trying to reason with a man who didn't see reason. Despite my own anger and hatred for the man I couldn't kill him. I couldn't lower myself to his level. I hoped Ann-Marie had a plan and I prayed that it would put everything right again, put Henry back where he firmly belonged, in the past. I was powerless to stop Henry who was stronger than me in my weakened state and could easily overpower me.

He had the advantage of being able to wander off into the daylight without fear of being arrested. I didn't have that luxury. And again the question of how I was going to contact Ann-Marie echoed round my head.

"You have not heard a word I have said. I wanted revenge.

I lost everything I had that day. Everything!" He spoke with renewed fervour. "Nothing meant anything anymore." He turned on me, rage like a beast inside him and, grabbing my clothes, forced me back against the wall almost lifting me off the ground.

"And it means a whole lot more now?" I said, through gritted teeth as my leg issued a retort of pain. Henry released his grip and crouched before me.

"No. You are right. I have finally said goodbye to her I am ready to move on. All thanks to you." Despite his confidence there was still a distant note in his voice, a sadness. "You have given me the opportunity. No one knows me anymore. I can start to live again, with a clean slate. Whereas, you my friend can pick up from where I left off." I could hear the contentment. "See how cruel life can be?" With that he laughed out loud and it reverberated round the chamber.

I knew that if Ann-Marie, Aunt Rose and Heather didn't come through for me then my future was looking grim. My parents would face the world knowing their son was a murderer, a lie, but no one would know that.

The laughing ceased. "Making your acquaintance has been," he paused, "interesting, but as you know, I need to dash. After all, I have a life to lead. Thank you for making the magic work." With that he picked up one of the lanterns and strolled confidently towards the exit of the chamber. "I will leave the other one, do not get too comfortable though you never know who might find you here." He laughed as he disappeared.

I tried to get up quickly but the pain cut me down and I reeled over on the ground.

"AAARRRRGGGGHHH!! Damn you, YOU, YOU!" I shouted knowing it was hopeless. Nothing I said was going to change the situation and my words resounded off the walls until they faded. In only a few days I had gone from an average 'Joe' on the street, to a murderer.

A sudden thought of recognition hit me like a bolt from the blue, an understanding of what he meant. 'He's going to tell the police where to find me' I said out loud as if I needed the clarification. The once secret dwelling wasn't going to be that much longer. I had to move out post-haste. But where?

I didn't know what the time was or exactly how long I had been down in the tunnels, what I believed to be a short period could have been hours, and it could be daylight outside. My heart sank. Once again I was thinking the worst case scenarios.

I eased myself to my feet trying to take the weight on my good leg before hobbling to collect the remaining lantern for easy navigation through the tunnels back to the entrance I'd used to get in. The more I walked the duller the pain became in my leg as anxiety started it cruel journey through me and I contemplated my next move.

At the entrance door I noted a yellowish-haze of streetlight shining bright through a crack at the doors edge, I could also see it was raining. I breathed a sigh of relief that it was still dark.

I pushed the door with my shoulder knowing it wouldn't be easy, but it should move, but it wouldn't budge. With gritted teeth, I pushed harder, nothing. Still the door would not move. Studying carefully through the slight crack, I could just make out the shape of something heavy against the door.

"Shit, shit, shit, shit." I turned and looked back the way I'd come. I thought of all the possible ways I could get out. All those bricked up exits that would have once been so useful, now closed off permanently. No way was I going to clear any of them in the few hours I had left. Even if I did, I didn't know if there was anything the other side of them that would allow me to escape.

"The theatre," I said as a thought came to me. "I can get out through the theatre. No one will be there at this time. I can get out through a fire exit."

I was talking to myself as if expecting answers that would confirm my ideas.

Once again I headed into the darkness proceeding along this now well-trodden path. It occurred to me the amount of time that was passing, although still dark outside, I didn't know how long it would remain so. Or how long I'd have before the police would be notified of my whereabouts, if at all. Maybe he was bluffing, maybe the police would think he was making a bogus tip-off.

Just in case, I quickened my pace, pain or no pain I had to get out of here, adrenalin kicked in and my hurt leg faded to the back of my mind. I'd underestimated Henry, he was clever, calculating. Henry knew the theatre would be my only way out, and my heart sank as the thought of possible capture became a real possibility.

27

As I reached the bottom of the steps that would lead me into the corridor where it had all begun, my heart sank to my feet. I was tired and scared. Scared of all that had happened and how things were looking set to turn out.

I was tired and before ascending the ladder I pulled a twix from my jacket pocket, the energy boost I needed, whilst I hoped the police were not waiting for me.

With my hands on the metal ladder, I took a deep breath and made my way up, praying I was not entering the lion's den.

It was a slow ascent as every muscle was screaming at me to stop. The lantern in one hand hampering my progress and clattering against the metal rungs. I dared to think about resting when I got to the top but knew I shouldn't as I didn't have the luxury of time. I heard a couple of snacks fall from my pockets and I cursed, knowing they might be essential later.

At the top I thrust the lantern through the opening and onto the floor, I hadn't realised how heavy it was until that point, the relief running riot through the muscles of my arm as I relaxed, almost slipping from the ladder, exactly as Henry might have done the night he died.

For the briefest moment it occurred to me that maybe that might be best as my future looked so gloomy, but I fought the notion, knew I needed to carry on if I were to change that.

Hauling my weary body through the hole, I collapsed on the floor and, for a few minutes enjoyed the sanctity of rest, especially as there appeared to be no one waiting for me.

My legs and arms tingled with relief, making it even harder

to motivate myself to move again.

"Can't stay here all night," I said out loud, and wearily rose.

I thought I knew the theatre well enough now not have to worry about the lantern so blew it out after placing it behind some boxes out of sight. Leaving the corridor, I made my way to the stage door.

The silence at night was eerie and the dim light that filtered through the dirty windows of the dressing rooms only added to the atmosphere. I remembered the stories of ghosts that were sometimes seen. Great stories, I had always thought, but now I was here late at night, on my own, I wasn't so sure. I hastened my pace.

At the stage door I was relieved at having not encountered any paranormal activity. I pushed against the bar that held the door closed. It wouldn't budge. I tried again, still it wouldn't budge. I had never before noticed the chain that held it tight, but then again I had never been in the theatre after it was locked up. I knew of only one other exit that I could gain access to and that was in the auditorium, a fire exit to the left of the stage. Would that also be chained?

I headed through the stage door only to be met with a massive black void that was the stage, no outside light penetrated this space. Precariously I crossed, what I hoped was, an empty performance area, carefully placing one foot in front of the other, hands outstretched searching for any obstacles that may be laying in wait. I thought I knew the stage well but the total darkness confused my senses, making progress slow. Suddenly I thought about my location on the stage and wondered how close to the apron of the stage I was, there was a four foot drop if I misjudged where the steps that I needed were. Deciding it would be safer I got down on my knees and searched the floor with my hands until I found them.

I found the wall that led to the double doors which concealed the fire exit. My luck was against me, the fire exit doors were also chained and padlocked.

The doors to the auditorium would be chained so that way was useless. I had to think of another way out. I sat down on the floor, too weary to think on my feet. My thigh felt warm but at least the pain had gone. Mentally I mapped out the whole theatre in my mind, trying to think of any possible exit, the pitch black of the auditorium as my only companion.

My options seemed to be running out quickly.

Some areas of the theatre I knew well, others not so well. There was a basement that had been sealed off until recently - that was no good as the access to that was behind the kiosk in the foyer, beyond the chained auditorium doors - and I wasn't sure it had any street access. There was access to the roof, although I wasn't sure where, as I'd never been up on the roof. I'd never had a reason to.

All the windows had bars on them so that wasn't any good either. Time was passing. I knew there were clocks in the auditorium but it was too dark to see any.

'The lighting booth'. I slapped my forehead with the palm of my hand. Why didn't I think of it before? There must be keys somewhere in there for the fire exits. I made my way with renewed enthusiasm to the lighting booth, but with the renewed enthusiasm came the aching of my weary limbs, bringing with it some pain. I used my hands to guide me past the rows of seats.

The door had a keypad lock but I knew the code and once I'd established my starting position, keyed in the code. Inside I felt around the wall for the light switch. The flourescent tubes blinked into life, illuminating the lighting and sound desks with the banks of amplifiers and monitors, as well as other electronic equipment. I had to shade my eyes temporarily from the sudden glare. The booth looked a bit of a mess to the untrained eye, however, Mark knew where everything was and everything had a home.

Surveying the box, I looked for keys or, somewhere obvious

where they would be kept. I wasn't sure where to start. I didn't expect them to be easily found, just convenient. Mark was very careful about security. I sat down in one of the chairs behind the lighting desk and thought about the most suitable place close to hand, nothing seemed appropriate, there were no drawers, the shelves were full of coils of wire, bulbs, and other replacement parts.

After some futile searching I went into his little office which looked a complete disorganised mess, nothing sprang to mind and I guessed I was just wasting my time so gave up and left the booth, switching off the light. I had to give my eyes time to adjust again to the blackness, closing them and counting to ten. Whilst counting I could feel the theatre breathing, feel its life pulse through me, there was something relaxing and secure about it. But with options running out the roof was looking like my solution. I considered the obvious places where an entrance might be and headed to the backstage area to check these out, using the wall as my aide, until I reached the stage again.

I did recall seeing a fire ladder running down the side of the building on the outside but don't remember ever seeing it come close to the ground. If I could find my way on to the roof then maybe I could use it to get away, it was my last hope other than the tunnels again. All that was left was to find the roof access. I was sure I'd seen Mark coming out of one of the dressing rooms with some roof felt in his hands once. I just had to remember which one, I racked my brains, searching for that memory.

"The back dressing room", I stated confidently. There was a door to another area where the power boxes were.

I was walking briskly along the corridor when, quite suddenly, it turned very cold, every hair on my body stood on end. I turned slowly although I didn't know why. In front of me was one of the ghosts that I'd heard about, running towards me at break neck speed. I froze in terror. The lad, twelve or thirteen, ran right through me and turned right, disappearing into the wall where a door, that led to a walkway suspended sixty feet above the stage, used to be.

Story has it that the lad was a runner for the back stage crew. Usually the runner was a young lad who wanted to work in theatre, and this is how he earned his 'stripes'. They never got paid unless actually used and then it was at the discretion of the crew or actors. He'd take any notes or props to the other side of the stage if required, which was not very often. This particular night the boy was carrying a prop to an actor who had forgotten to set it on the wrong side of the stage. The actor had signalled to one of the crew, asking the runner to bring it across, which he did.

Unfortunately for him one of the boards on the walkway was loose and as he trod on it, it gave way and he fell to the stage landing awkwardly on a piece of set narrowly missing one of the other actors. The boy died instantly. Now from time to time he had been seen, repeating that fateful journey, always disappearing into the wall, which had been bricked up almost immediately. After that incident the runners then had to go out the backdoor of the theatre along the street and in through the fire exit.

I shuddered, recomposed myself and carried on.

Locating the door from the dressing room I went through to the hidden area, finding the light switch by accident, finally a bit of good luck. The steps to the roof access were obvious, suddenly I lost the fatigue I felt and hastily made my way up, knowing I would soon be in the open.

The door onto the roof, whilst being securely fastened with bolts on the inside, was thankfully not padlocked.

Once on the roof the view was incredible, but I didn't have time to enjoy it as the impending dawn became obvious as the night sky started to soften into an orange glow, with the dawn chorus starting to chatter.

Walking around the perimeter of the building, I found the fire escape ladder fixed to the east side of the theatre, but it started on a little roof area about five feet lower than the main roof

"Great! More jumping." I was concerned for my leg. Whilst I was aware I was limping, the pain was bearable, and I wanted to keep it that way, jumping, or rather landing, was not going to help that.

I sat down on the ledge of the main roof and lowered myself as much as I could towards the lower roof, then gently let myself go, landing as softly as possible on my good leg.

'The next bit should be easy.'

Climbing down the ladder I felt the first few spots of rain. It didn't bother me that much as it was the least of my worries.

However, at the bottom of the ladder it became clear why I hadn't been quite sure where it met the ground, it was fifteen feet short of it, in a recess hidden from street view.

I couldn't believe my luck. 'Was nothing going to be easy?' I clung to the ladder, considering my options, which were few, if any. With a sigh I eased my left foot off the bottom rung, planting it as firmly as I could against the wall beneath. I then released each hand carefully tightening the grip of the remaining hand, until it was placed firmly on the rung below, feeling my body weight shift lower. I repeated this, leaving my right foot, and bad leg, on the bottom rung as late as possible. I then placed my right foot below the bottom rung so my backside was poking out into the early morning air. I hovered like this before moving my left foot further down the wall. It seemed to be working with both hands on the second rung up.

Suddenly my right foot slipped, my balance shifted and I went crashing against the wall, my face making contact with the rungs of the ladder. "Shit, shit, shit," I said, aware of the noise I was making.

I hung there like laundry out to dry as the rain chose that moment to get heavier and my hands, already tired, began to lose their grip. I took one last glance below, the fifteen foot drop seemed like a hundred and panic swept through me as I prepared myself for a shock of pain as down I went with a thud.

With gritted teeth I swore, not knowing which part of my body to grab first, even though the important thing was that I was out of the theatre and on the ground with no police in sight.

Getting up, I felt a shooting pain in my left ankle, making it barely possible to put my weight on initially. I took a few deep breaths to fight the wave of nausea that look set to sweep overwhelm me. I was cold and tired and just wanted to scream, releasing all my pent up frustration. I had to keep telling myself it was going to work out in the end. Hobbling around I tried to put my weight on my left foot and slowly it became possible, although it still hurt like hell and took my mind of my right leg. Limping my way along Clarence Road to the High Street, I put my hood up again to conceal my identity. There were a few people about, and I scrutinised everyone from beneath the shadow of the hood, wary of anyone approaching me.

After heading towards the Town Hall I proceeded along Victoria Avenue.

The only thing that slowed my progress was the limping, on reflection I had to laugh at myself, or I would go crazy, the way my luck was panning out.

It took ages to reach Ann-Marie's house and my left ankle had loosened up sufficiently, despite feeling swollen inside my shoe. The street was already starting to bustle with people leaving for work.

I had to lay low until I was sure her mother had gone to work. In an instant I realised it was Sunday; I'd seen the Sunday papers in a newsagents on my way but hadn't registered. Damn! Then it occurred that I didn't know what her mum did for a job, she hadn't been there yesterday. Maybe she worked in a shop? I didn't know what to do and without a watch couldn't tell what time it was. However, as I watched the street scene unfold I knew it must be after nine as parents started to take their kids out, dressed in football kits. I tried desperately to think what to do next, I couldn't call on Ann-Marie her mum might call the police.

I wanted to feel warm. I wanted a nice hot drink to thaw me out. I wanted a hot bath. I was not having any of it. I retreated to an alley a little way from her house on the opposite side of the road. Far enough down to be out of sight, but close enough to view the comings and goings of her house. There I waited. I hoped her mum would go out for something, anything, just so I could call on her. I felt like an unwelcome boyfriend waiting to see his beau.

It was not long before I started to shiver, and began to feel an eternity was passing. Suddenly her mother came out wrapped up warmly, she closed the door and relief washed over me. My ankle had started to seize up so I walked up and down the alley to keep warm and loosen it. When she was out of sight I made my way to the house and rang the doorbell.

Ann-Marie opened the door. "It's flipping freezing out here," I said, doing my best to stop my teeth chattering.

"Come in," she said urgently, smiling.

Inside the warmth immediately infiltrated me making me shake as feeling came back into every part of me.

"I've seen him, seen him in the flesh." I was like an excited school child. "And he's nothing like I imagined. he looked," I thought for a good word but couldn't find one, "normal." My chattering jaws made the words hard to understand.

"Do you want a cup of tea?" She asked before adding, "I imagined him like some deformed monster."

"That would be great, thanks. Do you want me to do it? I can't believe how cold it is out there," I rubbed my hands together.

"No, I'll do it. You haven't been out there all night have you? It's just that Aunt Rose said you could have stayed with her. If you'd come back I was to send you round."

'Great', I thought.

We made our way into the kitchen. I took off the coat and left it hanging over the banisters. The warmth of the house was soothing but I couldn't control my shaking, my cheeks felt as if they were burning as the heat returned, my chinos were soaked through; so I stood by a radiator to enjoy its' heat.

"I think that would have been preferable. But I spoke to him," I said urgently. "He said he wants to start again, as if it was the most normal thing in the world. Now! He doesn't regret anything. He doesn't think he has done wrong. In his head, what he did was justified. He made me sick. He enjoyed what he did."

"Aunt Rose, or rather Heather has found a way. It's powerful magic, it's going to take the power of the heads of all the local covens, all seven of them. They normally wouldn't but Heather says, under the circumstances, they want to put things right, you're quite lucky. Crimes against children they will not tolerate."

"Thank god. I don't need to do anything do I?" Ann-Marie didn't answer. "Please tell me I don't."

"Heather says you need to bring something personal of yours, it's got to be something you hold dear to your heart, something that represents all the good in you. And ..."

Ann-Marie broke off . She put two mugs on the work-surface, then feeling round for the teabag jar, put one in each and poured the hot water.

"And what? I do don't I, have to be there?"

"And they need him there too."

"Henry! You're joking." I said flabbergasted.

"He needs to be present so they can send him back."

"But how? I mean I can't just invite him over." I couldn't believe it, more obstacles. Every time I was getting closer, the end would get further away. I pulled out a chair and sat down heavily rubbing my ankle.

"Extrume Derm Har is what they have to perform."

"What?"

"That's the name of the enchantment."

"Right," I scoffed. "Any particular place?"

"There is a small clearing by the old scout hut in Belfairs Woods, that's where."

"The WOODS!" I exclaimed. "How are we, how am I going to get him to Belfairs Woods?" This went from the sublime to the ridiculous. I sank deeper into the chair, hoping that inspiration would attack me.

"There is one more thing."

"What?!" I was almost afraid of what was coming next.

"It still has to be done before the eight days is up,"

"But I thought…"

"Aunt Rose says that after the eight days they won't be able to do anything to correct what has already happened. It's almost like it all becomes set in stone and his physical presence here cannot be changed."

"This is hopeless. Not only do I have to get him to the woods but I cannot fail."

"You'll do it, I know you will." I felt Ann-Marie's hand on my shoulder for reassurance.

I sighed. I didn't know what I was going to do now.

"When will they be there?"

"They said it will have to be Monday night, they can't take the risk of doing anything during the day, they'll be there for nine o'clock."

I sank into my own thoughts, considering how I was going to get Henry to the woods, and in time.

28

The doorbell rang out as if an alarm clock was ringing inside my head, its horrible harsh electronic buzz suddenly breaking me from my thoughts. Ann-Marie was already halfway to the door before I realised. I rose from my seat like a protective father wanting to scrutinise potential suitors. I hoped it was Heather or Aunt Rose.

Standing in the kitchen doorway the front door was just visible and through its large glass panel I could make out a figure in dark clothes and wearing a hat. Ann-Marie was at the front door with Mojo at her side, he was barking which seemed unusual for him.

My imagination came to life, an electric shock making every nerve of my body tingle with anxiety. I wanted to shout out, tell her to come away from the door but the figure would hear. I reached forward as if by some miracle I would be able to pull her back into the safe retreat of the kitchen. Too late.

I heard her call out.

"Who is it?"

My heart sank down to my feet. I scanned the kitchen for a weapon, believing it to be Henry. I wanted to defend Ann-Marie and myself.

There was nothing, no knives on display. Hastily, I searched the kitchen drawers, pulling each one open in turn, hoping to find exactly what I was looking for, which I would know it as soon as I found it.

A rolling pin. No. A steel rod for sharpening knives. No. A carving knife – I beamed – yes, that would do. I brightened and then thought again. I couldn't kill him, no matter what he'd done, I couldn't become a murderer as well. I believed in an eye for an eye but my own morality would not let me commit murder. I placed the knife back in the draw and pulled out the steel rod instead, at least I could render him unconscious or at least give myself an opportunity to secure him in someway. I had to avoid killing him.

I made my way back to the kitchen doorway, weapon in hand.

The front door was opening. Mojo was now quiet. In my haste I had not heard the ongoing dialogue. Whoever it was had gained Ann-Marie's trust and was now crossing the threshold.

I steeled myself for the march to the front door, tightening my grip around the weapon. I stopped dead in my tracks as I saw a police uniform. Ducking back against the doorway as quickly as I could I hoped I hadn't been seen.

My breath was coming fast and I only just remembered in time that I was holding a weapon in my hand as it started to slip from my grasp.

My heart began pumping blood round my body so fast I thought I might pass out.

'Get a grip', I told myself. I took slow deep breaths and leaned as far forward as I dared to listen to the ensuing conversation.

"....days ago," said Ann-Marie, innocently.

"And you haven't seen him since, that's right?" The police officer stated matter of factly, while scribbling down in his notebook.

There was a glass fronted picture on the wall opposite the banisters of the staircase, about halfway along the hallway, and I used this like a mirror viewing the scene by the front door. The police officer, aware that the question answerer was blind, took furtive steps, this way and that, to gain a view into each room that he could, distrusting the answers he was getting, also aware that he was not in his rights to search the premises without the owner's permission.

He glanced at the picture and for a second I thought he may have seen me. I pulled back even further, my pulse racing. I knew he couldn't see me physically from where he stood as the hallway, crooked round the staircase, but did he catch a glimpse of my reflection in the picture. I held my breath, waiting for him to make a sudden movement in my direction. But none came.

He was staring intently in my direction and I could feel a pearl of sweat start to roll down my forehead across the bridge of my nose and hang at the tip for the briefest of moments before falling to the floor.

"Is there anything else I can help you with, officer?" Ann-Marie's question took the police officer's focus from the picture.

"No. No, thank you. If you do see your friend, it's important you contact us. I probably don't need to tell you how much trouble you'll be in if you don't," he said menacingly, knowing that she probably would not give away a friend.

"I will."

"Thank you, again." He glanced once more down the hall in my direction before turning to the front door. Opening it halfway, he hesitated, then added, "remember these are serious charges he is facing, he needs to be stopped before someone else gets hurt."

"I understand." Ann- Marie's innocence was so convincing, like a church bell breaking the morning silence.

Finally the door closed and he was gone.

I relaxed with a sigh and the steel rod crashed to the floor. The sound reverberated round the kitchen but I felt safe again with the threat abated.

Ann-Marie came down the hall towards me with Mojo at her side.

"That was close, I didn't think he was ever going to go."

"Me too. Do you think he believed you?"

She walked over to the kettle and switched it on again. It only took a few seconds as it had already boiled.

"I don't think he did. He had no proof anyway. But how did he know about me?"

"I think when me and Henry were sort of one, we knew things about the other. Shared a connection. You must have been one of the things, in me, he picked up on." I paused. "I'm sorry, I didn't mean to, if I'd realized he was going to incriminate you, I wouldn't have come here. I stupidly thought I'd be safe." I sat down, deflated.

"It's okay. Anyway, I haven't seen you," she emphasized that word, "in the last few days. Have I?"

"What?"

"I'm blind. Remember? I can't see anything, so I didn't lie exactly."

I smiled. The irony in her statement reflected exactly how Ann-Marie viewed life, simple, and everything is surmountable, whatever it is.

We stayed in the kitchen for a while and talked, normal talk, something we hadn't ever had the chance to do but, in the midst of all the chaos, knowing what we had to achieve, yet it seemed natural.

After lunch the mood changed slightly as reality came oozing back.

"How am I going to get him to the woods, Ann-Marie?" I tried hard to hide the emptiness in my voice.

"I don't know."

We sat there pondering the question.

"Look, I'd better be going, he can't be too far away. Hopefully! Where and when do we have to be in the woods?"

"Aunt Rose said nine o'clock in Belfairs Woods by the Secret Sunken Garden, it's about... I think she said about two hundred yards behind the old scout hut, to the north of the wood. The trees are really tall and thick so it can't be seen that easily from above. At the bottom there's a clearing with a stream running alongside. They'll be there about nine o'clock tomorrow night.

They'll wait for you."

"Tomorrow night. nine o'clock." The time flashed in my head like a large neon sign. "Okay." I was fast feeling like a soldier on a relentless mission for my country, except that this was for my life, my freedom. I rose from the chair and headed to the front door. Deep down I knew I should wait for nightfall, but I had wasted enough time already, and I didn't know where I was to find Henry, I didn't even know where to start looking.

"Wait," shouted Ann-Marie from the kitchen, as she made her way towards me. "Take my phone with you. At least we'll be able to keep in contact this time. I'll get you a torch as well, you'll need it tonight. Aunt Rose left it for you. Mum did find it strange though when she saw it."

"Thank you. You think of everything don't you?" I took the phone from her, placing it in my pocket, and waited while she got the torch. I put on the borrowed coat again. "See you later... hopefully." I swallowed.

"Course you will. You have to be positive."

I smiled. "Yes." I sounded daunted. "Can you look after this?" I took the silver plectrum that hung around my neck and placed it in Ann-Marie's hand, holding it there for a reluctant second feeling a connection with her, my gratitude for everything she had done thus far. "I don't want to lose it. At one point during my fight with Henry I thought I had. It epitomises the love of my parents, how much they care and everything that life held for me... before all this. I want to know it is safe and cared for." I paused as reality of the situation hit me. "And if I end up in prison I want you to keep it as thanks for all your help." Emotion started to well up inside me, the true implications of what my future held, should I fail.

"What is it?"

"It's a silver plectrum, a gift from my parents on my sixteenth birthday." Suddenly I was naked and vulnerable without it. I watched Ann-Marie turn it over affectionately gently caressing it with her fingers.

"What's engraved on it?" Her question took me a little by surprise.

"It just says 'To the best son, happy 16th birthday, Love Mum and Dad xx'."

After a pause, Ann-Marie closed her hand tightly round the plectrum and chain that it hung on. "I'll look after it. I guess you actually play then?" She questioned, I nodded my response absent mindedly before verbally confirming. "Maybe you can play something for me when this is all over." She held it so lovingly that I couldn't help feeling close to her. I let a sentimental silence sit between us for a second.

"Okay, you're on." I opened the door. It was still raining outside so I threw the hood up over my head. One thing about the rain is that it made it easier to conceal my face without looking out of place.

I looked back at Ann-Marie. "Thank you," It was like we were saying our 'goodbyes'.

"Go quickly," she said, urging me out of the door and closing it behind me. How did she know I was looking at her?

I was like a lost soul again, standing in the wilderness between life and death, not knowing which direction to go, or what I was looking for.

At the end of the footpath I debated which direction to take. Turning left, I started to walk briskly, all the time turning over the past few days in my head. My ankle had loosened up and my thigh was just a dull ache. I was now on the hunt for a clue, an indication of how I was to locate Henry. Needle in a haystack sprang to mind.

All the while a picture seemed to be forming in my head, an idea, although a part of me doubted it would work, but there was always a possibility. It relied heavily on past events and that there was still some sort of connection.

During our time as one, we had glimpsed and taken in

information about the other's lives. Henry, seemingly knew more about me than I about him, maybe that was because I had shut myself down and not allowed myself to be part of what I didn't want to be part of. Maybe I needed to explore that, open my mind, and allow his part to wash over and consume me.

I didn't know how to start but then thought Aunt Rose might. The more I thought about it the more convinced I became that she would be able to help me.

With a spring in my step I changed direction and headed to her house, I knew what road it was in. Even if I didn't know the number I was sure I'd recognise the house when I saw it.

As I crossed more and more roads I became aware of the large presence of police cars. Each time I saw one I dipped my head even further down to conceal my face.

Suddenly one slowed, drawing to a halt a hundred yards in front of me. I slowed as my heart beat faster. I would have to walk past, pretending to be innocent. Tension filled my shoulders. I subtly glanced round for other ways to go, avoiding the inevitable. It was the only route now without arousing suspicion.

I drew closer. My perception was that the world was focussed on me, all eyes staring right at me.

'Just keep walking, it'll be fine,' I muttered under my breath. As I drew level, the police car pulled away. With relief, I moved onwards as fast as my injuries would allow.

In Aunt Rose's road I scanned the houses looking for a green and yellow door and it wasn't long before I saw it. I knocked, and, within a minute, Aunt Rose answered.

"Come in dear, I wondered when you would arrive."

I was surprised. "You did?"

"Yes dear."

"I have just been to Ann-Marie's she said I have to get him to Belfairs Woods." I answered rather lamely.

"That's quite correct…"

"But I am not quite sure…" I interrupted her.

"How to find him?" I nodded. "That's why I was hoping you would come round, I have just the thing that will do the trick. Heather is very knowledgeable on these things. Now, take a seat and I'll put the kettle on." With that she closed the door behind me and went to the kitchen, leaving me in the hallway. Taking my coat off I hung it up on a coat hook near the front door and went into the lounge to take a seat.

"There we go. Just give it the right amount of time to brew," Aunt Rose said, placing a tray on the table, a few minutes later. She took a seat in the armchair opposite, organising the cups on their saucers.

"I saw him, actually spoke to him."

"Yes, Ann-Marie told me." I must have looked bemused. "She rang me before you arrived."

"Oh." Was all I could respond.

She lifted the lid of the teapot and stirred the contents, the aroma filled the room. "Yes, I think that is ready now." She poured the tea. All the time I watched, lost for words, still caught by the fact that she was always one step ahead.

She handed me a cup. "Now, drink this tea dear, it's a special herb tea. A yarrow root infusion that will help concentrate the mind and help improve the psychic connection and retrieve some memories. Just relax and drink. It's not to everyone's taste but don't let that put you off."

I did as instructed, too amazed to say anything.

Putting the cup to my lips, the sweet aroma flowed up my nose, a pleasant lemon aroma with a hint of something else I wasn't sure of. As it touched my tongue it was sharp to taste, making me want to spit it out. Reluctantly, I swallowed. It went down my throat, filling my whole body with a warm tingle. I could sense every muscle relaxing instantaneously. This was good stuff.

Aunt Rose spoke to me in her soft warm tones easing me

into her will, encouraging me to recall every detail I could about Henry. Slowly my mind drifted, focussing on Henry. I began to feel his presence, sense his torrid mind.

I felt the cup being taken from my hand. The rest was just a blur of images.

The carriage. His wife. The shop he worked in. The tunnels. His mother and father. The theatre. The first time he met Violet. My flat. My face in a mirror.

The pictures flashed up faster and faster.

"Ugh." I was bolt upright, breathing heavily, facing Aunt Rose.

29

"Just relax, Daniel, let it do its job." Rose's voice was soothing and beckoned no resistance.

I started to feel hot as little pearls of sweat formed on my forehead. The back of my t-shirt felt moist. Shuddering, I looked at Aunt Rose, who smiled warmly.

"Relax and let your mind wander. It will slowly start to become clear, you will have a better understanding of Henry."

I slumped back into the chair as a strange tingling tickled my brain. My body didn't feel like my own anymore, every limb felt disconnected. My sight phased between clarity and haziness. Then suddenly I had an awareness, like a bright penny shining in a dark room. I could see everything, it was all clear now and I could feel Henry's presence again, but in a different way. I knew what he was thinking and more importantly I could see where he was.

I could see shapes, blurry at first, but then the focus sharpened. Images of places I knew, and was familiar with, yet I couldn't quite place them.

It hit me, Victoria Circus train station, Platform 1- it had to be! It was the first stop on the line heading to London. From there he could go anywhere. Was this now or was this a past memory I was seeing? I wasn't sure. Then the picture changed and I saw a newspaper headline, one I recognised from my journey to Ann-Marie's about the new Southend-on-sea Football stadium. It was today, was he still there? I had a thought on how to find out.

The clarity brought a sense of feeling back into my limbs

and I tried to get up but the room briefly spun and I fell back down again.

"Easy Daniel. This is powerful and it takes a while for your body to get used to it."

"But I think I know where he is." I slurred my words as I tried to get up.

"That is good." Aunt Rose offered her help which I gratefully took.

"Thanks. Aunt Rose, have you got a telephone directory I can borrow?" My body still felt punch drunk, however, the adrenalin buzz was starting counter it and I soon found myself engulfed with a renewed energy.

"I think I have somewhere. Let me think. Oh yes, I know where it is."

I had a sort of plan that was starting to ferment and was eager to implement it. I allowed a smile to creep across my face. He thought he was going to get away with it but he was wrong. I was going to take back my life.

I still felt a little light headed as I thumbed through the pages of the telephone directory, looking for C2C services. I found their customer service number and dialled. It was Sunday, early afternoon, so I hoped there would be someone to answer the phone.

"Do you mind if I borrow your phone," I said rhetorically, apologetic as I waited for the call to be answered.

"No dear, it's fine." Aunt Rose cleared away the tea things from the lounge.

"Thanks," I added, drumming my fingers against my leg as I waited impatiently for the phone to be answered.

Finally, after about twenty rings someone answered. "C2C, good morn... afternoon," came the dulcit tones of a Lancashire woman.

"Hello. I was wondering if you could contact one of your stations for me." I almost stopped their but instinct told me

---

they'd say 'no' so I quickly added, "It's just my brother hasn't got his mobile on him and we need to get hold of him urgently, he was due to get a train about now from Southend Victoria Circus Station going to Liverpool Street. Only there's been a family emergency and we need him home as soon as possible."

"I'm sorry, you'll need to contact the station," was the rather unsympathetic reply.

"Can't you transfer me?"

"I'm sorry, no," the woman replied curtly.

"Well do you have the number?" I asked. Some people just wouldn't give more than the bare minimum of information.

The woman sighed heavily. "Hold on a moment."

"Thank you." There was a brief silence where I could hear the shuffling of papers on a desk. "Have you got a pen and paper I can borrow please?" I called to Aunt Rose, who was in the small kitchen at the end of the hallway.

"Of course dear," Aunt Rose said, as she brought them out to me in the hall.

"Thanks."

There was a clicking sound on the line. "Hello."

"Hi," I said.

"The number you want…" I quickly wrote it down, repeating each digit, then hung up to dial the new number.

Again it took a long time to be answered.

"Southend Victoria. How can I help?" The voice was abrupt but polite.

I explained the situation as I had done previously. The man on the end of the line was reluctant and I had to plead with him that it was urgent. My desperation started to trigger my imagination and I made the scenario more detailed, even the hardest of people, I thought, would have to concede to my story.

I was put on hold as in the background I heard the call for 'Mr Henry Highway to come to the ticket office' repeated three times over the station tannoy.

A couple of minutes passed. I waited and listened to the background noise. Questions started floating round my head. Was he there? Had I got it all wrong? Did I just want to believe? Make myself feel better?

"Just transferring you." Then I could hear the ringing tones of another phone.

A hesitant voice answered, "hello?"

"Hello Henry. Didn't think you'd hear from me again did you?"

After the briefest, "I thought the police would have arrested you by now," was the surprised reply.

"I'm learning. From you." I was trying hard not to sound malevolent.

He laughed. "I would really like to chat but I have got a train to catch."

"You might want to think twice about that. See if I'm going down, I'm going to take you with me. And did I not tell you the police are looking for two people now. Not just one. See they've been to my flat and they found your belongings, and that last murder you did will tie up nicely with the others, your fingerprints will see to that. Then there's always your DNA."

"My what?" Henry for an instant sounded concerned.

"Oh yes. See things have moved on a lot since you were last around. So you see there really is no way you are going to get away free."

There was silence. I could hear him breathing, along with the background noise of the station.

"You still there Henry?" I asked. "Concerned now?"

A very faint, "yes and no," was the stark reply. He regained his composure. "Well, they still have to catch me. They are hardly going to believe your story, a killer back from the dead after eighty years. They will lock you up in an asylum."

"I haven't got to tell that side of things, just that I had an accomplice. That will be enough, I think I can give a pretty good description of you, it won't take long to pick you up and my stash of money that you're using won't keep you going for long." I heard a man blowing a whistle ready for a train to depart. I could hear the unease in his voice. He thought he could walk away. I had just turned all that around. I wasn't sure what his next move would be.

"I'll take my chances, must dash got a train to catch."

Before he could put the receiver down I quickly added. "Remember this, how do you think I knew where to get hold of you?" This was my last rebuff.

I didn't know how long I was going to have this power, in which case he would be lost, just another face in the crowd.

The phone went dead. He'd hung up.

"Damn!"

"What is it dear?"

"He's hung up." I slammed down the receiver to a look of consternation from Aunt Rose.

"Sorry," I said, ashamed.

I didn't know what outcome I expected, but this wasn't it. I went back into the lounge and paced the room. Thoughts, ideas, rushing round my head like speeding traffic.

If I couldn't lure him to Belfairs Woods by deception I would have to use force, I knew where he was and that was where I was heading.

"I'm sorry to ask but do you have a car I could borrow? I'm going to have to take him to Belfairs Woods forcibly but I need a way of getting him there,"

"No dear, I've never driven,"

"Damn! Well, I've got to go and get him anyway before he gets too far away."

"Heather has a car though. Maybe I can give her a ring and see if she can meet you somewhere."

"Yes. Thank you. I'll leave you this number so you can get hold of me." I took the mobile that Ann-Marie had given me out of my pocket and dialled Aunt Rose's main phone, then did 1471 to get the number, writing it down on the paper she had given me. "Thank you. Thank you for everything," I said, before leaving the house to head towards the station.

I had the length of the journey to work out how I was going to hold him captive, if he was still in that vicinity, as he was powerful.

It was getting dark again, rain clouds making it appear like night. It wasn't actually raining but I knew it would not be long. My leg and ankle had faded from my conscious mind as I rallied my thoughts to Henry's capture. The limp I had acquired was the only sign of my injuries. Every step it seemed I was getting a little faster. My breathing was heavy. In my mind I felt confident that Henry had not boarded the train, it was a strange sense that I had but I was glad of it.

I knew there were a few ways that Henry could go from the station if he hadn't boarded the train. My first thought was that he would hide in the tunnels. This was his only safe haven, he didn't know anyone else so he had nowhere else he could go. Unless, he had told the police about them?

At the station there was no sign of him, however, I still felt his strong presence and guessed that this meant he was definitely not on a train, miles away. But how close was he?

Quite suddenly a strange, uneasy feeling engulfed me.

"Oh shit!" I realised exactly where he might go, the only other place he could possibly know about, Ann-Marie's house.

Adrenalin fused every nerve in my body into action and I started to run, pain smarted in my leg but I shut it out. I had no time for it. He might already be there and this scared me. I had put Ann-Marie's life at risk by not thinking through my actions. She'd helped me more than she had to and this was how I repaid her.

I was already hot from my walk to the station but now I was starting to sweat, I pulled off the hood of the coat and undid it, an automatic reaction, I was not concerned with the consequences, only with getting to Ann-Marie's before Henry. I was oblivious to everything else going on around me - focussed on the mission at hand.

Road after road I crossed, glancing at the traffic. Her house wasn't that far from the station, just a little further than the town hall but it felt like miles now, my breathing started to labour as I realised how unfit I was.

When I turned into her road, there was no sign of Henry, although I could feel his presence stronger than before. Dread filled my body. I slowed to a walk as I neared the house so I could think of my next move and get my breath back. Should I go to the front door or the back door?

The back door. It seemed the sensible choice. If he was inside already I needed to surprise him. If he wasn't then I didn't want to alert him to my presence. I ducked down the alley, following the course of it to Ann-Marie's garden, I could see the back door, the glass panel in it was broken and the door slightly ajar, my heart sank.

For a moment I pondered whether to enter or call the police. I wanted the best solution for Ann-Marie but also I didn't want to risk not getting Henry to the required place Monday night and, if I called the police that might be the result. I was in a dilemma.

I clambered over the fence and made my way to the back door cautious in case I was being watched, my footfalls crunching on the gravel.

The familiarity of the room layouts gave me an advantage, but not a great one.

With my back against the wall I looked into the kitchen, observing, looking for Henry and searching for a weapon that I could use, something to defend, or attack with. There was nothing in sight. I knew where the steel rod was so inched my way forward, back still against the wall, I reached out and pushed the door open. It moved silently.

Glancing into the kitchen I couldn't make out anyone inside, I entered to the sound of crunching glass under foot. 'Damn' I thought and hesitated before continuing. I knew Henry would be expecting me; there was no need to make it any easier for him though. I also had Ann-Marie's life to consider.

I looked up the hallway, no sign of any movement, and after taking the steel from the draw edged my way along it to the bottom of the stairs, glancing upwards, wary of being watched. There was no sign of him and a strange eerie silence settled on the house. I wondered about Mojo, I should at least hear some movement from him, especially if Ann-Marie was in trouble.

Unless!

No I could even contemplate that scenario. Hopefully the silence signified that she had gone out. I hoped.

Outside the lounge door I steeled myself for a swift entry, counting one, two, three, before rushing in.

Nothing.

I started to relax, confident that there was no one in the house. I left the lounge and went upstairs, still cautious, but more at ease. At the top I looked into the bedroom at the back and the bathroom to my left, they were clear. This just left two doors, Ann-Marie's room and the spare room. Warily I pushed the spare room door open, it glided back easily until it stopped against the wall, I had a clear view inside, it was empty.

Finally, Ann-Marie's room, I hesitated. Stretching out my hand. I placed it on the door and pushed gently. It inched open slowly, gradually showing the room.

Again, it was empty.

She had gone out. Thank god for that.

But what of Henry? I could sense he was close.

Bam!

I was on the floor. My head throbbed. I tried to push myself up off the ground but felt another blow to the back of my head.

My eyes closed, and I slumped on the floor.

30

As I came round I found myself laying face down in Ann-Marie's room, hands and feet bound. Someone was standing in front of me, the black brogues dirty and scuffed.

A voice grabbed my attention, clearing the fuzziness from my head

"So, did you really think you could sneak up on me?"

My head started to throb and a queasy feeling erupted in my stomach. I tried to remember what happened but was disorientated as my head thumped loudly in my ears. After a minute the fog started to clear, although the thumping didn't want to go.

"Henry?" I said, attempting to roll over so I could see him, but with my hands tied behind my back all I could manage was to lay on my side.

"I was all ready to leave and then you had to spoil everything. Finally I had decided that maybe it was time to get on with my life, as best I could. Start again, leave the past firmly on your shoulders and walk away. You had to spoil it!" Whilst he appeared calm, his eyes showed anger.

"Yeah, well I want my life back. You had your chance," I said, trying to edge my way to the nearest wall so I could sit up and, hopefully, shake the nausea that was starting to take hold.

"Everyone is allowed to make mistakes. Forgive and forget. Is that not what the Lord says?" I detected the sarcasm in his voice.

"What? Providing someone else takes the fall, is that it?" My hatred and anger finding its voice as I finally managed to sit up,

266

the nausea subsiding slightly.

"Sometimes situations arise, and you just have to make what you can of them." Henry sat down on the bed watching me. "Now, I have two problems." He paused deliberately then got up and kneeled before me. "You, whom I can easily eradicate with a simple letter... telephone call to the police. Simple. They are not going to believe your story. However it does pose another problem and that is they may be tempted to follow up on your description of me. If, as you say, they believe two people are mixed up in this. So, I should really finish you off. However, the other problem is the girl, I do not know how much she knows,"

I was about to speak when he pre-empted my question.

"The girl, Ann-Marie, is safe... well at the moment, unfortunately she was not here when I brok... arrived, shall we say? Which is lucky for you."

"Lucky for me. How do you make that?" I started to struggle with my bindings.

"Well as long as she is still alive," he came in closer to me, "then I need you to help me find her."

I lurched forward in a feeble attempt to attack, knowing full well it would be futile. Henry just jerked his head back, got up and turned his back on me.

"You don't think I'm going to help you do you? Anyway, how should I know where she is? Last time I saw her was this morning. She could be anywhere now,"

"Yes, I am sure that is what you would have me think." He turned and faced me again wearing a smug smile.

An uneasy feeling washed over me. Did he have a trump card? What was it?

There was silence as he stared at me intently as if weighing up the consequences of his actions. If only I could get free I'd wipe that smile from his face. Struggling as much as I could I couldn't loosen the bonds that restrained my hands.

"Have you met Ann-Marie's mother?" he said rhetorically.

"What?"

"Have you met Ann-Marie's mother?"

Full realisation of the game he was playing hit me like a steam train. I stopped struggling with my bonds and stared speechlessly at him. I glanced around the room expecting to see a body lying somewhere.

"You will not find her in here,"

"What have you done with her?" Of course, he hadn't done anything with her, if he had, he knew there was a strong possibility I might not go along with whatever his plan was. Also, he might not have her at all. I couldn't see the clock on Ann-Marie's bedside table from where I was so I had no idea what the time was. It was dark outside but it could still be about 3pm, in which case it would be a couple of hours before she came home. Then again, it could be the middle of the night for all I could tell.

"I have not done anything to her," he paused, "yet."

Good. That meant it was late afternoon and she hasn't got home yet, there was still time for me to try and resolve this matter before she arrived home.

"But I might, it really depends on how helpful you are going to be." He walked over to me, grabbed my shirt and pulled me to my feet. My leg and ankle smarted and for a second the room spun making me feel woozy. He was powerful. Even standing, I was helpless, feet and hands restrained.

"Come with me."

My eyes widened with fright and my heart sank as he turned to walk away. She was home. Henry grabbed my wrist and dragged me along behind him, hopping, trying to keep up, using the wall to balance when I felt myself start to topple over. He led me out of Ann-Marie's room, down the hallway to the back bedroom.

Ann-Marie's mother was gagged and bound to the bed. She was awake, her bleary eyes widened as we came into view. She looked as if she had been struggling with her bonds. Tears stained her lightly made up face, her neat brown hair stuck to her cheek.

Henry waved in a rather sick way and I countered by thrusting my weight against him, as if it was going to make a difference. He lost his balance briefly but stayed upright, whilst I hit the door frame and then fell hard on to the floor.

A crack resonated around the room and I howled in pain as nausea swept over me like a blanket, tears filled my eyes, snot and mucus seemed to amalgamate on my face as the pain fully registered.

"That was not very clever was it?" Henry said, looking down mockingly at me on the floor.

I couldn't believe I had been so stupid. As the pain ricocheted through every muscle in my body it became unbearable, and my eyes started to close as my brain shut down, and although the adrenalin kicked in, killing the pain the impulse to close my eyes and sleep was unrelenting.

I felt my face being slapped and wearily opened my eyes.

"Now, now, get up we can not have you falling asleep." Annoyance registered in his voice.

Then, grabbing both my shoulders, he pulled me up, my face contorted with pain, I felt too sick and numb, I wanted to close my eyes, my legs became like jelly. I saw Ann-Marie's mother's terror.

Henry dragged me back to the front bedroom. I started to shake as I was forced to tolerate consciousness. Sweat covered my whole body as it dealt with my injuries. Suddenly the bonds that held my wrists were cutting into my skin.

Sitting me down on the bed he checked my arm and hand.

"That really wasn't very clever was it? Now are you going to help?" he quizzed maliciously, convinced I would do his bidding.

The pain intensified and, as I tried to scream, he held his hand over my mouth.

My choices were slim. He had the upper hand. I could risk losing my life but not Ann-Marie's or her mother's.

I grimaced. "Okay, okay," I said, as best I could with Henry's hand over my mouth.

"Good. Now if I take my hand away, you are not going to scream are you?"
Too weary to fight, I nodded my acquiescence.

"Now where is Ann-Marie?"

I wanted to curl up and cry, shut out the pain.

"Come on, where is she? We can stay here all night if we have to, I am sure that arm will become unbearable sooner or later." He squeezed it for good measure.

I didn't want to tell him. I didn't know for sure where Ann-Marie would be. I tried to fight the pain, the result of trying to be some sort of hero.

I couldn't see a way to avoid telling him what he wanted to know, I wasn't strong enough.

Then in the midst of the fog, clarity started to form.

If her mother was home, then this must be evening possibly night-time. Then why wasn't Ann-Marie home? She said she was always in when her mum came in otherwise her mum worried. She must be with Aunt Rose.

Aunt Rose must have pre-warned Ann-Marie about this situation, she was always one step ahead, unfortunately not far enough to stop Ann-Marie's mother from coming home. The first thing Ann-Marie would want to have done would be to come home or call the police. Why hadn't she?

They could have ended her mum's suffering in an instant if they called the police, Why hadn't they? Maybe they didn't know the full extent of the danger except that it wasn't safe for Ann-Marie to come home just yet, maybe her mum hadn't been expected home so early, maybe she was going shopping.

My thoughts formed a plan, a plan that, hopefully, maybe, they wanted me to think of. It was one way to get exactly what we all wanted, but without Henry realising that we were playing him, instead of the other way round.

"I don't know where she is at this precise moment," I said, fighting to stay conscious as the adrenalin slowed and the pain started to course back.

I felt a slap to the face.

"Wake up, this is no time for sleep. Where is she?"

"I don't know…,"

"Don't play games. You are playing with her mother's life." He had me by the scruff of my neck shaking me violently to keep me awake.

"Let me sleep… I'm tired."

"Not until you tell me where she is… Come on… Daniel,"

I was finding it harder and harder to stay conscious. The pain seemed miles away, now I felt tired, maybe it was the shock kicking in. I wanted to sleep.

"Daniel. Where is she?"

"I told you I don't know." My words sounded distant even to me.

Finally, losing patience with me, he let me fall onto my side, on the bed.

"It's a shame Daniel she seemed like a nice lady too. Oh well, if you are not going to tell me, I have no choice." He walked towards the door. As he reached it I mustered up every last bit of strength I could.

"Wait," I said deliriously.

He stopped, turned and faced me.

"I am waiting."

"I don't know where she is now." He about-turned and started to walk out of the room again. "But I do know where she'll be Monday night about nine-ish," I quickly added.

He walked back into the room and leaned over me.

"And where will that be?"

I took a breath. I was slowly losing the battle to stay awake.

"The woods, Belfairs Woods,"

"Where? It's a big place," he stated gruffly.

I felt as if I had been out on the drink for the last twenty four hours, I was having problems saying my words.

"Behind the scout hut, the sunken garden."

"The what? Where?"

"North of BelfairsWoods, scout hut, sunken garden."

"Why would she be there at that time of night?"

"I can't remember... spirits... gatheri... spii..."

"What do you mean?"

I felt another slap to the face before blackness washed over me.

31

Daylight broke through the window, hitting my face. Groggily, I stirred, slowly taking in my surroundings. For a split second I was unable to fathom why I couldn't move my arms and legs freely then as pain registered in my wrist and ankle images of the day before came flooding back to me.

There was no sign of Henry and I listened carefully for an indication that maybe he was in another part of the house, all was eerily quiet. I still felt a little sick and as I rolled about trying to make my way to the edge of the bed, the pain in my arm checked itself, and my whole body felt stiff as if I done ten rounds with Mike Tyson. I tried to sit up but couldn't get the momentum I needed because of the soft mattress so, after a few attempts, which sapped my energy, I stopped trying. Every time I had moved my bindings tightened on my swollen wrist, reminding me how painful it was. Suddenly I remembered Ann-Marie's mother. I needed to see how she was. I also wanted to sleep for a week.

Taking deep breaths I gritted my teeth and forced myself to try and sit up. It was no use, I needed to swing my legs round, but something prevented me from doing so which confused me as pain made my head ache. Slowly I twisted round as best I could and caught sight of what looked like a thin green washing line, tying my feet to the bedpost.

The straining and movement brought on a new wave of nausea, a cold sweat engulfed my body making my clothes stick to me. I became uncomfortably cold.

I heard the front door slam shut and I looked towards the

bedroom door, any minute expecting a visitor, Henry. Nothing!

I focussed on my bindings, trying to think of a way to get free. I had to get free no matter how much pain it caused. How? I was never a boy scout so didn't carry around a handy little pocket knife. I didn't smoke, so no lighter either, sometimes I was my own worst enemy.

My attention was drawn to my trouser pocket. The mobile phone that Ann-Marie had given me was now vibrating, set to discreet. Desperately I tried to manoeuvre my body in the hope that I could pull it from my pocket. Every new movement caused a shot of pain to ricochet round my body. No matter what way I twisted it remained out of reach. The phone stopped vibrating.

I heard footfalls on the stairs. I ceased moving and settled as comfortably as I could.

"Afternoon," Henry said, cheerfully, walking into the room. "Glad you could join us." Suddenly I wondered how long I had slept for. Had I missed the deadline?

Even with the nausea, I realised how hungry and thirsty I was, as I saw Henry carrying a cup of tea.

"Don't suppose you've got one for me, have you?" I grimaced.

"You suppose right. What, do you think I want you to keep your strength up? I do not think so. Do not worry, it will all be over soon." He walked over to the window and looked out. "Lovely day. Sun is shining, a little cold otherwise very nice. So how about you explain a little more clearly where I can find Ann-Marie?" He sat in the wicker chair.

"Why should I? As you say I haven't got long, so I'v…" Ann-Marie's mother sprang to mind.

"You forget about our guest in the back bedroom."

I kept my mouth shut, not sure what I had told him last night if it was still only Monday. It was a blur.

He walked back over to the bed and stood in front of me.

"Now, I could make things a little nicer for you, if you promise to help that is. I will even make you tea, maybe even a bite to eat. Dry bread anyway, would not want you passing out on me now. The deal though, is this, if I give you food and drink you show me on a map where in the woods you are meeting you friend, Ann-Marie tonight, and..." he paused. "... explain a little more clearly why."

It was Monday, I hadn't missed the deadline. I was weak and needed sustenance and, in some respects, it was going to get me exactly what I wanted, Henry into Belfairs Woods and then straight back to hell, so I agreed on the proviso of food and drink first.

Ten minutes later he returned with bread, tea and a map of the local area. Placing them on the floor he untied the washing line that anchored me to the bed post. Then sitting me upright untied my hands and refastened them in front so I could at least feed myself. As the knots were loosened blood flowed freely again giving me pins and needles, bringing with it a refreshed bout of pain from my injuries. As he grabbed my wrist to tie it up again the pain almost made me pass out with nausea like a tidal wave. My muscles ached and my wrist was swollen with a yellow bruise starting to form.

"There you go. Enjoy." He placed the food on the bed next to me and went and sat back down in the wicker chair, drinking his own tea, watching me warily. The pins and needles continued for a few more minutes whilst I ate, which was awkward yet possible.

It was a slow process eating and trying to combat the nausea at the same time, but knowing I had to keep my strength up, I continued. This deal was going to get me what I wanted and I wasn't about to struggle and make my life harder.

After eating and drinking I laid back down on the bed, the nausea abated and I rested my head on the pillows, feeling refreshed and more coherent.

I took stock of the situation, taking time to study my wrist, guessing that it was either fractured or broken. I couldn't tell which, but knew it hurt like hell.

Henry watched me as if it were just a lazy Sunday morning between two friends sharing breakfast. After some time he approached me, bent down and picked up the map, opening it and placing it across my legs before hauling me into a sitting position, which caused me some discomfort.

"Where is this scout hut you speak of? I know… knew the woods quite well. Violet and I used to go there for walks…" He looked thoughtful, loving, caring almost humane. "… but I do not remember any hut or sunken gardens."

"The scout hut was only put there about forty-five years ago. It was only by accident that the secret garden was found. One of the scouts was out exploring one day when he fe…"

"I do not want a history lesson, just the details," he said, getting agitated at my reticence.

"Do you want me to tell you or not?"

"Do you want Ann-Marie's mother to suffer?" He pointed in the direction of the back bedroom.

"No."

"Well then, get on with it."

I looked at the map. It was an ordinance survey map showing the wood in great detail. I'd never looked at the wood on a map and it seemed a little strange and disorienting at first until I got my bearings.

I found the car park and the trail that led north-east near to the sunken garden and the stream that flowed by it, then I put my finger where I believed the gardens to be.

Henry picked up the map folding it so it showed only the immediate area, placing his finger where mine had been and walked out of the room without another word.

I flexed my back and shoulders easing life back into the stiff muscles. I caught sight of something trailing out of Ann-Marie's wardrobe. Suddenly I realised what it was, the tie from the canvas bag that we had taken from the flat days before.

If that were the case I knew there was a knife inside it. I began to pray that he hadn't noticed it or even snooped around. I still had to get to it though. That was not going to be easy.

Henry seemed to be gone for ages as I lay on the bed waiting. I wanted to attempt to undo my bindings especially now they were in front of me but I didn't know how long I had before he returned. If he returned and saw me fiddling with them he would surely make them tighter placing my hands once again behind my back. If I didn't try then he might forget, but I might not get another chance. I had to try.

I used my teeth to gnaw at the knots. A tear trickled from my eye as once again the pain bit into me and I let out a stream of muffled curses to fight it. Finally, with perseverance, I managed to untie the first knot. It was not easy with my injury rendering my right hand useless. I was beginning to sweat again, pressure from the injury and fear of getting caught. He was good at knots.

I felt the vibration in my pocket again and although I was now in a position to answer I also needed to get free. I continued biting at the knots until, finally, the second knot gave way. It hadn't taken as long as the first and I expected to hear Henry any second. However, my luck seemed to be holding fast.

I picked at the rope that held my ankles until it too fell away. My sweat soaked shirt clung to me and I wriggled to get away from the dampness, however, that was the least of my worries.

My legs were stiff after so long and when I tried to stand on them as quietly as possible they gave way. For a split second I thought my chance was over. I listened. Nothing. Making my way to the wardrobe, I had to cross in front of the open door. I checked the coast was clear. There was a shadow moving in the back bedroom. I prayed that Ann-Marie's mum was alright. Silently I opened the wardrobe door.

Sure enough Henry's things were there. Rummaging swiftly through them I found the knife which had been wrapped up again in its rag. The only place I could possibly conceal it was in my sock and up my chino leg, carefully resting the tip of the knife in my shoe. Replacing everything back in the wardrobe I closed the door quietly.

Back on the bed, I re-tied the restraints making sure I could undo them easily but also trying to make it look as though they had never been undone. I relaxed once more breathing heavily from the exertion.

The phone rang again. This time I could answer it.

"Hello," I whispered, all the time listening for footsteps in the hall.

"Daniel? It's me Ann-Marie."

"I can't talk much," I said, ever wary of getting caught.

"Where are you? Are you at my house?"

"A-ha." I was watching the bedroom door.

"Aunt Rose said I wasn't to go home, there was danger there."

"She was right." I wanted to say more, but the more I said the more I risked being caught by Henry. Did she know about her mother? Should I tell her?

"You can't talk, is that what you're hinting at?"

"A-ha."

"Is my mum ok?" There was the question I dreaded.

I thought about this question for longer than the others, I didn't want to upset her.

"A-ha." The tension in my voice I believed would give away this little white lie, but I didn't want to worry her.

"Can you get Henry to the woods tonight?"

"A…" I heard foot steps in the hall. I quickly put the phone in my pocket, ending the call first.

Henry appeared in the doorway. "Looks like we have got transport for tonight. So we just need to wait." He came closer. "You might as well make yourself comfortable. It's going to be a long wait for you." He smiled smugly. "Oh, when I say we, I meant me and Karen." For a moment I wondered who he meant and then it clicked into place. He started to leave the room then stopped.

"Better make sure you are tied up nice and tight we do not want you getting loose do we?"

"No, of course not," I added sarcastically. Fear raced through me as I thought he would realise I had untied myself.

"And I think a gag is in order."

As he untied my wrists he eyed his work, questioning it, then shaking his head, he re-tied my hands behind my back. I struggled initially, but he warned me not to. I realised the implications and acquiesced. Henry left the room.

A while later I heard a commotion going on in the back bedroom and could only surmise that Karen was struggling, she was probably scared even more because she did not know the full story and I wondered how much she did know?

The front door closed and the house fell silent.

I gave it a few minutes before cutting myself free with Henry's knife which I could still reach and manoeuvre easily enough to cut my bindings.

Limping to the back bedroom I found it vacant. I sighed from the effort, my ankle was stiff and although my thigh barely registered any discomfort the muscle still felt tight. He'd taken her as collateral.

Downstairs I made myself something more to eat as my nausea had been replaced by hunger pangs. I needed my strength later so this respite was important. I also found a bandage and painfully strapped up my wrist tightly. My ankle was loosening up the more I walked and I paced the kitchen.

It gave me the opportunity to gather my thoughts and formulate some sort of plan. I needed to get to Belfairs Woods. How though? It was ten miles away and I couldn't use public transport for risk of being caught.

While a second round of toast was doing itself nicely, I checked the garden shed. Through the glass I could see a mountain bike, a man's one. I thought it was a bit strange, but it was what I needed. I searched the kitchen for the keys to the shed whilst eating my toast and dropping crumbs everywhere. I located them hanging just behind the back door.

It was a struggle to get the bike out as I couldn't apply any pressure to my wrist and, therefore, knew it was going to be tricky cycling with only one good arm, but I would have to try regardless. Braking would be interesting as I only had the front brake. I had no choice. It was as simple as that.

An hour later I left via the back alley, which was only just wide enough to get the handle bars through. At the edge of the alley I checked the coast was clear, pulled the phone from my pocket and checked the time, 3.57, it was later than I thought.

Normally I could cycle ten miles in an hour or so. I had five hours. Plenty of time. Suddenly a revelation hit me that I could just go to Aunt Rose's that would be simpler. Why hadn't I thought of that? Maybe I should walk? Sod it, I'll take the bike.

I got on the bike and exited the alley turned left. At first I was a bit wobbly until all my muscles had warmed up. There was no wind about which made the going easier and I rested my hurt wrist in my lap. It was dark again and I had no lights so kept to the pavements.

With only the front brake I couldn't afford to go too fast for fear of not being able to stop quickly. The bike had twenty-one gears but with only one hand I could use seventh, fourteenth and twenty-first. It was enough.

Aunt Rose's house was deserted and I didn't want to waste anymore time so I headed straight for the Belfairs woods.

I was making good progress and started to relax as I cycled along Blenheim Chase, enjoying the passing scenery, forgetting for the first time that I was a wanted man. I cycled past the junction of Flemming Avenue and spotted a police car parked up. I locked eyes with the driver for an instant then gritted my teeth and hoped they wouldn't recognise me, whilst trying to speed up.

I heard the rev of an engine and saw the reflection of flashing lights in the windows of the houses to my left. Looking over my shoulder I saw the car hurtle out of the road.

'Please just go past, please'.

It drove past me and for a split second I thought it might carry on going but suddenly it braked sharply in front of me, blocking my progress.

With my bad wrist I didn't have time to stop and I careered into it, sprawling headlong over the bonnet the bike rearing up underneath me. Before I knew where I was I felt hand cuffs being placed on me as my rights were read to me. I cried out in agony as my wrist smarted from the pressure being applied by the handcuffs. It happened so quickly I didn't have time to react or argue.

32

A few minutes of thoughtlessness had caused me to get caught. I couldn't get to Belfairs Woods and I needed to be there, to complete whatever the plan was. What the outcome was going to be now, I didn't know. All I knew was that I was in the back of a police car and under arrest for crimes I hadn't committed, knowing I was going to spend the rest of my life behind bars.

If only I'd taken more care. If only! I sank deeper into the rear seat until I was shocked by a shot of pain from my wrist, then everything else started to hurt. I let a further tirade of statements ransack my mind. If only I'd stayed off of the beaten track. I knew so many back streets. I'd had time. It would have been easy for me.

How were they going to perform the ceremony without me?

I was taken to Southend-On-Sea Police Station, an old building with new offices added on to the side with no thought for the character of the facade. It had always been associated with the police in one form or another.

When it was first built the local magistrate had it as his residence, a prestigious and formidable building, having an impressive grand double oak door entrance with an ornate stone archway and larger than life windows. In time it became the courthouse for the whole of the county, with the help of a lot of internal remodelling - the cellar forming the prison cells. Then it became staff quarters for the police training centre.

Now it was back as a police station and offices with new holding cells on the grounds, along with a new training centre and car depot.

We pulled up to the security gates, I saw hoards of photographers. I was surprised how quickly word had leaked out. Or was it a case of 'they had their man and they wanted people to know that the streets of Southend were safe again'.

I tried to hide my face from the wall of flashes that blinded me but it was no use. The gate took forever to open and the policemen didn't seem in a hurry to drive through.

I went numb to all the pain I felt as despair flooded over me. I was in a kind of trance, not really aware of anything anymore, trying not to believe this was real. Viewing it as if I would be able to play it back at some later date.

The car parked up and the back door opened up and I was unceremoniously pulled out.

"Aaarghh," I cried in pain.

"Shut up!" One of the officers grunted. I was scum to them. They had no sympathy for me. Why should they? I was accused of atrocious crimes, I could feel the distaste and hatred they had for me.

I wanted to explain but knew it was useless. My world was lost, my life gone.

Leading me inside, I could still hear the clicking of cameras going off, trying to take every last picture before I was hidden from view.

My poor parents. The next day they would see the headlines in the papers and hear it on the news. How could they face their friends again? Everyone was soon to know that their son was a killer, a murderer of innocent young girls. They'd be forced to move, vacate the home they had made, all those years of memories, good memories savaged by recent events. They'd have to leave everyone and everything behind, all because of me.

Inside I was told to sit, I did so and they handcuffed me to a rail fixed to the wall, there was just me in the cold, empty waiting room.

"Daniel Stephens," a man said.

"Yes."

"Custody Sergeant Harris," he gruffly introduced himself as he reached behind me and undid the handcuffs before pushing me towards the counter. "Not going to give me any trouble are you?"

"No. Aargh!"

"What happened to that?" He observed my swollen wrist.

"I fell." I wanted to tell the whole story, I was innocent, the real killer was still out there, loose and about to kill again later that night. How many times had they heard that? I didn't know what to say, I really believed that they wouldn't listen to me. They'd have me committed. I had to try something

"Listen," I commanded but was met with cold eyes that dared me to speak. "Please, you must listen there…"

"I don't have to do anything." The custody Sergeant yanked my arm harder as a form of rebuke and I was brought to heel at the counter.

"Ouch. Careful." But the steel in his eyes made me aware that he didn't care about my injuries.

"After we've booked you in, we'll get the doctor in to look at it." Harris was curt but polite as he took various details, question after question, fingerprints, belongings, belt, shoelaces before being shown into a cell. The door slammed shut and the bolt being driven home was like the final nail in the coffin as the sound reverberated round the hard, white-washed, cold, cell walls.

There was a bed in one corner, metal bucket in the other. Cold and lonely, I sat huddled up on the bed. Scared, I started to cry. I could understand how even the toughest might fall to pieces in here. I sat staring at the door, wishing, praying that someone would come and take me away and say it was just a bad dream. Nothing! Other doors were being opened and shut, a commotion was going on outside but I could only listen to the sound of dread. My fate.

A little while later the bolt slid across and the door opened.

"This is Doctor Fingle, he's come to look at your wrist," Sergeant Harris barked.

In walked a middle aged man in a tweed jacket carrying an old fashioned doctor's bag. The officer stood guard at the door, truncheon ready in case of trouble. He wasn't going to get any, I knew that, but he didn't. He had probably experienced a few rough customers in the past and was ready for anything now. The doctor put down his bag on the floor and sat on the end of the bed.

"Can I see your wrist please?" He was polite but offered no bedside manner. Probably only doing his job because he had to not because he wanted to. Wanting to help a killer made no sense, as far as he was concerned I deserved everything I got. He felt around my wrist, moved it this way and that as I snarled in pain with each movement. He didn't need to ask whether it hurt, but he did all the same.

Then, after a minute or so, he said, "I don't believe it's broken, just fractured, I'll bandage it up for now. There is not a lot else I can do. I can't give you any pain killers so I suggest you just rest it for the time being." His cold and emotionless voice rang out.

"Can't you give me anything, please?" I said meekly.

He thought for a second and after confirmation from the custody sergeant finally conceded that I could have one for now, after asking whether I was allergic to anything.

"Also, I need to tell you something, there's someone else."

"Save it for the interview room," Sergeant Harris commanded. "Come on Doctor Fingle."

"But it's important."

"Shut it, I said."

I couldn't stop the tears forming in my eyes, my cause was lost now, no one was interested in what I had to say.

The doctor spoke to the custody sergeant about the medication I was allowed, I only half listened, I didn't care anymore.

He shot a glance at me as if to say I was the scum of the earth. I felt ashamed, but I hadn't done anything wrong. It wasn't me.

The door slammed shut again and the bolt shifted into place. I was alone, except for the noise of other prisoners coming and going from time to time. It was like time had been suspended and meant nothing anymore.

The trap door in the main door slid open, the custody sergeant stood there, he placed a cup of water on the tiny shelf, next to it was a tablet.

"Take this."

"What is it?"

"Just take it and shut up."

I stood up gingerly, took what was offered and did as I was told. Then he was gone again. This time I paced the cell, only a few feet across and not much more in length. They certainly didn't want you to get too much exercise in here.

All I could do was wait.

A meal was served to me at some point. It didn't look very appetizing and I had lost my appetite, so only picked at it. I lay down afterwards and drifted into an uneasy sleep occasionally woken by the noises outside my cell, now resigned to my fate, the fact that all hope was gone.

A group of witches stood in a circle. They were wearing ceremonial gowns, the only light visible was from large candles standing a foot tall on the ground in front of them. A strange stillness hovered in the vicinity. I could see the dark shadows of the trees still in the dim moonlight and could hear the wind winding its way through them, yet not even the slightest draught hit this sheltered spot. The flames from each of the candles burned brightly and rose to an extraordinary height, each seemed to glow a different colour, blue, green, red, an unusually bright yellow, mauve, orange and white.

The witches were standing behind the candles, chanting, large pendants were visible round their necks, each one reflecting the colour of their candle's flame. I couldn't understand what they were chanting. They all seemed to be saying different things.

A shape had been drawn out on the ground, from the angle I was seeing it, it looked like a seven-pointed star, each witch with her candle at a point.

In the septagon that marked out the centre of the star, a figure lay still on the ground bedraggled and rather worse for wear. Then it stirred as the chanting grew louder. Gradually shoulders lifted off the ground, followed by the head, it was a man. He took a second to look round the circle of women, who all now had their arms stretched out about chest height.

Each witch seemed to have a separate purpose in this task, their own part to perform in this ceremony. The volume of their voices grew louder. Their actions took on different forms. A couple of the witches held their pendants out from their chests, another hovered hers above the candle in front of her, four different coloured flames escaped from it in bursts of light, shooting three feet into the air then back into the pendant. It then emitted an immense beam of multicoloured light into the centre of the septagon.

A fight in one of the cells woke me from my slumber. I remembered the bizarre dream, the vividness of it, the smell of it. I tried to sit up but found my body too weary, every muscle felt like it didn't belong to me. Suddenly the room started to spin like a roulette wheel, nausea choked me. I could see the bucket in the corner but could not raise my weary body.

What had they given me? Was this my demise, payback by a doctor for the cruelty that someone else had acted out in my guise. I tired to scream but found the effort too much.

Darkness again.

The figure in the centre attained full height. It was Henry, I could see him clearly. He looked directly into my eyes, anger in them, alive for all to see. He went to move from the centre but was thrown back by the bright beam of light. He fell to the ground, then got back up, this time not trying to move from the septagon that held him. He shouted something that was inaudible.

The candles erupted into a blaze of light, as if fuel had been poured over them. Seven columns of light shot high into the air, joining together to form the tip of a pyramid above Henry. The tails of these columns joined a split second later then the ball of light hovered in the air for a few seconds more. The chanting grew to a crescendo. The candles shot out another flame that stretched towards the centre of the septagon, all meeting at the same point, within Henry.

Pierced by the burning flames, Henry screamed in pain, arms reaching upward towards the sky.

The chanting started again, this time in unison. 'CASKIMOTAR', they were saying, quietly, effortlessly, picking up speed and rhythm as it grew into a thunderous sound that echoed around the woods. The witches pointed at Henry, palms face down, fingers following the flow of the arms. The flaming ball that hovered above him changed its form to an arrow and shot to the ground to meet the rest of the flames, somewhere within Henry.

Henry screamed louder, so loud I thought he was going to burst my ear drums. He looked at me, pity in his eyes, I began to feel guilt. I looked deep into his eyes.

I wasn't sure if I was dreaming. I looked round breaking off the stare. Everything seemed real, every noise, every colour, the intoxicating smell. To my right Mojo was sitting on the ground, leaning against my leg, Aunt Rose to my left. She appeared taller than I remembered her. I couldn't see Ann-Marie.

Where was Ann-Marie? I panicked.

I scoured the area hoping to catch sight of her, sitting under a tree somewhere.

Suddenly I was awake again. "AAARRRRGGGGGGHHHHHH"
I screamed. Every part of my body elicited pain, cramps
contorted me into a ball where I lay. I tried to reach out to the
door of my cell, attract attention. I screamed again, my insides
on fire with pain.

The door of my cell burst open.

"What's all this bloody noise?" Sergeant Harris commanded.

He stopped suddenly, as his face turned from anger to
concern, wondering what he should do.

He rushed to my bedside, but found himself retreating as the
heat forced him away.

The pain was immense, gritting my teeth I closed my eyes,
clasping my hands tightly into fists, trying to shut out the pain.
None of which helped.

Once more I reached out for help from the officer, who
stared on disbelievingly. Tears streamed down my cheeks.

"Tell them I'm sorry," was all I could say.

My heart felt it was going to burst, pounding harder and
harder against my ribcage. I felt myself being thrown against
the wall, and I passed into unconsciousness.

It felt like only minutes but finally I came round. My first
reaction to scream from the pain.

"Arrgh!" I stopped suddenly.

I didn't feel any pain.

Suddenly I wondered whether I was blind as I couldn't see
anything. Was I dead? Finally, I was dead! 'What a blessed relief'.

I lifted myself up, numb from everything, rolling my left
wrist round pleased that I could feel no pain.

"Is this what death is like?" I asked aloud, waiting for
something to happen.

Suddenly my head hurt, a thumping pain. I felt a bump on
the back of it.

Something wasn't right.

Standing up, I put my hands out. I could feel walls. I inched my way forward, I kicked something, something stacked against the wall. As I was feeling my way around a light came on behind me.

"You okay Daniel? There's been a powercut." The voice was familiar.

"Mark?" I asked hesitantly.

"Yeah, you okay?"

"Fine." I didn't know whether I was dreaming or it was reality.

"You sure?"

"No, I'm not sure. This may sound strange but where am I?"

"You're in the theatre, there was a power cut..."

"Is it Sunday?" I asked hopefully.

"Er, yes. Why?" he couldn't hide the sarcasm.

"Yes," I said jubilantly, pinching myself to make sure I was really here. "I don't know how but...yes, you did it."

"What?" Mark quizzed.

It was Sunday again, I was back in the side corridor. Whatever Heather had done it had worked. I made my way towards Mark, his torchlight and the open doorway but just before I escaped through the door I thought for a moment. Then grabbing the torch from Mark I went back to where I had been.

"What are you doing? You alright?"

"I'm fine." I smiled to myself.

I scoured the walls, glancing at the graffiti, until I found what I was looking for. I placed my hand on it, whilst searching the floor for something hard, anything, I found a piece of an old chair, then rammed it into the plaster destroying the incantation. I watched as with every strike another piece of plaster crumbled and fell from the wall.

"Oi! What you doing? Some of that graffiti is years old." Mark stepped angrily towards me, but I'd stopped before he made contact.

"I know." I was done.

"What you smiling for?" Mark studied the mess I'd made.

"Nothing, absolutely nothing."

Angrily he told me to get out and I ran so fast I thought I'd meet myself coming back.

Running down the stairs I could hear talking. 'Yes', I was definitely back. My head was still brimming with all the events of the last eight days. I couldn't control my relief that it was all over.

"What happened to you Daniel?" Susan, one the girls, asked.

"What?"

"You look as though you won the lottery."

"Nothing so small," I said sarcastically. If only they knew.

It was no good, I couldn't stay there any longer, I had to leave, there were things I wanted, needed, to do that couldn't wait.

I rhetorically asked if I could go and, before Fiona had answered, I heeled off into the darkness of the auditorium finding my way back stage to pick up my jacket and heading out through the stage door.

I ran faster than I'd ever done before. Breathless and exhausted I was outside Ann-Marie's house within fifteen minutes. I stood on the other side of the road trying to get my breath back. I studied it like a great marvel of modern architecture. It was raining and I was getting soaked but I didn't care, it felt great to be alive. The curtains weren't drawn and I could see both Ann-Marie and her mother sitting down talking in the living room. I was so relieved.

Would Ann-Marie know about the past events? I wanted to say thank you, but was too afraid to knock. What would I say? Would she wonder who this strange person was?

Aunt Rose. She must remember. Either way I wouldn't feel so much of a fool if I went round there and introduced myself. If she didn't know I would make something up like I had the wrong house.

Half an hour later I was ringing the doorbell to Aunt Rose's house.

The door opened.

"Daniel, I was expecting you, come in, you're soaked."
I did as I was told. She took my jacket and hung it up, I left my wet shoes by the door and went and sat in the lounge as instructed.

Aunt Rose brought in a towel and a pot of tea. After pouring the tea she settled down in her armchair. I went to put the cup up to my lips and hesitated. She saw.

"It's alright dear this is normal tea."

I smiled. "So you do remember. How about Ann-Marie?"

"My dear boy she won't remember. As you can guess everything went well, Henry is back where he belongs, and time is back as it was. There is one thing though."

"What's that?"

"You must destroy the incantation before it causes anymore trouble."

"Already done," I said, pleased to be one step ahead of Aunt Rose for a change.

"Good."

"One thing though, I saw it all happen. But don't understand how? And, I couldn't see Ann-Marie. I could see Mojo. Yourself, even if you seemed a little taller, you were both standing next to me. Where was she?"

Aunt Rose smiled. "Deary, you were viewing it through Ann-Marie's eyes. She told me how she could see when you shared contact." I nodded my agreement. "Well it appears a little of that remained."

"But she's blind, and then she saw through my eyes."
"Daniel, she held what you hold most precious and that enabled her to see temporarily as if you were there, that is the power, strange as it may be sometimes."

I felt round my neck and found my silver plectrum, holding it tightly.

We sat in silence. "But what about me being there?"

"That..." she paused. "... talisman, for want of a better

word, represented all the good in you and that is what gave you the connection to each other that night. Heather said that if you could not be there then the witches only needed something that represented the good in you. But, it had to be true."

"If I had been told that I could have just laid low for a while, instead of taking risks." I was getting agitated when I should just be pleased it had worked.

"Daniel, if you didn't have anything that represented your true self then yes you would have had to have been there. Ann-Marie was told this but she was also told that she was not to ask for anything to be given to her, you had to relinquish it because you wanted to, because you cared, and trusted her. Magic is strange, it relies on faith and goodness to work, so, to force the passing of a treasured possession is manipulation and that can be disastrous."

Inside I was a mix of feelings and emotions, Aunt Rose patiently let it all sink in until the doorbell chimed out.

"Do excuse me."

"Yeah, sure." I reached to the tray and took another biscuit. I was about to take a second bite when I heard a familiar voice. I stood up to go into the hallway, but they were already coming into the lounge led by Aunt Rose.

"Daniel this is Ann-Marie and her guide dog Mojo."

"Pleased to meet you," she said in a friendly voice.

"This is her mother Karen."

"Pleased to meet you," I said.

We all sat down, Karen, Ann-Marie and myself, on the settee, while Aunt Rose went and made a fresh pot of tea.

"Have we met before? There is something about you that is so familiar. Something in your aura." Ann-Marie said curiously. I didn't know how to answer this and said nothing.

"I don't think so." I lied.

"Do you mind if I touch your face?"

"Sorry." I exclaimed rather too harshly.

"It helps her form a picture in her mind. Blind people some-times do this," Karen interjected, covering my awkwardness.

"No, no I … I don't mind." I leaned forward slightly and the silver plectrum dangled loosely. It felt strange as Ann-Marie fingered my face delicately, studying the contours, building up a physical image in her mind. As she touched my ears I smirked.

"Sorry," She said.

"No, it's fine, just tickled that's all."

"What's that?" Her hand had found my silver plectrum. Her fingers toyed with it tenderly, feeling the inscription on the back.

"It says…" I started but Ann-Marie finished the sentence.

"To the best son, happy 16th birthday, Love Mum and Dad xx" I sat opened mouthed, and even her mother looked surprised.

"You can feel that?" I asked.

"No, it's… it's just familiar."

My heart raced as I wondered if she remembered anything else. She touched my face again.

"You've got a nice smile." I smiled harder, trying not to blush. "Thank you."

"A promise?" Ann-Marie finally said, her brow furrowed as she tried to remember something.

Aunt Rose shuffled into the room carrying a tray. "Here we go, a nice fresh pot of tea. How are you Karen?"

"You know me Rose, I'm always good. Although…"

Ann-Marie interrupted her mother. "You promised you'd play me something."

I was stunned and I could see Aunt Rose looking on in bemusement, whilst Karen was just bewildered at the statement.

"I'm sorry David," Karen tried to apologise for her daughter.

"Daniel." I corrected.

"Sorry Daniel. Ann-Marie you must be confused with someone else."

Ann-Marie looked unsure, her mind registering a dim recollection, a latent memory. But I knew I had.

"Yes I would love to."

Aunt Rose smiled at me, a knowing smile. Karen just looked incredulous.